Young Warriors
Stories of Strength

YOUNG WARRIORS

Stories of Strength

edited by

Tamora Pierce and Josepha Sherman

RANDOM HOUSE 🏠 NEW YORK

Library of Congress Cataloging-in-Publication Data
Young warriors / edited by Tamora Pierce [and] Josepha Sherman.
    p.   cm.
SUMMARY: Fifteen original short stories by various authors relate the exploits of
teenage warriors who defeat their enemies with cunning and skill as they strive to
fulfill their destinies.
ISBN 0-375-82962-8 (trade) — ISBN 0-375-92962-2 (lib. bdg.) —
ISBN 0-375-82963-6 (pbk.)
1. Fantasy fiction, American. 2. Short stories, American. [1. Soldiers—Fiction.
2. Self-realization—Fiction. 3. Fantasy. 4. Short stories.]
I. Pierce, Tamora. II. Sherman, Josepha.
PZ5.Y8518 2005   [Fic]—dc22   2004016432

Printed in the United States of America 10 9 8 7 6 5 4 3 2 1

RANDOM HOUSE and colophon are registered trademarks of Random House, Inc.

CONTENTS

YOUNG WARRIORS

Stories of Strength

INTRODUCTION

Tamora Pierce

FOR MY FIRST-EVER TRY at editing an anthology, I wanted both a co-editor who was an established professional, like my friend Josepha (Jo) Sherman, and a theme we could both be comfortable with, such as that of young warriors. It was a theme very well suited to us both: Jo has spent much of her career thinking and writing about all kinds of warriors, while I pretty much specialize in girls and boys who, when called upon to defend things that are dear to them, find it within themselves to do just that, however difficult it may be. With all of our years of study on the subject, we were still fascinated to see how our anthology's authors viewed both warriors and the function of warriors, particularly when Jo and I chose to leave our definition of a warrior wide open. Here a warrior is someone who takes a stand resulting in conflict that she or he feels obligated to face.

This entire examination of warriors and their choices picked up resonances from our current period of world upheaval, in which we are forced to ask hard questions about the nature of war, of those who order it, and of those who fight it. Like most books, this one picks up the flavor of our time, so that in these stories you will find the idea of the warrior and of what makes one, particularly a young warrior, thoroughly explored. The writer's viewpoint may be primarily comic—as in the stories of Esther Friesner and Mike Resnick—or dramatic, but you will be asked to do some serious thinking by every writer. Each story reveals the writer's peculiar relation not only with the image of the warrior, but with the reality.

Since warriors often make sacrifices to achieve their goals, our young warriors must do the same. Brent Hartinger's hero discovers his best solution will call for him to surrender ambitions of wealth and glory. Janis Ian's young scholar will be forced to surrender youthful dreams and innocence alike. India Edghill's young bride, if she is to achieve her desires, will have to give up a normal life, while Lesley McBain's girls will face exile among strangers. Doranna Durgin's hero will face the warrior's test, to see what she is ultimately made of, as so many young people do when they are forced into battle.

Some stories will make you question the traditional image of the warrior and what the warrior does. Are you able to recognize the warrior's heart in someone who doesn't fit the traditional bill, such as Esther Friesner's Helen, the much-swapped most beautiful woman in classical Greece, or the Stirlings' mermaid, or my own goatherd? Might there be a time when a warrior must not do what policy, tradition, or faith demands, when it is possible to lose by winning? You will read Mike Resnick's story of enemies who discover they have more in common than they have with their own people. Margaret Mahy shows us a magician who fails to recognize a true warrior because that warrior doesn't fit the standard definition.

In this anthology are those who have trained to be warriors and have chosen to turn aside from that path, as well as those who have never trained for it, yet picked up weapons to defend those they loved from some looming threat. In Laura Anne Gilman's story you will encounter a frightened yet polite young aborigine, a builder, who understands that if he is to succeed as a warrior, he needs to think as well as act. In Janis Ian's tale a would-be soldier discovers the truth about the troops he aspires to join and learns to use his wits as a weapon, confronting an ancient evil alone in the woods. Mike Resnick's warrior-to-be, clad in secondhand armor, goes out to prove his skill as a fighter, only to question his goals with a stranger.

While the stories are dressed in the costume of historical and fantasy fiction, they hold the same hard questions we ask ourselves after every news broadcast. Is India Edghill's native girl who takes up alien weapons to defeat an oppressor exacting vengeance for her dead, or engaging in terrorism? Is Pamela F. Service's religious heroine, who lures a foreign commander and his guards into a rocky desert, a rebel insurgent, or a national defender? Is it a crime to hide a fleeing prisoner from the enemy who seeks to kill her, or an act of heroism? And what do you call Bruce Holland Rogers's warrior who understands that he is afraid to die? One of the subtle questions Margaret Mahy asks is, who is the truer patriot, the immigrant or the scion of the upper classes who cares only for national security on his terms?

Ultimately, how do we reckon the costs of battle? Is the damage worth it? Is what we give up of ourselves worth it? Which is better: to be the heartless battlefield reaper at the beginning of Holly Black's tale, unaffected by the dangers and the death around her, or the shattered, grieving woman at its end? Bruce Holland Rogers's hero comes to see the cost of war, but how can true peace be won?

There are other, nonhuman powers in some of these stories, powers that give the young protagonists a nudge—or in one case, pretend to give the young warrior what he desires, only to deliver a surprising twist. Once again these powers are there to make you think through the ideas our authors have placed before you. Each story has its own outcome, but you are left to make your own conclusions about the rightness or wrongness of that outcome. This is what each of our young warriors has to do. This is what we have had to do as writers and editors, and it is what we hope you will do: only think. The world could change completely, as it does in one of these stories. Our landscape could remake itself. Who would have the mental agility, the vision, and the pure courage to turn her or his back on the past and face the battles of an unknown future, as Rosemary Edghill's priestess does? To use the weapons of mind and hands to remake the world? How many of us could make the choice my own hero does, to see that her old life is over and she must make a new one?

In a way, we ask all of our children to be this kind of warrior: to face the future, to fight its battles, and to know when fighting is not just unnecessary, but harmful. In this respect all of our children are these young warriors, preparing their weapons and, more importantly, their minds. We owe it to them and to ourselves to see to the sharpness of our own minds by testing them on the visions of others, to see if we aren't ready for a new way of looking at war and those who fight it.

THE GIFT OF RAIN MOUNTAIN

Bruce Holland Rogers

I LAY ON MY BACK, watching the little patches of blue sky that I could see through the jungle canopy. My brother Baxmal and Chulchun, an older warrior, had climbed into the trees to spy on our neighbors. Baxmal had threatened to clout me with his war club if I tried again to join them up there. "You're too clumsy. You'll shake a branch, and someone in the city will see you. Then we'll all be dead."

"Why would they kill us?" I had said. Scaled Jaguar, ruler of the city, was our ally.

"That just proves that you don't think like a warrior yet," Baxmal said. That stung. He was only a few years older than me, but those years had broadened his shoulders, and his arms were much thicker and stronger than mine. I was almost as tall as he was, but he took pleasure in treating me like a child. I wasn't a child—I had trained with a spear and shield—but I wasn't allowed to carry a weapon yet. I was a runner. I served the warriors with my speed and endurance.

Baxmal had said, "A warrior knows that this world is full

of treachery. He keeps his eyes and his mind open." He nodded toward the city. "Already we have seen strange things."

"Like what?"

But Baxmal wouldn't tell me. Chulchun was even less
talkative.

So I watched the sky, as I did every day when it was our
turn to come here to the mountainside and spy on the city
below. My view was boring. At least my brother and his companion could see people walking from the houses to the fields,
or from the palace to the temples. I watched nothing more
interesting than ants or lizards on the tree trunks. Once a pair
of macaws flashed through an open patch of sky.

I spent my time imagining how it would be when I was
a warrior taking captives in battle. Our family was poor, so
there wouldn't be any feathers on my shield at first. But I'd
be quick on my feet. Before they knew I was coming, I'd be
among the enemy, hitting them with my club. *Kaak! Kaak!*
Spears would bounce off my shield. I wouldn't have to use my
own spear, I'd be so fast. I could rely on the blunt side of my
club. *Kaak! Kaak! Kaak!* Just like that, I would have three captives sitting dazed at my feet before the main line of our warriors had even joined me in battle. Lord Tayomam would see
how I was fighting. After the victory, he would reward me
with so many quetzal feathers that my shield would be as daz-
zling as any highborn warrior's. I would be invited to the
palace to stand behind my bound-up captives and accept
Lord Tayomam's praise before the captives were taken off to
the temple to die. When I walked through my neighborhood,
I would hear girls in the shadows of their houses, talking to
their sisters: "There he goes, the warrior Mactun!" "Don't get
your hopes up," their mothers would say. "He's going to marry
into a noble family, a great fighter like him!"

Thump! Something hit my leg.

"I said, stand up!"

Baxmal stood over me. He had struck my thigh with the butt of his spear. "You can finally make yourself useful, if you wake up!"

"I'm awake!"

"If I were the enemy, you'd have never heard me coming."

"I heard. I knew it was you." I got to my feet.

"Here is a message. You must take it straight to the palace. These words are for the generals and Lord Tayomam himself."

That got my attention. Before, I had always taken messages to one of the captains, and the messages were rarely anything other than that Baxmal and Chulchun were coming behind me. My brother liked to make me run out ahead of him, with a message that amounted to nothing, just because he could.

"Are you listening?" My brother leaned in, his face close to mine. "A procession of warriors came into Scaled Jaguar's city. They were unopposed and came first to the temple. Then to the palace. Their leaders were two men in feather robes, and they were received in both places. Food and water were brought to the warriors, who number six twenties or more. They are the people of Smoke Bat."

Baxmal might not have believed that I knew how to think like a warrior, but I understood. Smoke Bat was the ruler of a distant city. He was our enemy, the enemy of all our friends. Or so we had thought. Scaled Jaguar now seemed very friendly with him. And that was a lot of men. Six twenties of warriors would be more than a raiding party.

"Repeat it back to me."

I did. I had it memorized already. I knew what each detail meant. My message would be an early warning of betrayal and invasion.

"Now go!" said my brother.

In some of the old hero stories, there are runners who fly like a bow from an arrow to deliver their messages. But I would not be able to fly like an arrow until I had made my way through the jungle on the mountainside and down to the path. Vines and branches barred my way. The mud was slick. I hurried as best I could, ducking low branches and climbing over lower ones, descending. I rehearsed my message in my head as I went. *A procession of warriors. They went first to the temple.*

Pig.

Their leaders, two men in feather robes, were received in the palace.

Pig.

Six twenties of warriors. Or more. Smoke Bat's people . . .

I parted palm fronds that grew at eye level. I stepped into a small clearing, and the peccary grunted.

I froze. It was an old boar with a scarred snout, not five arm's lengths away down the slope. One of his tusks was broken, but the remaining one looked like a yellow knife.

The pig grunted again, softly. Slowly I looked around for others. I didn't see any. That would have been bad, stumbling into a herd of them. Not that this one didn't look formidable enough by himself.

I stood my ground. I looked for something to throw, but there was only mud, leaves, and tangled roots. If he charged, which tree would I try to climb?

Idiot! I had smelled him before I saw him. I hadn't been paying attention to what was right in front of me.

The boar hadn't moved from where he stood. There were

more scars on his head, and one on his side could have come from a spear. He was old. His legs trembled. I took a step back. "Peccary," I said softly, "I'm young and fast. You'd have to chase me uphill. You don't want that, do you?"

I backed into the palm fronds, hoping that he wouldn't rush me in those first moments of my retreat, when I couldn't see him any longer.

He was still grunting softly. I retreated up the slope. When I couldn't hear him anymore, I detoured around him. At last I couldn't smell his musk.

That was stupid. I hadn't been thinking like a warrior at all. I was thinking all about my message, rather than noticing what was before me. What if I had stumbled onto something more dangerous than a solitary old boar?

Then I truly had a warrior's thought. What if I had rushed into the arms of my enemy?

If I were Scaled Jaguar and I were planning betrayal and a surprise attack, I would anticipate that my plans might be discovered. I would watch the roads.

If Scaled Jaguar's guards were hiding near the road, I'd be caught if I ran like a runner with an important message. I could follow the river instead, but Scaled Jaguar would have probably posted guards on the river, too.

It would be better to go straight through the deep jungle and avoid the roads, but that would mean going where hardly anyone ever went. I'd have to go over Rain Mountain.

There was no priest to bless me for such a journey, but the more I thought about it, the more necessary it seemed. The risk of encountering a witch or a spirit did not seem any worse than the risks of following the road or the river. Going through the jungle, I wouldn't be able to run, but my route would be more direct.

I crossed a stream, paused to drink, and thought once more about the choice I was making. If Scaled Jaguar's people were my enemies, they would definitely try to kill or capture any messenger. Whatever spirits I encountered on Rain Mountain might or might not oppose me.

I chose.

The jungle of Rain Mountain was like the jungle anywhere. The same trees and lianas. The same mud. The same butterflies. But it was different, too. The same birds called to one another in the forest canopy, but the silences between their calls were longer. The wind up there in the canopy seemed different, too. It wasn't steady. It came and went, as if the wind were roaming its territory like an animal. Or a spirit. The patches of sunlight that reached the forest floor seemed especially bright. The deepest shadows were especially dark.

I tripped on a root and fell. I got up and hurried on.

A voice said, "Where are you going, that you're in such a rush to get there?"

I stopped and looked all around me. I didn't see anyone. My heart started to pound. I continued.

"I said, where are you going?"

This time there was a young man standing directly in front of me. I nearly ran right into him.

"Oh," I said. "I didn't see you."

"Not until I wanted to be seen," he said. His smile was relaxed, not at all threatening. He was about my brother's age, it seemed. Not much older than me. "Tell me why you are hurrying."

He could be one of Scaled Jaguar's warriors, I thought. But his hands were empty. He wore no armor. Then I noticed his eyes. In his young man's face, his eyes were the eyes of an old man. They were eyes that would detect a lie.

"I carry a message for my father," I said. It was not a lie. Lord Tayomam was father to all his people.

"So there is news in the world of men," he said. Two deer, a doe and a buck, came out of the shadows and stood on either side of him, near enough that he could have reached out to touch them. "Come, stay with me awhile." He gestured toward the door of a stone house that I hadn't seen before. "We will drink and eat and smoke a cigar."

"You are a gracious host," I said, for I gathered that this was no mere spirit. "With your permission, I must decline. My father needs me."

"You are a loyal son," he said. "But if you will stay with me but a moment, you will find that I am powerful over many things, visible and invisible. I could give you a gift of armor and a fine spear."

"I thank you," I said again. But I repeated, "My father needs me."

"Go, then," he said.

I hurried on. When I looked over my shoulder, the place where he had stood was empty.

Not long after, who should I see in front of me but the same young man with old eyes. "I do like to hear news of men," he said. "Come, you are wet with sweat, and breathing hard. In the cool of my house, you can rest and refresh yourself." Again he gestured at the door of a house that looked just the same as the one I had left behind.

"I must decline," I said.

"If you will but keep me company for a while, I will give you these." From the shadows, he picked up a set of wood-

and-leather armor, and a shield. There was a spear, too. A very fine one. I was tempted.

At the same time, the beings that owned mountains were known for their wit and trickery, and the owner of Rain Mountain would be no different. The safety of my people depended on the message that I carried.

"Lord," I said, "I thank you. But I must continue, for my father needs me."

"Go, then," he said.

The third time that he stopped me, he again offered me armor, a spear, and a shield. But this shield was covered with green feathers. I couldn't stop myself from saying, "It is beautiful." But I could not carry such a shield without having earned it.

"Come into my house," he said, gesturing toward the shadows, where I saw what looked like the same stone doorway as before. "You will give me news. Then, when you accept my gift, you will take with it the reputation it demands. All will know you as a great warrior."

That was tempting. I licked my lips. How much would it delay my message to sit down with the owner of the mountain? Not much, perhaps. But what if Smoke Bat and Scaled Jaguar were even now marching to attack? "Lord," I said, "my father awaits me."

"You serve him well, since you will not be tempted. Your message must be important." For the third time he said, "Go, then."

The owner of Rain Mountain did not appear before me again as I descended the far slope of his domain. I came into my city from the fields, so I appeared at the palace without an escort. The guards were a little surprised, therefore, by my arrival from the wrong direction, and alone. Still, they admitted me. A captain heard my report, then brought me to the first general, who heard it and had me repeat it for a second general. Then both generals made me wait while they reported to Lord Tayomam. Then yet another captain summoned me to a cool, dark room where the generals and Lord Tayomam received my report one last time.

"And why did you not come by the road?" asked Lord Tayomam.

"I thought that the enemy might be watching the road," I answered.

Lord Tayomam nodded, gave the captain a brief glance, and then began to speak to the generals about their plans as if I were no longer there. The captain took me to a room where he gave me water, a gourd full of atole, and some tamals to eat. He left me.

My work as a messenger was done for now. Later Baxmal and Chulchun would return as other watchers went to relieve them. I could go home.

However, I couldn't stop thinking about that feathered shield.

I had crossed Rain Mountain most of the way and the owner had not shown himself. I was beginning to think that the feathered shield would not be mine after all. Then, suddenly, there he was on the path before me. "Where are you going this time?" he asked.

"I bring a message to my brother," I replied. It was true. I had asked my mother if she wanted me to tell Baxmal anything. "Yes," she had said. "Tell him the wood he brought me for cooking won't last half as long as he said it would. I need more!"

The owner invited me to join him in his house and tell

him all that I knew about the goings-on of men. He offered me a gift: a captain's shield and the reputation to go with it.

Captain! Oh, how wonderful it would be to lord it over my brother!

The offered gifts just kept getting better!

Better and better . . .

"I thank you, Lord," I said. "But I must continue and deliver my message."

The next time that he stopped me, the owner of Rain Mountain offered me a general's cape. I almost took it. The third time, what he offered was the manikin scepter of Lord Tayomam's line.

I looked at the gift as he offered it. He held the scepter as if it were an ordinary stick of wood, not the emblem of divinity on earth inlaid with colored stones.

"I am not of noble birth," I said.

"With this," the owner promised, "you would be."

I would be a ruler of men, the warrior above all warriors. The warrior in charge of a battle that was about to begin.

I reached out to touch the scepter.

But what did I really know about being a warrior, much less the commander of a city? My people were about to be attacked. Who was I to replace Lord Tayomam at such a time? Perhaps part of thinking like a warrior was also knowing one's limits.

"No," I said, withdrawing my hand. "Though your offer is most generous . . ."

"You are wise," said the owner of Rain Mountain. "There is a greater prize yet than being a great lord of men. Do you want to know what it is?"

What did I care now? I had pushed his offered gifts beyond the limit of what I could accept. "O Lord of the

Mountain, tell me. Tell me what is greater than to rule over men."

"To live in peace," he said. He smiled. "Come, then, and visit with me awhile. Tell me the doings of men. Tell me about these messages you have carried. We will eat and drink and smoke. And then I will give you the gift of peace. City will not fight against city. There will be no raids, no sieges . . ."

No glory for the warriors, I thought. No praise for the takers of captives.

No risk of putting on armor, facing an enemy, and dying.

Tears brimmed in my eyes. This was a thought I had kept hidden. I had almost hidden it from myself. Of course I had imagined that once I became a warrior, I would kill; I wouldn't be killed. I would take captives; I wouldn't be taken captive and sacrificed. Of course I would not be one of the many warriors who died.

I knew that every young warrior must think this way.

Some young warriors were wrong. Some died.

Many died.

The owner of Rain Mountain must have looked into my heart to see my thoughts. I said, "Really? I could live in peace?"

He smiled. "Come into my house." He put his hand on my shoulder to guide me toward the doorway. "We will drink and eat. We will talk and smoke, and talk some more . . ."

Time for a mountain is a different thing from the time of a man.

I drank from the gourds of the owner. I ate strange and delicious meats from his bowls. I smoked his cigar, which smelled of flowers. It seemed that we passed an hour or two together. I told him of the coming war, and also of the message I was carrying to my brother. He laughed. He laughed both times.

When I came out of his house, it was into the light of dawn. That surprised me. Could I really have spent an entire night in conversation? I turned to remark on this, but the owner was gone. In the shadows, there was no stone house.

I continued down the mountain. I sought the place where Baxmal and Chulchun had hidden themselves and spied. But I couldn't find them. And when I climbed into the trees to peer down at the city of Scaled Jaguar . . .

There was only jungle. Dense jungle everywhere, over what had been fields. Trees covered the palaces and temples. They looked just like tiny hills.

The roads back to my own city were overgrown. Jungle came down to the banks of the river, as if no one had ever cut firewood there. In the valley of my home, it was the same as with the city of Scaled Jaguar. Everything was overgrown. I could find no sign of any other human being.

Birds and monkeys called to one another.

I was alone.

This was the Lord of Rain Mountain's gift of peace.

BRUCE HOLLAND ROGERS

BRUCE HOLLAND ROGERS lives and writes in Eugene, Oregon, the tie-dye capital of the world. He speaks Spanish, and his visits to Mexico and Central America have inspired his interest in the pre-Columbian cultures of that region. "My mesoamerican fantasies are only loosely based on real cultures," he says, "just as Tolkien's work is loosely European. It seems funny to me that heroic fantasy writers largely stick to European settings when we have the entire world's traditions of magic and heroes to explore."

Bruce's fiction is all over the map. Some of it is science fiction, some is fantasy, some is literary. He has written mysteries, experimental fiction, and work that's hard to label. Bruce has won the Pushcart Prize, two Nebula Awards, and the Bram Stoker Award. He is probably best known for his short-short stories, some of which appear online at www.shortshortshort.com. He is married to Holly Arrow, a professor of social psychology at the University of Oregon. You can learn more about him on his personal Web page at www.sff.net/people/bruce.

THE MAGESTONE

S. M. and Jan Stirling

FARE TOSSED THE BUCKET of kitchen scraps over the *Osprey*'s rail, then paused to stare out across the heaving green-gray waters, fascinated. He'd never before been more than a day's walk from the farm where he'd been born, and now it seemed like a vanished dream. Even seabirds didn't come out this far. It was like walking on the beach searching for clams and driftwood, yet not like it. There he walked on the water's edge and looked out across it westward; here the creaking, pitching round-ship was a tiny wooden chip lost in an endlessness of foam and salt-smelling spray without form or direction.

Fare reached into his tunic and pulled out the strange stone his mother had given him the night before he'd left, holding it out until the chain pinched the skin on the back of his neck.

The chain's silver, he thought. Worth more than the stone, but . . .

The stone was gray, ridged in subtle patterns that hinted

at a multicolored shine, like the inside of an oyster shell almost worn away by the sea.

"Your father found it in a fish's belly and carried it for luck," his mother had told him, putting it in his hand. With a soft smile, she'd folded Fare's fingers over it. "He left it with me, for luck in childbed, when he left on his last journey. It kept him safe while he carried it; let it do the same for you."

He sighed at the memory. It had been lucky that his uncle had come to take him as an apprentice trader. The work was just as hard and constant, but at least it was a change from the south end of a northbound ox. And in a few years he wouldn't have to do all the scut work, which, as the youngest and least experienced hand, was presently his lot.

"Thanks, stone," he said, grinning—he was just fifteen summers this coming solstice.

Beyond the stone, water parted around the blunt bows of the little ship, forming a smooth swelling V . . . and in it a face, looking back at him.

Startled, Fare gasped, letting the stone fall back on his breast as he grasped the rail and leaned out for a better look. The face slid away, down the wake of the ship. Yellowed strands of kelp swirled, hiding it from him as it slid away. He raced to the stern, dodging bales and barrels, staring into the water, hoping for a better look. But even the clump of kelp had disappeared.

It had been a girl's face, the features slightly bloated, with strange eyes that seemed to gleam like metal. But she had been fair in spite of that.

She must have drowned. He'd seen bodies washed up on the strand.

"What did you see, lad?" his uncle Comgall called from the steering oar. His big weathered hands gripped the tiller with an easy flexing motion that belied the strength it took. "A seal?"

"The body of a woman, Uncle!"

"Where?" Comgall asked.

"Aft, now, in our wake!" the boy said, pointing.

Comgall shook his head, making a gesture to ward off her angry ghost. "There's nothing we could do for her, lad, but put her back in the sea. Back to work!"

"Uncanny," one of the sailors muttered. They were coiling a length of tarred rope together, but the man looked up at a single patched square sail instead of speaking to Fare's face. "Best forget it."

Fare nodded. *But she didn't seem dead,* he thought. *Those silver-green eyes . . . they were uncanny.*

He repeated the gesture his uncle had used, one against half-world creatures.

Neesha followed the small ship, letting its wake pull her along beneath the surface, listening to the grumble of its passage.

She had been scouting this sea-lane for her troop, looking for trouble in the form of their enemy, the Creesi, whose incursions into her people's territory had begun to take the form of piracy against humans.

Not that her people cared about humans. They just didn't want those curious and dangerous creatures to start hunting their kind. No doubt that was just what the Creesi planned. *Typically dishonorable,* Neesha thought bitterly.

What to do? the mermaid thought. There'd been magic on that tubby little scow, strong magic and wild. All her people could sense such, whether they could use magic or not, and the touch of it had drawn her close. But never in her wildest imaginings had she expected to see the lost magestone itself!

Report it? Then: *No.* Odds were the ship would be gone, unfindably. Mother Sea was wide.

For longer than she'd been alive, the Creesi, a merfolk tribe of outcasts and madmen, had fought her people. It was in a battle with them that the stone had been lost, and with it a great deal of their high mage's strength. He himself had disappeared seven moons ago. The lesser mages said he was being held on an island by humans, which was surely impossible—he'd die if kept on land.

I'll take it myself! she decided. *And bear it home triumphant!*

"Lir's Shoal," Comgall said, looking at the lighter green of shallow water over sand. His glance went to the west, where the sun gilded scattered cloud. "We'll anchor here for the night and make Kernow on tomorrow's tide."

Stone-and-wood anchors splashed over the bow and stern.

"You take watch, lad," Comgall said to Fare. "And no napping, mind! Wind, wave, or Saxon can come on you quickly."

Fare felt himself swell with pride as he took a great spear from the rack by the single mast and made his way forward to the bows; Comgall and the three seamen wrapped themselves in their cloaks and settled down to sleep. The sun cast a last glittering road to the west; then it was moonlight and starlight, half seen through high scudding cloud.

Neesha settled low in the sea and watched, ignoring the slight sour taint that seepage from the bilge gave the water around the ship. When she sensed that the seamen's sleep was deep enough, she began to work the oldest magic known to her kind: the luring of a sailor into the sea.

It was tricky to work the spell on one human only, and she gritted sharp teeth in concentration. Suddenly her own small magic felt lifted, supported by something stronger.

The stone's helping me! she thought in wonder. Legend told that it had a will of its own. *It wants to come home!*

The human standing in the bow shook himself, yawned—and then dropped into the water in a swirl and gurgle of bubbles, the spear he'd been holding falling from his hand and vanishing in the darkness of the depths. The mermaid grasped his ankles and pulled him down. When they were deep enough so that even if he awoke he'd not make the surface before he drowned, Neesha pulled herself up his body to find the stone, hanging outside his tunic, glowing faintly. The light was bright enough to reveal that he was only a boy, probably no older than her own fifteen summers. The mermaid knew a moment of regret.

Steeling herself, Neesha reached for the stone—and was met with blinding white light and pain. Her mind screamed in agony; it was like being stung by thousands of jellyfish at once.

For a long moment she couldn't see, couldn't move, and only just kept herself from mind-calling to her mother—a cry that would have been heard by any merfolk in the vicinity, and there were likely more enemies about than friends.

Reaching up, Neesha grabbed the boy's foot and tugged him back to herself. She felt his chest move and she started, then looked at him more closely. His nostrils were flaring as he drew breath . . . but it wasn't water that flowed into his lungs; she could see a thread of bubbles bursting from his lips as he exhaled.

He's alive! she thought, with a spurt of fear. *Magic!*

Frowning, she reached for the stone again, slowly. As she

approached it, sparkles of pain flowed over her hand and the stone brightened threateningly. Neesha withdrew her hand and stared at the human. The stone's glow faded; she blew bubbles as she considered the situation.

Legend didn't lie.

The stone most definitely seemed to have a mind of its own. Right now, that mind was made up about this human. *It wants to stay with him,* she thought. The stone brightened, as if agreeing with her.

Why? she wondered angrily.

Wielded by her tribe's mage, Shashu, the magestone had created wards that kept them safe from all predators; it had been the luck of her people. Now the Creesi robbed and killed them with impunity. It was said that the Creesi had allied themselves with human pirates—proof that they were mad.

In an instant, it all came clear in her mind. This boy could go where she could not. If Shashu was being held on an island, the boy could bring the stone to the mage and help him escape.

Allying oneself with a human, though . . . She shuddered. *I'll bring him to my war chief,* she thought. *Let her decide.* At the thought, the stone's glow faded away. *What does that mean? That I should go alone with this boy?* The stone brightened. A yes? *Then I'd be killed and you'd be in enemy hands!*

This was stupid. For all she knew, the stone glowed and faded in a random fashion, and asking it questions made no difference. She *should* report back, as was her duty, dragging the stone and the human with her.

Then the boy awoke.

What a dream! Fare thought. A very real dream, for he felt the wet cold of the depths and saw the strange face of the drowned girl before him. But he was breathing, and he felt as relaxed as if he were still in his hammock.

Then the trance broke, and he knew the dream was real. Before him was a mermaid, and she was trying to drown him! He lashed out with his fist, but she bent backwards, smacking him hard with her tail and sending him spinning through the dark water, the breath knocked out of him.

In the blackness, Fare didn't even know which way was up, and he couldn't breathe. The spinning had left him dizzy and sick. He began to thrash about in panic. Suddenly he was struck again—this time on the back of his head—and for a moment he knew nothing.

Neesha could almost feel sorry for the human. Despite her youth, she was the best in her troop in the combat art of Shi-se, and he was alone and defenseless. It was obvious that he couldn't see beyond a few feet in the dark water. But she didn't want to feel anything for him; she just wanted the stone. So she struck him again, trying to dislodge it; if he died in the process . . . how sad. She spun in the water, winding up for a killing blow.

The next thing Neesha knew, she was floating, feeling as if she'd run headlong into a cliff, with varicolored bubbles seeming to pop in front of her eyes. After a moment, she realized that the human was thrashing his way to the surface, and from somewhere she found the strength to go after him. She couldn't let him surface here, so close to the ship.

Grasping the boy by his belt and collar, she whisked him out to sea with powerful flicks of her tail. Neesha assumed the stone would see to it that the human kept breathing, but hoped it wouldn't.

When she thought they'd gone far enough, she surfaced

and let him go. The boy sank briefly, then rose, spluttering and coughing. Neesha waited to see what he would do.

Fare gave a hoarse, involuntary cry as he tried to thrash away from the staring mermaid. Her yellow hair hung in ribbons, to cling to her naked shoulders, and even in his panic, Fare remembered the stories the older men had told him about lovelorn sea maidens. Surely if she'd just wanted *that*, she wouldn't have dragged him out to sea. Maybe she wanted to watch him drown. His chest heaved as he coughed and struggled to stay afloat, and to fight down terror as he kept choking. He was drowning and sensed darkness closing in.

Suddenly he felt calm. The fear was still there, but less overwhelming, as if he'd felt it yesterday instead of just now. His arms and legs began to move in an organized way that brought his head above the waves. Still, the water's cold leached his strength from him.

Without thinking, he grabbed the mermaid to keep himself from sinking, and she allowed it. Her eyes shone like a cat's in the moonlight.

Looking into those staring eyes, he snapped, "What do you want?"

"You help," she said, and her voice was like a song, although her Brezh was strongly accented.

Fare blinked in surprise, then half laughed, half sobbed. "Help you?" He gestured at the emptiness around them. "How can *I* help you?"

A look of impatience crossed her exotic features. "Not here! On land. Pirates hold my . . ." She paused, obviously searching for a word. "Chief. You help save, I let you go."

Once he was on land, why would he do anything she wanted? Fare sensed a trick here.

"Pirates on island," she said, as if reading his thoughts.

Ah! I knew there had to be something, Fare thought. Even so. "Why would you trust me?" he couldn't resist asking.

Cautiously the mermaid reached out and touched the stone around his neck with a webbed and taloned finger.

"The stone? You want this?"

She cocked her head and stared, then nodded once.

"If I give it to you, will you swear to take me back to my ship?"

Again that slow nod.

Fare reached for the chain to draw the stone over his head. There was a crackle like lightning, a flash and burning pain. He screamed, and sank helplessly. A hand reached down and drew him up. He and the mermaid stared at one another.

The mermaid sighed. "You help," she said, resignation in her lovely voice.

Fare shuddered. "What do you want me to do?"

What indeed? Neesha wondered. This was madness! One mermaid warrior and one human boy against an island full of pirates and Creesi murderers. All because she *thought* it was what the magestone wanted.

All right, I know the magestone wants it.

Neesha pointed to the stone. "This help you. Give you breath below."

He looked at her uncomprehendingly.

Holding her hand above the water, she said, "Breathe." Then, with her hand, she mimicked diving. "Breathe, no fear."

"Easy for you to say," he muttered.

Neesha ducked beneath the surface, stretching her senses. Finding what she sought, she called a pod of the cousins to her, and soon she and the human were in the midst of a chittering, rollicking throng of dolphins. Neesha explained what she wanted and gained their delighted consent. Mischief of any kind was always to their taste.

Fare tightened his grip on the mermaid. The frolicking pod looked somewhat alarming in the dark.

"They help," she said to him. "You hold here." She guided his hand to a dolphin's sturdy fin. "Put . . ." She made a flickering gesture with two fingers.

"Legs?" he asked.

"Over." She reached down and tugged his leg over the cousin's body. "They take us."

"What—" he began. But the dolphins were off, and he was underwater and unable to ask *What do we do when we get there?*

As they neared the island prison of the mage, Neesha emptied the pool of her mind, listening for other voices.

To her amazement, there weren't many Creesi near the island—perhaps ten in all, widely scattered. Fear grabbed her; they must have gone a-raiding in force, and here she was, miles from where she should be.

Neesha forced her mind back to the problem at hand. *Ten is more than enough to be a problem. . . .* She probed deeper. Most were sleeping—over half in drugged dreams, she found to her relief—while four kept watch. Those who watched didn't converse and she sensed anger and deep bitterness attached to their private thoughts.

Only four. Maybe this could be done.

There was a taint in the water that the cousins found disturbing, and so did she; it was at once oily and bitter.

Moving carefully toward the wakeful guards, Neesha found that she was also approaching the source of the awful taint that soured the water. They came to a massive rock and she clung to it, gazing through the moonlit waters. At last she spied her quarry, four brawny mermen with heavy bronze tridents and nets weighted with lead sinkers around their waists.

Doable, she insisted to herself. Then she studied the area as she'd been taught. The Creesi floated before the mouth of a cave, and the seabed before it had been cleared of all cover. Only the cliff face itself could give them a chance to get close without being seen, but even that was feeble cover. The magestone was proving astonishingly potent, but it couldn't make them invisible.

Neesha considered. First she must rid herself temporarily of this clumsy human. So far, the outflow of rancid water had disguised her presence, but the thrashing progress of her companion was bound to attract notice.

Pressing his hands to the rock that sheltered them, she leaned close and said into his ear, "Stay."

He looked at her, then nodded. Relieved, Neesha swam off.

Fare watched her go, then turned his attention back to the guards, only vaguely discernible in the faded light that came and went with the waves above. There was a faint sparkle along the cliff side, and on staring hard at it, he realized it was the mermaid.

What is she thinking? Fare wondered. Was she planning to attack them? Ridiculous! The guards were easily twice her size! Even though he could still feel the bruises she'd inflicted on him, he was certain she was no match for one of the mermen, let alone four. He forced himself to grip the rock tighter, fighting the urge to help her. If she did have a plan, attracting attention to himself would surely ruin it. Hating the necessity, he kept still.

* * *

Neesha clung to the cliff, pulling herself closer to the quarry, freezing whenever she thought she'd attracted attention, then moving stealthily forward. Finally she was close enough. Reaching into the natural pouch in her belly that would one day hold her young, she plucked out a blowpipe, and from a quiver attached to it, a specially treated sea-urchin spine. She paused, centering herself. She needed to be fast; she needed to be accurate. Her life depended on it—and perhaps the lives of her people.

She aimed and forced a precisely calculated amount of water through the pipe, propelling the dart toward her first victim. There was a slight *tock!* as it struck his neck; then his muscles froze and he floated quietly, drifting. Another . . . and another. Then the fourth guard turned and saw her. Startled, he flung his trident at her, then snatched the net from around his waist. The mermaid curved around the trident as she brought the blowpipe up. Her shot went wild, and the guard bore down on her, strong and swift.

He flung out the net but she spun upward, avoiding it and delivering a painful slap to his hands. He rolled in the water, reducing the force of the blow. Recovering, he swept his tail at her. Neesha evaded it, but only just. As he came around again, she plunged a dart into his tail. The net caught her tail fin and she rolled in panic, only drawing it tighter. Before he could pull her in, the drug began to take effect. He gritted his teeth, fighting it, and reached out; he slowed, then stopped.

The young mermaid hung in the water, exhausted, and watched consciousness fade from her adversary's eyes. In the distance, the cousins played, and the other Creesi still dreamed, heedless. Relief flowed through her, washing away fear. She dragged off the net and let it drop.

Now to see where this cave leads, she thought.

* * *

Fare was already on his way to her, knife in hand. When he'd seen the guard attack, he'd sprung out of hiding. Two of them might overcome the fellow, big as he was. Then, as suddenly as it had begun, it was over—the guard drifting in the current, the mermaid motionless in the water. Was she hurt? Then she looked up, those silvery eyes flashing in a moonbeam as she shrugged out of the net and gestured him forward.

As soon as they entered the dark passage into the cliff, Fare knew there was something wrong. The water was foul, and there was a feeling about the place that made the back of his neck draw tight. At any moment he expected something vile to grab him. After what seemed an eternity he saw light. Looking up, he saw the flicker of torches through the murky water.

A face, upside down, loomed before him. A pale face with the eyes of a man tortured past sanity. A clawed hand reached for him, and Fare cried out, thrusting himself feebly backwards. The mermaid flashed between them, catching that deformed hand. She looked over her shoulder at him and gestured that they should surface.

Neesha drew Fare toward the side of the pool and surfaced carefully. The two of them listened. They looked around and saw nothing alarming. The pool was well below the torches, and she thought it must be deeper when the tide was in, for the rock was wet a long way up.

Then she froze. A single manacle was clutching the mage's tail at its narrowest point, just below the great fan, holding almost half of it above the water. The fan itself was split and shattered, the supporting bones fleshless in places.

The scales on the tail were twisted and buckled where they'd dried in the air. Neesha moaned, sickened at the sight. *No wonder the water here is foul,* she thought.

She had come to rescue Shashu. Now, remembering the mad look in his eyes, she thought they might be too late.

Rage, pure and fierce, coursed through her, and she turned to the human boy. *Humans* had done this, offending even the heartless Creesi. No wonder she'd sensed anger from them. Anything that could wreak such torture on a living being didn't deserve to live. Neesha drew back her hand to strike.

"I'll climb up and see if I can loose the chain," the boy said, unaware of his danger. He turned to look her in the eye. "We've got to save him if we can."

She lowered her hand and nodded, ashamed.

Fare climbed the slippery rocks, his stomach in knots. He knew pirates were killers, but this! This was unclean, and a sin against the gods. It made him feel ashamed of being human.

Then he was looking over the edge of a gently sloping ledge. Catching his breath at the suddenness of his exposure, Fare looked slowly around, then blew his breath out in a long, slow stream. No one was here. He pulled himself up and looked around.

One of the links of the chain that bound the merman was slipped over an iron rod sunk into the rock. Fare almost laughed with relief. No lock! He went to the rod and tried to pull the chain up and off. It came almost to the top, then stuck. After straining for a while, he let it go and sat down, panting, to consider the matter. He needed slack. He was about to call down to the mermaid when he heard footsteps.

* * *

Amator, the pirate chief, stepped over the sleeping body of the guard. *When you wake, dog, I'll have the flesh off your back,* he thought. "Worthless, motherless, sea wrack," he muttered.

When times were good for pirates, things fell apart. The men could see no reason not to get drunk and stay that way. And Amator knew from experience that you could only press them so hard about discipline and keeping watch. At this post especially.

They didn't understand that he wasn't worried about being attacked from this place. He was worried about losing their prize prisoner. The fish-man's magic had brought them untold success on the sea, and the Creesi had given much aid in that regard.

But now they had withdrawn, angry at his treatment of the prisoner.

"Plotting," he mumbled, and realized with a grin that he was drunk, too.

Let 'em plot, he thought. *There's nothing they can do.* It was the prisoner who raised storms or calmed the sea. And it was Amator and not the fish-men who held him captive. He'd do as he pleased with the ugly unnatural animal. And if the Creesi didn't like it, they'd soon find out who was in charge and what was what!

Amator leaned over the pool, put his great, scarred hands on his knees, and shouted down, "You there! Show yourself!"

Shashu's face rose slowly from the water, his staring eyes filled with hate and pain.

"Have you decided, thing? Will you do as I've asked?"

The mage didn't answer.

"Such a simple thing," Amator sneered. "Teach me to raise storms." He shrugged, grinning. Then, at the expression of loathing on the prisoner's face, he grew angry. "Too proud to answer, eh? Maybe I've been too kind. Let's dry you off a little more and see what you think then, eh?"

Amator moved around the pool to the iron rod and lifted the chain off with a casual grunt of effort.

Fare rushed from his hiding place behind a fold in the cave wall, shoving the pirate over the cliff and into the water with a mighty splash. The boy himself fell, striking the sharp rock wall on the way down and scraping off half his tunic and much of his skin. When he hit the water, he turned to face the pirate, whose head rose out of the pool with a roar.

Before Fare could do anything more, Shashu's two withered arms closed about the pirate chief, and he vanished beneath the water.

The mermaid surfaced and looked at Fare without expression. Then she said, "Come." Wincing, he pushed away from the rock wall. She put an arm around him and pulled him out of the sea-cave.

Dawn had come, and morning light illuminated the awful scene before them. The merman, his eyes filled with nightmares, held the drowned pirate as though never meaning to let his tormentor go.

Neesha glanced at the human boy, wondering what to do. If she took the magestone from him, he would surely drown. If she gave the stone to Shashu, the mage might use its power on anyone who came near him, not knowing friend from foe. *Or it might cure him,* she thought.

The cousins had stopped their play and were approaching them. They circled Shashu, exclaiming in chirps of concern over the state of his tail. Some of the younger ones nudged the pirate's body and the mage lashed out at them, causing them to flee with panicked cries to their mothers.

Neesha quickly explained to the dolphins that the body was that of one who had tortured the mage. The cousins were silent for a moment, swimming solemn circles around the wounded merman, weaving an intricate pattern. Their stately progress seemed to calm Shashu, and slowly his grip on the human body lessened.

Fare nudged Neesha and pointed upward. With a frown, she brought him to the surface.

"The dolphins are your friends, aren't they?" he asked, wiping seawater from his eyes. "They'll do what you tell them, right?"

Neesha smiled at that. The cousins did what they liked. "Maybe," she said.

"Have them tow him back to your people, using the chain. That way he can't hurt them. You, uh, *have* a place?"

Neesha nodded. It was a good idea. She even thought the cousins might do it. They were sympathetic creatures, and the mage's condition had plainly touched them.

"Take me back to my ship. I'll give you the stone and we'll say good-bye. All right?"

She considered this. In some ways it went against the grain: humans were the enemy, every bit as much as the Creesi. But this one had helped.

"Yes," she said simply, then turned and dove back under the water.

The cousins were eager to help, and crowded around demanding that the chain be tied around "ME, ME, ME!" Neesha chose the strongest and used the pirate's sash to tie the chain around the dolphin. Then she watched them swim away, the mage still clinging to the pirate's body, looking back at her with haunted eyes.

*   *   *

When she popped up beside Fare again, the startled boy gulped water and began to choke. She held him up until he got himself under control.

"I didn't think you were coming back," he said.

She blinked. The thought hadn't occurred to her. *But no,* she thought ruefully, *the stone wouldn't like that.* She was convinced it wouldn't surrender itself until the human was safe. Neesha smiled. The human's life was a small enough reward to give; she didn't begrudge the stone that.

It had taken them a while to find his uncle's ship, till near midnight. The mermaid brought Fare close, but stopped when she saw his uncle Comgall leaning over the rail.

"I can make it from here," he whispered. Biting his lip in fear of the consequences, he lifted the chain over his head and offered the stone to her.

Her lips parted and she accepted it reverently, pausing before she put it around her own neck.

"I have to ask," he said, and she looked at him, tilting her head. He drew in a strengthening breath. "May I kiss you?"

She laughed once, then covered her mouth, but her eyes were merry as she looked at him. She dropped her hand and, smiling, nodded.

Fare leaned forward and, closing his eyes, very gently kissed her lips. He drew back, startled, and she was gone.

After a moment, he called to the ship. Laughing and cheering, the seamen threw him a line and drew him on board, slapping his shoulders, covering him with a blanket, and demanding to know what had happened.

"I kissed a mermaid," Fare said.

His uncle considered him. "And how was that?"

"Cold, fishy, and very wet."
The men roared with laughter.

Far out in the water, Neesha raised a critical brow. *Hot*, she thought, *musky, and very dry*.

S. M. AND JAN STIRLING

S. M. STIRLING was born near Metz, in France, in 1953. Since then he has lived in other European countries, North America, and Africa, and traveled extensively elsewhere. His first novel was published in 1984; since 1988 he has been writing full-time, and his latest novel is *Dies the Fire*. His interests include the martial arts, history, anthropology, archaeology, and cooking.

Jan was born and raised in Massachusetts, never expecting to live anywhere else. Then she married S. M. Stirling in 1988 and moved to Canada. From there they moved to New Mexico, where they now live with their two cats. She also never thought of writing until she married Steve. But, she says, there's something about being around writers and computers. After two rather humbling years of trying, her first story was published in a Chicks in Chainmail anthology and her stories have been published in several anthologies since.

ELI AND THE DYBBUK

Janis Ian

IT WAS GETTING ON toward midafternoon of the eve of the Sabbath when Eli met the dybbuk.

The dreamy-eyed son of Mordechai and Ruth was walking along the edge of the Tsar's forest, searching for stray bits of wood his mother could use to build the fire up before sundown, for after sundown all work would be forbidden until darkness fell again. Although why keeping warm was work, Eli did not understand as yet, for he'd only studied Torah a few years now. He kept a careful eye on the sun as he calculated the remaining daylight hours. It wouldn't do to be late.

He had an armload of wood already, wood the Tsar allowed villagers to glean, and if he could just find a few more pieces, he could run home well ahead of sunset. Perhaps there'd be enough time to play with the soldiers' horses before his mother called him to dinner.

In accordance with Jewish law, Eli had become a man just a little over a year ago, when he'd turned thirteen and been bar mitzvahed. His parents were already talking about marriage, his mother dreaming of a girl whose parents would be wealthy enough to support the newly wedded couple while Eli stayed in the shul and studied. She dreamed he would become a great, learned man.

The trouble was, Eli didn't *feel* like a man. He felt like an impersonator, a child dressed up in a man's body. Years of running up and down the hills had made his legs sinewy and strong; chopping and stacking wood had left his arms muscled enough to win pretty consistently when the boys wrestled. But his face was another matter; he had a high, narrow forehead and the watery eyes of a scholar-in-the-making. And it was difficult enough being fourteen without feeling like his face and his body belonged to two separate people!

He loved to feel the wind as he pushed it aside when he ran through the hills. He loved to wrestle; in fact, when the great strongman Zishe Breitbart had passed through the *shtetl*, Eli had been thrilled to be chosen as the one who held the great athlete's iron bars before he bent them. But he also loved to read, stories of heroes mostly—David facing Goliath, Judah Maccabee smiting the Roman legionaries. He daydreamed constantly; his ears were bruised with the verbal blows of his mother raining down upon them. *Eli, are you dreaming again while there's no water in the house?! Eli, where were you that you didn't hear me telling you to pick up the challah for Shabbes?!* Dreaming, of course. Dreaming of riding a huge stallion into his village, his chest covered with medals, his hand resting easily on the hilt of a gleaming sword. Dreaming of saving princesses, kingdoms, whole continents. He loved to dream, and nowhere in those dreams did he see himself married. It was easier to dream of joining the Tsar's army than to see himself with a wife and children!

Much to Eli's dismay, his parents went by the chronological seasons, not the seasons of the heart. They had already consulted the *shadchen* about brokering a possible marriage between himself and Leah, the girl next door. Since she was the only female close to his age for miles around, the arrangements had gone smoothly—except for Eli's part in them.

He mused on the problem as he walked, trying to approach it Talmudically. In the Talmud was stored all the great wisdom of the Jewish people. The rabbis would approach a question with another question. *They wish me to marry Leah,* Eli thought. *Well, what is the problem with Leah?* He considered it for a moment, and decided that there was only one small problem. On second thought, there were two. First, she wanted to marry a scholar, and scholars didn't ride off on white horses to save the universe. Second, Leah was not beautiful, and although Eli was ashamed that it mattered at all to him (for didn't the rabbi advise that one should seek a virtuous, obedient wife, and nowhere in the Talmud was there any mention of seeking a gorgeous one), he found himself wishing she looked just a bit less . . . Jewish. More like the girlfriends and wives of the soldiers he'd befriended: blond and big. Instead, Leah was dark-haired and small, so small that he wondered if her children would be healthy.

In every other respect, she was clever enough. She could already make latkes and blintzes that smelled good all through the house, and she sewed beautifully. But she seemed to have no other interests that he could see, and for Eli, who dreamed of sitting astride a giant stallion in a handsome uniform, the thought of marriage to a girl whose dreams began with latkes and ended with blintzes was too horrifying to contemplate.

So contrary to all tradition, when his parents told him he was betrothed to Leah, with the girl and her parents looking on, he'd stared stubbornly at the ground and refused.

"Why?!" his father had thundered after Leah and her parents had left. "Why?!" his mother had wept the next morning. But he could not explain that it didn't matter because in two more years he was planning to run away and join the army, so he refused to speak. Since that night, both sets of parents had continued to try to convince him, even spending every Sabbath meal together, but to no avail. His mind was made up.

Now, when he passed Leah on the path, she no longer smiled at him, but averted her eyes and hurried away. He was sorry for that, because she was a nice enough girl, but it couldn't be helped. One day he'd come back triumphant, with a saddle trimmed in gold and silver, and they would all forgive him. Of that he was certain. And he wouldn't need a wife then; he'd have his brother soldiers for company.

Of course, he'd neglected to mention this part of the plan to his parents, who loathed and feared the army as they feared the Cossacks, and all that went with them. Eli had heard stories of terrible pogroms in other towns, soldiers who thought nothing of impaling a baby on the tip of a sword and galloping around the village, waving it like a trophy. He found that hard to believe. The Cossacks of his town had always smiled at him as they cantered by. Some even knew him by name. Occasionally they'd let him help with the horses, though he only did this when his parents couldn't find out. He'd have to rush home afterward and clean the muck off his shoes, for he'd been forbidden to ever go near them. But he told himself that he was practicing for his future, and the soldiers seemed to like him. Eli was positive that as soon as he was old enough, they'd welcome him into their ranks like a long-lost brother.

It was in this manner, dawdling and daydreaming, that Eli bumped into Leah and knocked her down. He was walking fast to beat the sun, his eyes half-closed to better see the stallions in his future, when he collided with her back.

"Oof!" she exclaimed, falling facedown into the dirt.

Oh, no! thought Eli. *She'll think I did it on purpose!* Appalled, he rushed forward to help her rise.

"Are you all right, Leah?" he asked anxiously, peering into her face. Marriage or no marriage, they'd grown up together, and he genuinely cared for her.

Leah looked down at her wrinkled blouse and made smoothing motions with her hands, then slowly raised her eyes to meet his.

"Of course I am," she purred, arching her neck coyly. "My, Eli, what a big, strong man you've become!"

Eli stared at her in confusion. The Leah he knew would never speak to him in that manner! Leah was always shy in his presence, even more so these past few years. Though she clapped when he wrestled, she did the same for every other boy in the village. He searched her forehead to see if she'd bumped it badly, but there was no sign of a bruise.

"What's the matter, honey, cat got your tongue?" she purred. "I can get it back for you . . ." She smiled then, running her tongue along the edge of her lips, and moved forward to place her mouth on his.

Eli was so startled that he took a step back and fell right onto the ground. There he sat, in a most undignified position, stupidly staring at the girl next door who'd somehow become the woman from a bad section of town! Was she playing games with him now? The thought enraged him.

"I don't know why you're doing this, Leah, but it's not going to make any difference! I won't marry you," he said with finality.

Leah put her hands on her waist, tilted her head back, and roared with laughter. It was not the laughter of a young girl, though, but the rich, throaty laughter of a woman of the world.

"Marry! Who said anything about marriage?!" she chortled. "All I'm talking about is a little fun!" And with that, she sat right down in the dirt beside him and began to unbraid her hair.

Now Eli was truly horrified. Unmarried women did not unbraid their hair! Even married women only did that in the privacy of their homes, where only their husbands could see. Even the *goyishe* women, the non-Jews, kept their hair bound. Leah was behaving like the basest of women—what on earth was going on here? He began to rise, but she made a chopping motion with her hand.

"Stop right there," she said in an imperious tone. He stared at her, wondering what had come over the timid girl he'd thought he knew so well.

She pinned him with her eyes, and he was suddenly unable to move. He tried to rise, to run for help, but his limbs would not obey. Instead, he sat like a lump of clay, unable to do anything but breathe.

When her hair was down and hanging loosely over her shoulders, she slowly began to unbutton her blouse. Eli had never been so mortified in all his life. What would her parents think? What would *his* parents think?! It was beyond belief.

He made a small, strangled sound, and she grinned lasciviously. Abruptly, his limbs and his tongue were freed. Panting with relief, Eli jumped to his feet and backed away from her, but Leah rose and calmly walked toward him, still unbuttoning the blouse.

"Leah, Leah, stop! What is it, what's going on? You're not behaving at all like yourself—I'm going to get your parents right now!" Eli threatened.

She stopped and looked at him with a sneer, her features contorted, mouth twisted into a grimace of hate. "Parents?" she spat. "What parents? Those two pious lumps of lard in that dirt-floored hut back there? Those aren't my parents! My parents are long gone, and serves them right!" Then she laughed, a long, maniacal laugh.

The laughter suddenly stopped, and he seemed to hear another voice entirely come from her mouth, one that sounded a bit like the old Leah. "Help! Help!" it cried, and he didn't know what to do, because right away her upper teeth came down on her lip, drawing blood, and her mouth twisted back into a sneer. The change was terrifying to see.

Noticing his shocked expression, Leah composed her face, and for a moment Eli thought it had all been a trick of the sun—the cruel mouth, the furious eyes and narrowed lips. But then she shook her hips at him, darting her tongue out in the air, and the movement was so not Leah that for a moment he felt faint. She kept coming toward him, though, and now survival became paramount. His brain snapped back into gear with an awful clarity as it slowly assembled, then reassembled, all he'd just seen.

This was not Leah! This could not be Leah! Therefore it must be . . .

The thought was too horrible to contemplate. But contemplate it he must, because there it was in front of him. He was a man. He had to stand his ground.

He stopped trying to get away then and turned to confront her, trembling with a fear greater than anything he'd ever known.

"You're not Leah, are you?" he whispered.

She tossed her head, and the unbound hair seemed to have a life of its own as it settled around her face. "Don't be silly, Eli, you've known me all your life. Of course I'm Leah!"

"No," he stammered, "no, you're not. You're not Leah. You're not even human. . . . I know what you are."

She stopped moving forward then and rebuttoned the blouse. "Oh? And what exactly am I, then?" she asked, looking down at her fingers as they worked the buttons. "Exactly *what* do you think I am?"

Her tone, at that moment, was more threatening to him than her exposed bodice had been, and Eli took a step backward in terror. But then he remembered that one day he'd be a soldier and soldiers were brave, even in the face of supernatural danger.

"You're a dybbuk!" he spat with all the force he could muster. There, he'd said it.

"A dybbuk?" She laughed, smoothing her hair back into place. "You foolish little boy, you don't even know what a dybbuk is!"

That was it. The real Leah would never have made fun of him like that. She was the gentlest of souls. This had to be a dybbuk. He tried frantically to remember what he'd read about them. Dybbuks were dead souls who'd been too evil in this life to enter heaven. Instead, they wandered the earth until they could find another body to inhabit. A fierce war would take place between the evil soul and the body's rightful owner as each fought for possession. That would explain why she'd bitten through her lip when the real Leah tried to call for help.

Sometimes, he remembered, a dybbuk could be exorcised, but only by a rabbi skilled and experienced in such things. Their little *shtetl* had no one like that. He took a deep breath and studied her face. Leah's appearance, while not beautiful, was kind and gentle. This face had no softness in it. The thought of Leah and this . . . *thing* . . . fighting for Leah's body made him sick to his stomach.

She seemed to sense his thoughts. "So," she sneered, "you would rush back to town, alert the entire village, have me caught and caged like a wild animal?" She began to advance again, her arm upraised to strike him, but she suddenly stopped as her entire body began to tremble and twitch. She moved like a drunken marionette, lurching forward, then jumping back, her arms flailing, until looking out at him from frightened eyes was Leah, the real Leah. As he rushed toward her, he heard her cry out, "Eli! Eli! For pity's sake, help me! Help—"

One of her hands reached up with a jerking movement and covered her mouth, and the eyes changed back to another's, filled with rage and cunning. In one convulsive movement she tore open her bodice, exposing her breasts. Eli hastily looked away and began to pray.

"There, little *pisher*—go and rouse the village now! Bring them back here—bring them all! This is what they'll find— poor Leah, ravished by the boy who refused to marry her, used and then cast aside!" She laughed triumphantly.

Eli looked at her in dismay, and she moved toward him like a snake, rhythmically swaying her shoulders and hips. Her eyes glistened in the setting sun.

"Come on, honey, it's better this way. She was a boring child, such a do-gooder! Nothing but blintzes and challah all day long, and 'Mother, can I help with the soup? Father, can I get you your slippers?' What a bore she was! Oh, I promise you'll like it better with me! A little kiss, a little fun—no one will ever know." Again she pinned him with her eyes, and again he could not move. He continued to silently pray for someone, anyone, to rescue him from this demon. Surely God in His heaven would answer somehow!

There was the sudden clatter of horse's hoofs, and with a sigh of relief Eli saw his friend, the soldier Yevgeny, trotting up the path. Leah turned to look, and Eli, now free again, began running toward the horse, his arms waving frantically, shouting at the man to stop. Leah ran after him, beginning to loudly cry and wail.

"Yevgeny, help, she's mad!" Eli shouted. "Completely mad! I tell you, she's possessed by a demon!" Heaving and panting, he stopped beside the horse, with Leah not far behind.

"What's this, young Eli?" asked the soldier, noting the disheveled Leah and Eli's ashen pallor. "What's all this? I thought you people didn't go in for this sort of fun!" He smirked as Eli babbled loudly over Leah's wails.

"A demon, a demon has possessed her! You must help me!" he cried.

"A demon?" The soldier snickered. "Nonsense! You people have too many superstitions, boy. Just out for some fun, eh? And now that you've been seen, you have to make up some excuse, is that it?" He laughed again, then fixed his eyes firmly on Leah's bosom.

Eli stopped talking and looked up at the tall soldier on his fine horse, the man he'd so often admired. Yevgeny smiled at Leah, now silent, then said, "Come here, girl, let's have a look at you."

Leah slowly walked toward him, hips swaying, lips parted. He leered at her in return. "What's a pretty girl like you doing with a child like him?" Yevgeny asked, making a contemptuous motion toward Eli. "You should taste a real man, instead of wasting your time on this baby."

Eli couldn't believe it—a baby?! He was a man in every sense of the word, legally and physically. He was ready for marriage, and this idiot called him a baby? No, not an idiot. Yevgeny had been good to him, had always given him sweets and allowed him to feed and water the horses. Yevgeny just had no idea what was really happening. Eli wanted to protect him, to save him from the dybbuk, so he grabbed the soldier's arm and tugged at it to make Yevgeny listen. Instead, Yevgeny reached over with the other arm and dealt him a casual back-handed blow that landed Eli in the dust. The soldier looked at him sternly.

"Look, boy, I've let you play with the horses, but make no mistake—you're a Jew, and I'm a soldier in the Tsar's army. So when I say 'Quiet!' *you* shut up, and when I want a woman, *you* bring her to me on a silver platter. Or else, make no mistake, I'll thrash you within an inch of your miserable life!"

Eli couldn't help it; despite his being a man, hot tears rose to his eyes. First Leah, now this. Yevgeny no longer looked so fine on his big stallion. Taking a closer look, Eli saw that the cuffs of the uniform were frayed and the horse hadn't been properly curried, and suddenly Yevgeny looked only like a middle-aged man pretending to be brave and young.

Leah had said nothing during this exchange, but now she walked up to the soldier and began caressing his thigh. Her fingers moved higher, and the soldier's breath quickened.

When he moved to dismount, though, she abruptly sank her teeth into his leg and held on until he managed to knock her away.

"Aarrgh!" he roared as the horse reared back to attack. "You—you—you crazy Jewess!" He looked over at Eli and drew his sword, yelling, "Crazy! She's mad! You were right, boy!!"

Eli saw with horror that Yevgeny was ready to kill her, so he rushed toward Leah and knocked her down just as the sword whistled past her head. He sat on her so she could not move, babbling, "Please, sir, please; she's mad, it's true; she doesn't know what she's doing. I'll take her home right now, sir, her mother will know what to do with her. Just a child, sir, a poor unfortunate child; she'll not bother you again, I promise!"

The soldier paused, looked down at the tear in his pants leg, then at Eli sitting in the dirt, yarmulke askew, covered in dust and perspiration. He began to laugh. "Bitten by a crazy Jewess whose brave defender is a boy barely out of diapers! I guess this'll be a good one for the barracks." He drew himself up on the horse and sheathed his sword. "All right, boy, but keep her in the village, hear? One more misstep and she's dead!" With that, the horse turned and cantered away.

"Get off me, you great lump!" Leah hissed, twisting suddenly and throwing Eli off her back.

"What?! I just saved your life, you little fool!" Eli was getting angry now, the humiliation and fear eating at him, making him angry enough to forget that this woman was a malicious soul of great power.

"Hmph!" she snorted, tossing her hair at him. "I didn't need your help. I was handling the situation."

Eli looked at her in wonderment. "Handling the situation" indeed! She'd almost gotten herself killed, that was all. This dybbuk had the ego of a princess—she thought she knew everything!

Thought she knew everything . . . Suddenly, an idea came to him. The important thing was not to look scared. If he could be brave, maybe it would work. Thinking of Daniel facing the lions' den, Eli slowly rose to his feet and offered the dybbuk his hand. She looked at him suspiciously, but took it and rose, facing him.

"Look," said Eli with a trace of impatience, "I don't know where you come from—maybe a big city like Kiev—but things just aren't the same here. You don't know what you're doing. You don't know how to behave. You're going to give yourself away in five seconds once you get back to the village."

The dybbuk looked at him, surprise and annoyance on her face. "Don't know what I'm doing?! Why, I've traveled all over this country! I've had coaches, and footmen, and jewelry so fine you'd have to close your eyes to keep from being blinded! And I'll have you know that I'm smart, very smart, probably the smartest person you'll ever meet!"

Eli looked at her skeptically, then shrugged his shoulders. "Suit yourself. But things are different here, I can tell you that much. Without a guide, you'll be lost."

Intrigued, she searched his face. "And why, proud boy, are you willing to help me so suddenly?" asked the dybbuk. Then she looked down at her bodice and smirked. She gestured toward it with a satisfied smile. "Decided it was worth it, hmm?"

Eli fought down nausea and shrugged again. "Didn't say I was willing to help you. Just said you'd give yourself away."

Fire flared in her eyes. "Not if you'd show me what to do," she argued.

"And what do I get out of it?" he asked.

"Why, you stupid little boy—you get *me*!" She grinned, baring her lips and clenching her teeth as poor Leah tried to break through again with a moan.

Eli ignored the struggle and laughed. "You? Remember what the soldier said—I'm too young to know what to do with a woman as accomplished as you!" he told her.

Pleased at the compliment, the dybbuk smiled prettily and said, "Then what do you want?"

He cast his eyes downward, trying to look embarrassed, and shuffled his feet like a little boy. "Um . . . I . . . er . . ."

She smiled at him, a genuine smile, the smile of a cat who's finally cornered her mouse. "Come, speak up!" she said. "I'll strike a bargain with you, for I love a good game!"

Eli frowned. "How do I know I can trust you?" he challenged.

For one fleeting instant, the dybbuk actually looked pious as she gazed heavenward and said, "The Lord our God watches over everyone, as I learned to my eternal sorrow. Once I was like you, like her, but it wasn't good enough for me. I stole and I cheated, and I left my family and never looked back. My punishment is eternal, and the rules of it are stricter than any parent could impose. Though I inhabit another's body, I may not control her heart. What that heart would never do, I cannot force it to do. It would never break a promise; therefore, I cannot. We, too, are bound by certain laws."

Eli was intrigued. "And what happens if you try to break a promise?" he asked the dybbuk.

She grimaced, then said, "A fate even more terrible than this one. My name will be stricken from the Book of Life, and no one on this earth will remember me. It will be as though I never had been."

Eli thought that over; it sounded like a good enough idea to him, though he supposed the dybbuk wouldn't like it. "So once we strike a bargain, you have to keep it—or else?"

She nodded, then said with a leer, "But I'm a lot older than you, my boy. A lot. I can remember before your great-great-grandparents were born. The chance of your being able to put one over on me is slim. However . . ." She paused, thinking. "However, I was always a gambler. So here is my offer. You may ask me one question—only one, mind you! It must be something a human can answer. And if I don't answer correctly, I'll do everything in my power to grant your desire, and you will be free of me forever."

Eli turned away, pretending to be deep in thought while hiding his exultation. She'd taken the bait! He grinned foolishly to himself, and acted as though he were thinking it over for a few minutes. Then he turned back to the dybbuk with a sigh and said, "All right. It's a bargain."

They shook hands on it, and the dybbuk waited expectantly.

"Here is my question for you," said Eli, pausing dramatically. "It is this: *What is it that everything has?*"

Then he sat down to wait. The riddle had been told to him years ago by his great-grandmother; he was pretty certain it hadn't been repeated in the village since her death, but one never knew. He tried to calm his anxiety as he waited for her response.

"How many answers can I try?" asked the dybbuk, deep in thought.

Eli was startled; she was still trying to cheat! "Only one, of course!"

"Of course . . . ," she said dryly, and closed her eyes to ponder the question.

They sat that way for a long time as the shadows lengthened and Shabbes drew closer. For a moment, Eli worried about being out after dark; then he silently laughed at himself. Here he was, facing down a dybbuk, and all he could think of was that?!

Finally he saw her eyes flicker open, and she smiled, a bitter, malevolent, victorious smile.

"Oh, you silly boy! You thought that because I was a woman, I wouldn't be able to guess it, didn't you? Now, confess!"

Eli honestly said no, because he had never thought of the dybbuk as female, only as evil.

"Well, now I've guessed it, and you shall be my guide and protector for all your life!" she said smugly.

Eli was beginning to get annoyed. It was almost sunset. The candles would be on the table soon, and he was getting very hungry. "Then, if you're so smart, what's the answer?"

She laughed, clapped her hands, rose to her feet, and said, "Why, it's a soul, of course!"

And Eli, too, slowly rose to his feet, clapped his hands, gave a little bow, and then said, "No, it's not. That's the wrong answer."

The laughter died on her lips and she glared at him, her face turning red. "It is *so* the right answer!" she shouted.

"It is *not*!" Eli shouted back. "I said, 'What is it that *everything* has?' A rock has no soul. A grain of sand has no soul. That is *not* the correct answer."

And then he smiled, a terrible smile of righteous joy, as she slowly sank back onto the ground.

He looked down at her, no longer afraid. "And now I will have your end of the bargain, dybbuk," Eli said.

She looked at him warily. "What is it you want? I can

make you as rich as a Rothschild. I can make you as handsome as the handsomest prince. What do you want?" she asked.

He paused, arms at his sides, then simply said, "I want Leah back."

The dybbuk scrambled to her feet, grimaced at him, and angrily said "No!" Then she began running, running away from him as fast as she could, screaming "No! No! No!" And Eli, desperate to make her fulfill her end of the bargain, raced after her, but he could not catch her. She ran and ran, and he stumbled after her, but the dybbuk was running with the speed of a demon, while Eli was only human. He was panting and winded, about to give up, when there was an enormous clap of thunder, as though heaven itself had parted. Eli smacked his hands against his ears in pain, then froze as the dybbuk fell to the ground, where she lay as if dead.

He looked up at the sky; there was not a cloud in sight. Then he looked at the dybbuk, lying like a corpse. Slowly he approached the body, and standing as far away as possible, he turned it over.

Leah gave a small moan, and her eyelids fluttered open. Eli cautiously moved forward. He saw with joy that there was no sneer on her lips, no cunning in her face now. He helped her sit up, then held her as she wept against his shoulder, smelling her clean hair and marveling at the softness of her tears as they fell upon his skin. When the tears had run dry, he stood and helped her up. He looked into her eyes, and each began to speak at once.

"I'll never be a soldier or want a sword again—" Eli began.

"I never saw anything so brave in all my life as when you—" Leah said.

They looked at one another, startled, then tried again.

"Leah, I am so sorry for—" he said.

"Eli, I can't tell you how sorry I—" she said.

They stopped again, then both began to laugh. Leah put her arm through his and shyly whispered, "I saw everything, Eli. Everything! You were so brave, braver than any soldier could be! Weren't you afraid?"

Eli was about to say he hadn't been afraid, not for an instant, but he blushed at the thought of lying to her, who'd already been through so much that day. Instead, he pulled her close and whispered, "Leah, I was terrified . . . but I couldn't let her have you."

They went back to the path, and Eli gathered up his wood. Then, with her arm through his, they walked toward the little village, Leah braiding her hair and straightening her clothing as best she could. And the farther they walked, the further the details slipped from their minds, until Eli looked at Leah's tousled hair and dusty blouse and said, "Wow. That must have been quite a fall you took!"

And Leah looked at Eli's unkempt yarmulke and dusty shoes and said, "It must have been! I hit my head so hard I barely remember a thing! I don't know what I would have done if you hadn't come along."

And in that manner they entered Eli's home, where both sets of parents waited with anxious expressions. Seeing them, Leah's mother jumped up with a start, exclaiming over her daughter's appearance. "What, did you fall? Whatever happened here? Are you all right?"

"Yes, Mother, I'm all right," Leah replied, watching Eli place the wood in the tiny hearth. "I fell, so badly I can't remember a thing, but Eli found me and saved me."

Eli's mother looked at him in consternation, taking in

his torn pants and dirty shoes. "A fine thing, out there romping around like a hooligan, probably playing soldier with those filthy Cossacks again while we wait and worry. A fine thing indeed, Eli!"

Eli opened his mouth to protest, but his mother continued, now looking at Leah.

"And you, young lady! Running around like a boy, of all things. Look at your hair, look at your blouse! What will the neighbors say? You couldn't at least stop at your home to change?"

Leah prepared to explain—although she really had no explanation—but before she could say a word, Eli placed his finger over her lips to silence her. Slowly he took her hands in his. He led her to his mother, then said, "Mama. That's no way to speak to my future wife, is it? Come, let us share the Sabbath meal, and you can begin planning the wedding."

And the parents, not understanding what had provoked this sudden turnabout, could only weep with joy as they welcomed the young couple to the Sabbath table.

That is how, in one short afternoon, young Eli left his dreams of soldiering behind and became a true man.

Years later, walking with his firstborn son, Eli tried to explain why some men were soldiers and others scholars. "You see, my son, sometimes to *know* is a more powerful tool than to *do*. For those who *do* are forever bound by their actions, and those they act upon are bound as well. Whereas those who *know* can be more flexible, for knowledge occupies no space and knows no limits."

He could see that his son was losing interest, and thought perhaps this was all a bit abstract for a child who hadn't even reached puberty. He wondered how to regain the boy's attention. As they walked, Eli suddenly had a vague memory of a riddle he'd asked someone years ago. He slowed his steps, trying to recall the exact puzzle.

When it came to him, he smiled at the boy and said, "Joachim, here is a riddle for you. If you answer correctly, I will give you a sweet tonight after dinner. Listen. What is it that everything has?"

The child thought for a long moment, then lit up with anticipation of the sweet. "Oh, Papa, of course, the answer is 'A name'! Because if it doesn't have a name, how can we know it exists?"

And Eli laughed aloud and lifted the boy to his shoulders, and together they ran home to Leah, who did not know the answer to the riddle and did not need to know. For so long as there were Elis and Joachims in this world she would be forever safe, and no darkness would inhabit her soul.

JANIS IAN

JANIS IAN is normally a singer-songwriter, with two Grammy Awards, nine Grammy nominations, and twenty-two albums to her credit. She published her first song at twelve, made her first record at fourteen, and released a book of poetry (since reissued) at sixteen. Her father and grandmother were wonderful storytellers, and she grew up on the tales of Sholem Aleichem and her family's own stories of life in the *shtetl*. When not singing or writing songs, Janis reads, mostly science fiction and young adult books. Her two favorite books in the world are Madeleine L'Engle's *A Wrinkle in Time* and Orson Scott Card's *Ender's Game*, probably because they both feature young heroes, both male and female. Janis writes: "I love the idea of women as warriors, since my generation didn't really have them available as mentors."

Janis began writing prose stories two years ago; this will be her eighth published story. For more information, go to www.janisian.com.

HEARTLESS

Holly Black

O Moon! old boughs lisp forth a holier din
The while they feel thine airy fellowship.
Thou dost bless every where, with silver lip
Kissing dead things to life.
    —*John Keats, from* Endymion

ACROSS THE LANDSCAPE of the battlefield, men stared sight-
lessly into the sky, their armor black with blood, their steam-
ing intestines spread over the ground. Swarms of crows
covered them in a jumping, fluttering carpet. Camp women
scavenged among the corpses, cutting the throats of the dying
and looting the bodies for anything of worth.

Ada bent close to one man, his mouth already darkened
like a bruise on his pallid face. For a dizzying moment her
sight narrowed until all she could see was a gore-clotted eye-
lash, a stitch of livery, the twist of a pale worm. She gagged,
but a second quick breath steadied her. Ada was surprised the
stench could still make her choke. It reminded her that she

hadn't always been a camp follower; her hair hadn't always hung in knots and the hem of her dress hadn't always been stiff with filth. It reminded her of things better forgotten.

The army's food had already been cooked and distributed—boiled horseflesh, cabbages, onions, and what dried stores the Baron's men had managed to frighten out of the local churls. The camp women had a few hours before they must return to the fire pits, to scour the pots and begin planning for tomorrow. Ada had to move quickly if she wanted her share of what was left on the field.

The dead man had a good set of spurs, new-looking, with bronze details. She stripped them off his sabbatons and tied them up in her skirts.

The next man she squatted near was still breathing. His brow was sweaty, and his eyes moved feverishly under closed lids. She held her knife near his throat. She had been warned never to leave a man alive while you robbed him: he might wake at any time, and even a wounded soldier was danger- ous. Still, she hesitated. No matter how many times she told herself that it was like killing a sow, it still wasn't. Maybe it was the memory of compassion that nagged at her, the remembrance of what she had been before she'd bespelled her heart into her finger bone.

"Help me." The soldier's mouth began to move before his eyes opened. He spoke in a dreamy monotone.

Ada jumped back, the blade just nicking the flesh of his throat.

"Help me," he repeated. He didn't seem to notice that he'd been cut.

"No," Ada said. She'd had enough of knights and their commands. She had to feed them, to bind their wounds and be bothered by them when she sought only sleep. Just because she hadn't killed him quickly didn't mean she owed him anything.

"I am Lord Julian Vrueldegost."

She wondered whether or not he had been one of the men who had burned her village. At one time, that would have mattered to her.

"I'll die," he said. "Please."

Ada sighed. "And if I help you, what? You'll go back to your hawks and greyhounds, your hunts and feasts, your feather beds and spiced wines. And what will I go back to?"

He looked confused. "The Count, my father—he would double the size of your land. Please. My side feels as if it is on fire."

"What land?" She wished that he would just go ahead and die so that she could get back to robbing him, but instead she dipped her finger into a nearby pool of blood and smeared it across his neck. She brought her face close to his. "Play dead, your lordship, and hope none of the other women find you. They are even less kind than I."

The part of her that would have been pleased by his pleading and his fear was long gone, and with it the part that might have pitied him. She reached for the grubby string around her neck and felt the smooth bone hanging there. Her mother had cut off the end of her finger once the spell was complete, but Ada could never bring herself to get rid of it. Her heart.

The wind picked up, whipping at her as she walked back to the encampment. She thought little of it until she noticed that the leaves on the nearby trees remained still. Then something tore at her skirts, ripping them enough so that the spurs dropped onto a carpet of oak leaves and acorns. A cawing started overhead as a mass of black birds circled and began to land around her.

"Stop it!" she called. Her knowledge of magic was poorer than her mother's, but even she could see this was the work of some spirit. "What are you? What do you want?"

Invisible hands grabbed hers, pulling her in the direction of the battlefield.

"Show yourself," she demanded, sitting down on the cold ground and ignoring the crows. "I'll not stir from this place."

A shape leaped down from the branches above her. It had the head of a raven, but its body had the thin limbs of a boy, dusted here and there with feathers. She had never seen a manes up so close. It must belong to Lord Julian. Only a nobleman could afford the conjuring that trapped an ancestor into the shifting flesh of a spirit. Manes drank blood from their charges, she knew that much. She had heard that great ladies would sit at tournaments with their manes suckling voluptuously at their wrists.

"Hedge-witch," it said, coming closer on all fours and regarding her with unblinking eyes.

"Hedge-witch no more," Ada said. Without her heart, she couldn't cast even the simplest of spells. There were other, darker enchantments that *required* a bespelled heart, but she didn't know any of those.

The manes pointed to the bone around her neck. "I know what that is. You should hide it. One snap and your life is undone."

Ada touched the string reflexively. "I don't want to lose it," she said.

It turned its head quizzically and regarded her with black eyes. "Help my master and I will tell you a place you can hide it where it will be safe always."

When dealing with spirits, her mother had told her, it was usually easier to acquiesce. Ada picked up the spurs and began to tie them up in the remains of her dress. She made a mental list of what she would need for Julian: a blanket, some water, bindings for his legs, honey to slather over his wounds. Those things were easy to come by, especially with so many men dead.

When Ada returned to the battlefield laden with supplies, she found a crone hunched over Lord Julian, stripping off his gauntlets with knobbed fingers.

The woman looked up and Ada recognized her from the camp—Clarisse. People said she'd once been very beautiful. Despite the fact that she was bent with age, she still tied filthy ribbons in her hair and tinted her cheeks with the juice of berries, or sometimes with blood.

"What is this here? A lovely turquoise ring."

Ada narrowed her eyes. "That's a *signet*. If anyone sees you with it, they'll know it was stolen."

"Perhaps they'll mistake me for a duchess." Clarisse cackled. Then she suddenly clutched her wrist and dropped the ring.

Puzzled, Ada bent closer. Long red marks had appeared on the old woman's forearm.

"You did it! You summoned spirits to attack me!" Clarisse pulled a crude knife from her belt.

"What?" Ada stepped back. Her own knife was close to hand, but she didn't want to drop the things she was carrying to get to it. She considered explaining about the manes and then decided that would make Clarisse more suspicious rather than less. "If I could summon spirits, I would put them to better use than scratching old women," Ada said finally.

Clarisse clapped her hand to her cheek as if she'd been struck. "You wretch! I'm not *old*." She stood up and then looked around her, at the field of the dead and dying, as if she didn't know how she'd come to be in such a place. "Take him if you want him so much. My other suitors give me plenty of gifts." She began to stagger off, rubbing her arm.

Ada knelt beside Julian and watched Clarisse go. She was so stunned that she almost forgot about the ring in the dirt. It was the blue of the stone that drew her eye. Gingerly, she picked it up. The gold was heavy in her hand. She smeared away mud to reveal a coat of arms with three ravens on it.

"I'm just holding on to it for him," she said aloud as she tucked it into the folds of the sash at her waist. Then she started stripping off his gilt-inlaid armor. The leather-and-cloth padding underneath was stained with sweat and blood.

He moaned as Ada tugged him onto the blanket. Pulling his body over the field made her muscles ache. By the time they reached the burned village, she was exhausted. He had barely stirred.

Even in the dying light, Ada easily found the way to her mother's old house. She tugged at the blackened hatch to the root cellar. It opened in a great gust of soot.

"That's the best I can do," she said. "I can't carry him down the stairs, and you don't want me throwing him down."

A sudden gust of air made cinders whirl across the floor. The manes appeared and scuttled closer, pressing its beak so close to the wound that she wondered if its tongue would snake out for a taste.

"Julian's people will come," it said. "The crows have brought my message. Just get him down there. You only need help a little while longer."

"As you say." Ada pressed lightly on the skin just to one side of Julian's injury, but it was enough to make him awaken with a gasp. The manes cawed loudly, and she wondered what would happen to it if Julian died.

The knight looked up at her, disoriented and afraid.

"Your creature wants me to hide you. Can you stand?"

He reached up and touched a stray lock of her hair, running it between his fingers as if he were spinning it into thread. "I don't know your name."

She narrowed her eyes, confused. "Ada," she said finally.

"Ada," he repeated. "You have hair like my sister's. Jeanne. She will be twelve soon."

"I'm fifteen," Ada said. "Now get up."

He managed a thin smile. She could see his hands tremble as he rose. Pressing her shoulder under his arm, she led him down the stairs. He moved slowly, like a sleepwalker. The earthen room still stank of fire, but otherwise it was unchanged from her memory of it. By the dim moonlight, she could see well enough to wash his wound with the water she brought and to smear it with honey. He tried to hold still, but sometimes he shuddered convulsively, or gasped.

"The gash doesn't stink yet," she said. "That's a good sign."

Julian moaned again, flushed with fever, moving restlessly into something like sleep.

"Maybe it would be better to be dead," Ada said to no one in particular.

It was fully dark when she stumbled back to the campsite. Most of the men were sleeping on their pallets of rushes, but a few still argued over dice beside dying fires. As Ada approached her own blankets, she saw that one of the Baron's men was waiting for her. Her eye was drawn to where his red beard was split by a scar that ran from his chin to his ear.

"You've cheated us out of a prisoner, is that correct?"

"No," Ada lied automatically. She'd seen a girl hanged for stealing a silver cup and did not want to join her.

He snorted. Without warning, he seized her sash and ripped it. Her knife tumbled out, along with a few copper coins and the knight's signet ring.

The man leaned down and picked up the ring from the dirt.

"I found it," she said hurriedly.

"That old hag said different." He shrugged. "Where is the owner of this ring?"

"Dead. Clarisse found it on him, but I scratched her and took it. She means to repay me with trouble."

He grabbed hold of her hair and pulled her close to him. She could smell the onions on his breath and the rot of his teeth. "His body isn't on the field. Do you know who this belongs to, slattern? You've hidden the Count's son. The Baron wants a corpse by dawn."

She had known as much, but somehow had failed to comprehend the import of it. After all, what would it matter if Julian were the King himself when even a common man-at-arms was so far above her?

"He's in a root cellar in the village." She was pleased, just then, that she didn't have a heart to trouble her.

The man let go of Ada's hair, and she fell to her knees. He rested the heel of his boot against her throat. She felt her pendant of bone pressing against her skin and knew that it could crack along with her neck. She would die. But still she could not really be afraid.

"He's alone?" the man demanded.

"Yes," she gasped.

He removed his foot and she gulped breaths of air.

"Get up," he said. "You'll be taking me to him."

Ada pushed herself to her feet and allowed him to lead her to his horse. The dappled gray courser was chewing on the rope that secured it to a post. She noticed that it had already been saddled and that the man had strapped a sword and a crossbow to the leather belts across its rump. It did not lift its white muzzle as she fitted her wooden shoe into one stirrup and hauled herself onto its back.

The man laughed as he untied the horse and then swung up behind her, pushing his body against her back lewdly.

"Through the battlefield," she said.

"Very well, then." One of his hands held the reins, but the other snaked around to cup her breast. She knew that should disturb her, but the voice that told her why seemed so distant.

"What did he promise you?" the man asked. "Gold? Riches? A tumble?"

"Nothing," she said, with a shake of her head.

"You're a cold one," he said. His fingers dug painfully into her breast, kneading it. She winced. "Or a bit simple.

"Or maybe I'm mistaken. Maybe you're one of the Count's women, a spy. What do you think I would make of that?"

She shook her head again, as though she *were* simple and didn't understand him. She considered what would happen when Julian was dead and she was alone in the house with the man-at-arms. Would he kill her? She imagined him heating up her mother's old fire-tongs to find out for himself if she was a spy. She imagined other things. And still she was numb to dread.

Did she really care for nothing, not even herself?

Ada noticed the lack of a heart in a way she had not

before. She pushed around her thoughts like a child pushing her tongue into the sore space left by a missing tooth.

"I know a cure for your silence," he said as they picked their way over the field of rotting bodies.

She looked down at the field of corpses, their faces turned to burnished silver in the moonlight. They were beyond caring too. Dead.

Ada remembered how, long before the war, she had cried over the death of a cat that had ranged around their corncribs. Yet with the finger bone dangling around her neck, she had buried her mother without a single tear. She could not even remember where she'd dug the grave.

Surely it was better not to feel. What was the purpose in courting pain?

But then she thought of all the different sorts of pain, all the ones she hadn't been able to avoid.

She imagined taking the finger bone off her neck and snapping it in two. Even though that would kill her, she could not bring herself to care. That troubled her. She knew she should care. She shouldn't stand by and allow her own death. She didn't want to be dead.

Her heart was still missing, so she wasn't afraid when she broke the string around her neck with a sharp tug. The method for undoing the spell was simple. She didn't even flinch as she swallowed the bone whole.

Pain stabbed her chest, a thousand sharp needles, as in a foot kept too long in one position. She pressed her hands between her breasts and felt a steady drumming. Tears burned in her eyes.

Then, abruptly, she was overwhelmed by fear, fear that bit through her flesh to bury itself in her marrow.

This was a mistake, she thought. *I can't do this.* She started to shake.

The man-at-arms tightened his grip on her and laughed.

She thought of Julian, of the way that he had touched her hair. She didn't want him to die. She didn't want anyone to die anymore.

"You know where we're going, don't you? You haven't lost your way?"

They had come to the edge of the village without her noticing. Looking out at the remains of the houses, black and indistinguishable, she knew what she had to do.

"He's in there," she said. Pointing to where a neighbor had once brewed ale and kept chickens, she found that she could hardly breathe. It was harder to lie now, when she was afraid.

"Is he armed?" The man-at-arms shifted on the saddle.

She shook her head. "He's badly hurt. Defenseless."

"Dismount," he ordered.

She climbed off the horse. He drew his sword and jumped down after her. Trailing him to the house, Ada hoped he would go in first, hoped he would give her a moment to get away from him.

He signaled with his chin for her to go through the door. Once inside, he would see that she had lied. She hesitated.

"Get in there," he whispered.

She had hoped for more of an advantage, but there was no more time. Ducking away from his arm, she ran back to the horse and pulled the crossbow from the horse's rump. The bow was drawn tight, but she fumbled getting the bolt in place.

A loud shout came from the doorway. The manes had

appeared, cawing and capering, surprising the man-at-arms into giving her another few moments of time. She slammed the bolt into the notch and pointed it in his direction.

His eyes went wide and his mouth curled into a sneer. "Don't be stupid."

"I want to live," she said, and shot him.

The bolt hit him just below the throat. His scream stuttered as blood stained the front of his leather doublet. He reached up a hand and staggered toward her. Then he fell heavily onto the dirt.

Tears burned her eyes, streaking her cheeks with lines of salt.

She didn't know how long she had been there when she noticed Lord Julian stood behind her. His fingers touched her shoulder as she turned. He still looked pale, but his fever seemed to have broken. She noticed for the first time that he was young and that he needed a haircut. "Thank you," he said softly.

She nodded. She wanted to say something—to tell him that she hadn't done it for him, to ask about his sister, or to say that she was glad that he was awake—but she didn't know how to say all of those things at once, so she was silent.

The manes settled near the man-at-arms and began to tear at his wound with its beak.

"It's hard to see so much death." Lord Julian looked off into the deep shadows. "Was he the first man you've killed?"

"No," she said. "He was the last."

Julian paused at that. After a moment, he spoke again. "Do you recall when I offered to double your land?"

"You said your father would double it."

He smiled. "But you refused me. Let me make you another offer. Anything. A position in the castle? A commission? Tell me what it is that you want."

She wanted her mother to be alive again, for the war to end, for everything to be as it had once been. She wanted to scream, to weep, to shout.

Ada laughed out loud even as tears stung her eyes. "Yes, that's it," she said, leaning back to look up at the stars. "That's exactly it. *I want.*"

HOLLY BLACK

HOLLY BLACK was born in a decrepit Victorian house in New Jersey. Her mother, a painter and doll-maker, fed her books on ghosts and fairies that formed much of her later perspective on the world. She also developed a fear of the dark. Nonetheless, Holly spent a happy childhood cooking up imaginary witches' brews with her younger sister and tending to the needs of her pet rats. Adolescence brought Dungeons & Dragons, punk rock, boys, and an unhealthy habit of reading books until 3 a.m. During these years, Holly wrote a lot of poetry, a play, and a very bad novel.

When she was a bit older, she wrote the suburban fantasy novel *Tithe: A Modern Faerie Tale,* which was named an ALA Best Book for Young Adults and a New York Public Library Book for the Teen Age. She is also the author of the *New York Times* bestselling serial The Spiderwick Chronicles, illustrated by Tony DiTerlizzi. Holly now lives in Amherst, Massachusetts, with her husband, Theo; a motley assortment of animals; and too many books.

Holly Black's Web site is www.blackholly.com.

LIONESS

Pamela F. Service

AMANITARI LET THE TEARS flow over her dark cheeks. They coursed down the three scars like floodwater along dry wadis. The tears did not sting. It had been over two years since the scarification ceremony that had made Tari a priestess of the lion god, Apedemek. The scars had long since healed. But her heart had not.

The princess still remembered her anger and bitterness when the queen, herself a renowned war leader, had chosen not to train her daughter as a warrior or to make her heir to the throne of Kush. Instead, Tari had been sent to the desert temple to meekly serve the god of war while her brother, Kinidad, had been the one trained to fight wars.

While Tari learned rituals, Kinidad and their mother, the queen, had led the armies of Kush northward to fight the Romans, the hated foreigners who had conquered Egypt and now threatened Kush. Gloriously they had beaten the Romans, burning forts and carrying off booty. All the while, Tari had been left safe and furious in the desert temple.

But soon her fury had turned to resolve. She would not remain a useless pampered princess. If Apedemek, the lion, was the god of war, then she, his priestess, would learn the arts of war. Instead of burning incense and chanting hymns, she made the priests teach her how to handle horse and chariot, how to wield spear and sword, and how to shoot bow and arrow with deadly accuracy. Tari practiced for hours, then took long excursions into the African desert, her only companion the temple's sacred lion cub, Naga. Tari had taken fierce joy in her warrior training and felt pride in serving the mighty Apedemek, shown on the temple walls as a muscular warrior with a lion's head and wielding two great swords.

Now, with the news from the palace, all that joy and pride had dissolved. The queen had summoned her back to the capital, to the gleaming city of Meroe on the Nile. But she was not called to fight at her brother's side. Kinidad, her cheerful, reckless brother, was dead, killed by the Romans. Tari was now heir, and her mother wanted her kept safe in the royal palace.

During the long chariot ride over the desert toward the lush river lands, Amanitari's tears dried in the scorching wind. Her grief and fury remained. She had envied her brother, but she'd also loved him deeply. When she reached the palace, she didn't even stop to wash but strode into the queen's room, the now full-grown lion Naga padding at her heels.

"Mother," she said without ceremony, "how can you think of keeping me here when I should be leading the next attack against the Romans?"

The queen dropped the papyrus scroll she was reading and fixed the princess with her one good eye. "I can think of it, daughter, because I must. You are now heir to the throne.

I have already lost one child to the insatiably greedy Romans. I will not risk another."

"You'd rather risk losing a kingdom? The Romans have already gobbled up most of the world. We've got to stop them here!"

The queen sighed and stepped toward the princess. Naga, crouching at his mistress's side, growled. As Tari placed a hand on the lion's tawny head, the queen laughed. "I see the god Apedemek does favor you, daughter."

"He does, and he favors Kush too. But he won't if we give up and don't fight with all we have!"

"Oh, little one," the queen sobbed, folding Tari to her breast, "I'll never stop fighting. I lost an eye fighting the desert dwellers who are forever nibbling our lands from the east. And now I've lost a son to the Romans, who would swallow us from the north. I would lose my own life gladly if it would keep us free of their empire. But I will not risk our last hope for a great ruler. Someone must survive to lead Kush through the dangers ahead."

With anger faded, the two sat sharing tears and talking about the years they had been apart, about Tari's training and the battles with the Romans. The forces of Kush had taken several key Egyptian border towns, and thinking their victory secure, the queen had returned south to Meroe, leaving Kinidad in charge of the border. But then the new Roman general, Petronius, swooped down with fresh troops and reversed all of Kush's gains, even burning the holy city of Napata. In that battle, Prince Kinidad had been killed.

"Surely you aren't letting that go unavenged," Tari protested.

"Of course not! Already new troops are assembling. We

must try again to turn aside this ravening crocodile before it devours all the Nile and glides unchecked deeper into Africa. But no, you will not be going with those troops. Our family has ruled Kush for over a thousand years, and one of us must survive so we may rule for many years more."

"But . . ."

"No. I will leave soon to rejoin the troops. I am old and expendable. But you, priestess of the warrior god and heir to Kush, will remain our hope in Meroe."

Tari knew better than to argue further with her mother, but was far from accepting her fate. That evening she and Naga paced back and forth on the flat roof of the palace. The courtiers and servants respected her privacy, or at least respected the presence of her lion companion.

From there she watched the moon rise over the bluff to the east. In eerie silence, it lit the royal pyramids like so many faceted jewels set in silvered sand. One of those pyramids was Kinidad's now, though not the grand one he would have had as king. Perhaps that one awaited her. She shivered. Naga rubbed against her, and she caressed his head.

Beyond those pyramids lay the desert; she could sense it even from here. The desert—abode of lions and home of the temple to Apedemek. No, she would not believe that her warrior training and lonely desert vigils were only so she could remain safe in this palace and at last lie under a ruler's pyramid.

She brushed a hand across her cheek. Her scars bound her to Apedemek, god of war, protector of Kush. And she would serve him.

The next day, Tari formed and discarded several plans until a familiar voice in the courtyard below drew her to a window. The sound of Netakamani giving orders to a soldier flooded her with memories. In her mind, Tari could once again see Netak with Kinidad and herself, playing war games in the royal gardens or among the date palms and flooded fields bordering the Nile. They had been happy then, and always victorious.

"Netak!" she called joyfully. "Don't go! We'll be right down!"

Moments later she burst out of a palace door and threw her arms around her cousin. He hugged her back, then looked doubtfully at Naga. "When you said 'we' just now, I was afraid you'd been betrothed to some pesky princeling. But I see your companion is far more formidable."

Tari punched his arm playfully. "I've always told you that if I married any pesky princeling, it would be you. But at the moment I am promised to the god Apedemek, and you see what a fine chaperon he sends me with."

"Indeed, I will stay on my best behavior. But I'm so glad to see you! Though I wish it were a happier occasion that brought us together."

She sobered. "You were with Kinidad when he was killed?"

Netak nodded. "That Roman jackal Petronius swept down on us at Pselchis, rejected our terms for peace, and kept driving us south. Your brother refused to return the statues we'd captured and dedicated as offerings to the gods. Petronius attacked and burned the great temple at Napata as if it were some worthless shed! Kinidad died defending it."

Tari could picture her stubborn brother doing that, the same way he'd never given up in any of their games. Pushing aside memories, she asked, "And you are reassembling forces to return north?"

"Meroe's blacksmiths have been filling barges with new

iron spears, swords, and arrows, and new battalions have been training for weeks. I'll be leaving at dawn with the first contingent. The queen will follow in a few days. We'll pick up more recruits, supplies, and horses from river towns along the way."

"At dawn? Good. Then we will go with you."

He looked at her blankly.

"Naga and I."

"Do you have the queen's permission?"

"Of course not. But then, Kinidad and I didn't have her permission to join most of your escapades before. Just think of it like that, as another game, only with much higher stakes."

"But it's not a game. It's deadly real, and you're the heir to the throne now."

"That's precisely why I must go and finish what my brother started. Besides, I am more than just the royal heir. I am a priestess of Apedemek. You don't want to defy the will of a god, do you?"

Netak looked down into Naga's large golden eyes and mouthful of gleaming teeth. He laughed nervously. "Certainly not a god with such persuasive representatives. But your mother is formidable too."

"She won't defy the god either, particularly if I don't give her a chance."

The next morning, the sounds of a departing army shattered the usual predawn stillness. Horses, donkeys, and even a few war elephants protested being loaded on barges while soldiers shouted excitedly, and armor and weapons clanged. Workers hoisted supplies on board, townspeople called farewells, and in the chaos, one princess disguised as an ordinary soldier slipped onto the barge commanded by a distinctly nervous Netak. The growling occupant of one crate was promised freedom of the deck as soon as the boat was safely under way.

The trip northward seemed agonizingly slow to Tari, though when she let herself relax she enjoyed watching the banks of the Nile sliding by. Slowly the green fields and date palms gave way to drier land where the desert reached the river and villages were fewer and poorer-looking. In places, sunbaked cliffs brooded over the river and sent angry arms into the water, churning it white. Then, forced to land, the crews of the barges carried cargo and boats around the rapids until the river calmed again.

Tari enjoyed the company of the other soldiers, and though her identity was no longer secret, they treated her as a comrade. But each evening, when they pulled ashore to camp in wild desert places, she felt drawn away from the campfire gatherings. On the chill dry winds, she heard the distant lonely cries of lions.

She could feel Apedemek out there as well, and she knew she must obey him. But for the first time, she felt afraid. Before, war had been a game to play with other children, or moves to practice with friendly teachers. Now, with every day, it became closer, more real. Lives ended in war. Her brother's had. Would hers? Would all her dreams of duty and glory prove as dry as sand blown over long-dead bones?

In those chill moments she would find Naga at her side, butting his head against her, moonlight gleaming in his golden eyes. Comforted, she would return to the others, but even as they sat and talked around the fire, the specter of fear and doubt lurked behind her like the cold desert night. Would she know what the god wanted of her when the time came?

During the days, life was too noisy and immediate for

such worries. Then, in the golden calm of one afternoon, they came to what had once been Kush's northern capital, the sacred city of Napata. The Romans had battered its grand houses into heaps of rubble, and the great temple now lay a gaping ruin. Its charred and fallen roof left massive pillars stretching uselessly to the sky like the carcass of a giant beast, ribs bare to the scouring desert wind.

Netak showed her where her brother had died. There, at the high altar, the army of Kush had offered their captured Roman statues to the gods, and there the vengeful Romans had seized those offerings and slaughtered the prince and his guards.

Tari knelt on the flagstones, now broken and stained with soot and blood. Raising her voice into chant, she publicly vowed that this outrage would be avenged. Then, when none but Naga was close enough to hear, she whispered, "Great Apedemek, if my life is indeed yours, give me your strength and your courage. I cannot do this on my own."

They proceeded north, passing villages the Romans had left in ruins, until General Harsiotef, commander of this forward contingent, ordered them to shore, where they joined with forces that had marched overland. Assembling on a bluff that held back the eastern desert from the narrow strip of fertile green land fringing the Nile, they finally looked down on their destination. Below them spread the town of Primis, an irregular jumble of mud-brick houses. Aside from a few scuttling figures and roving dogs, the town seemed deserted. The obvious reason for this lay to the north, in the alien and menacing new Roman fort.

"They say Petronius provisioned the fort well before he returned north to Alexandria," Netak said as he joined Tari at the bluff's edge. "That will make a siege difficult."

"It would be anyway," Tari commented, "since the Romans could probably slip supplies through on the river. But what are our general's plans?"

"The queen and the rest of the army should arrive in a few days. When they do, he plans to attack and push every last Roman into the Nile."

Tari shivered slightly at the thought of her mother's arrival. But though she would surely receive a royal scolding, it would probably be little more than that. It was too late for the queen to send her back to Meroe. Most of the troops by now knew that the heir was among them. They would expect her to stay and fight as her brother had. But it was that thought that most frightened her now.

Trained as a priestess and a warrior, she was prepared to fight. But she had never actually done so. She had killed animals in the hunt, but never another person. Could she? And could she evade their attempts to kill her?

She dragged her attention back to Netak as he talked on about battle plans and pointed to strategic features of the land. "But whatever happens," he was saying, "we'd better launch the attack soon, because our spies report that Petronius and more troops are already headed this way."

A week later, however, the Roman reinforcements had still not arrived, while the boats of the Queen of Kush and the rest of her army had. As Tari had hoped, frenzied battle preparations shielded her from most of the queen's wrath, though the princess did her best to make herself useful elsewhere.

Mostly she distributed weapons and equipped the horses, but she kept clear of the elephants because her constant companion, Naga, spooked them into near frenzy. Most of the horses shied from the lion as well, but finally Tari found a fiery gray stallion that seemed to feel himself the lion's equal, taking Naga's presence in his stride. Tari chose him as her mount.

At last came the cold dawn she'd been yearning for and dreading. The sun god had not yet risen above the eastern desert when the forces of Kush began assembling in battle formation. The feeling in her stomach was as cold as the morning air, but Tari let that cold rise to freeze her face into a mask of fierce joy. She resolved that if she had to die, she'd do so in a way to make Apedemek proud.

As she scanned the assembled troops, her own feeling of pride blossomed. The shields and armor of the Kushites were mostly leather, not the pounded metal of the Roman armor that gleamed on the soldiers in and around the fort below. But her people were fighting for their land, not for the greed of some emperor who lived across the sea.

Again she hefted her iron-tipped spear and tightened the scabbard that held her sword of finest steel specially made for royal warriors. Nervously she reached over her shoulder and checked the feathered arrows in her quiver. Then she smiled at Netak, mounted at her side. In that moment, the flame of excitement and even courage felt real.

The battle plan had been explained to her, but when the charge came, she quickly lost all sight of plan and order. Elephants, chariots, horses, and foot soldiers surged around her. At first the Romans seemed to move with impunity behind their shields, as if they were large, scaled monsters. But in places their formations broke, and yelling Kushite warriors poured through. Everything soon became screaming, blood-splattered chaos.

When her spear first found a Roman victim, Tari felt the

shock go through her, almost as if she were that soldier. But she raised her shaking voice and cried "For Kinidad!"

Her second Roman, a foot soldier, she brought down with her sword when he tried to slit open her horse's belly, and over him she screamed "For Apedemek!" Over the third, a mounted warrior who fell to her arrow, she called "For Kush!" These cries, taken up around her, mingled with shouts of anger and pain, with the screams of horses and the bellowing of elephants. Cries of terror rose too as enemies fell to the claws of the lion battling at her side.

Tari lost awareness of everything but the fever of battle and the bloody hacking rhythm of her sword. Time had no meaning and the battle had no form, but gradually it seemed they must be winning. The forces of Kush nearly surrounded the fort, and some seemed to have breached a wall.

Then, subtly, something changed, the way a fine day suddenly feels ominous with an approaching storm. At first she couldn't tell where the change had come from. Then she saw it. Over the edge of the desert flowed a fresh flood of Romans. Petronius and his reinforcements had been closer than reported.

The newcomers more than doubled the Roman troops and soon had the forces of Kush pinned between them and the river. The Kushites' once victorious advance became a rout as they hacked and scrambled, trying desperately to live long enough to retreat. As the sun finally dropped into the west, only a ragged remnant of Kush's grand army straggled back to their desert camp.

Tari was numbly surprised to find herself among them. Not daring to think beyond the present moment, she tended to a shallow spear-gash along Naga's side, then applied healing ointment to the sword wound on Netak's shoulder. The queen, she was relieved to hear, had survived as well. Most of the blood on herself, she found, was not her own.

That night the fires burning in Kush's camp were vastly outnumbered, not only by the myriad desert stars but also by the Roman campfires on the riverbank below. Being the heir and now a proven warrior, Tari attended the council of the queen and the Kushite commanders, though at first her main struggle was not to slide into an exhausted sleep.

"What saved us today," General Harsiotef was saying when Tari quietly joined the council, "was mostly the setting sun. If we engage the Romans tomorrow, we shall be destroyed as surely as a windstorm destroys a grass hut."

"But surely we cannot give up now," another general protested. "Kush has never assembled such a massive army."

"And we have never met such an army either—incredibly well armed, well disciplined, and well trained. It's clear how the Romans have conquered most of the world. You saw what their catapults did to our war elephants, and how their metal shields compared to our cowhide ones."

"Are you suggesting that we admit defeat?" an angry voice said, and Tari suddenly realized it was her own.

"I'm suggesting, Princess, that we admit reality. Tomorrow Petronius will ask to parley, because he'd rather negotiate a surrender from us now than needlessly lose any more men. And we could kill more of them if we chose to fight, but how many of us would survive if we did?"

The queen raised her voice now from where she sat silhouetted by the fire. "If we treat with the Romans from this position of weakness, there is little good we can hope to gain from any treaty. They will demand whatever they want and leave us only those lands they deem too much trouble to hold."

"So what, then, are you suggesting, Your Majesty?" General Harsiotef asked deferentially.

"I am suggesting we pray that the gods show us how to make all of our lands more trouble than they are worth to Rome. But if they do not do so before tomorrow's negotiations, then I suggest we agree to what we must and prepare for years more of slow, painful war."

The council broke up shortly afterward, no one happy with the queen's decision but no one offering a better one. Tari and Naga retreated to the rope-strung wooden cot set up for her under a spindly thorn tree. But she could not sleep. She had proved herself today a worthy warrior of Apedemek's, but what good had it done? She was priestess of the god of war, yet not only was the war lost, so too, it seemed, was the peace. The greedy Romans and their aloof, arrogant gods would swagger over their land, treating a civilization thousands of years old as if Kushites were uncouth barbarians.

What kind of warrior priestess was she if she let that happen unchallenged?

Before the idea could become solid enough to seem ridiculous, she slipped from under her blanket; quietly donned her kilt, tunic, and shawl; and, leaving her armor untouched, strapped on her sword. Beside her, Naga, despite the rigors of the day, radiated tense, fierce energy.

The Kushite guards let Tari pass when they recognized her and her companion, and soon the two were slipping like shadows through the day's gruesome battlefield toward the celebrating Roman camp. From her higher ground, Tari scanned the fort's buildings, the surrounding campfires, and the torchlit wharf area. She wasn't sure what she was looking for, but she prayed that Apedemek would let her know when she had found it.

It was the river wharf that drew her, and she veered that way. Fewer sentries were posted there than around the fort, and praying for her god's hunting stealth, she managed to evade them. A number of Roman boats were drawn up to the pilings, where crates and bales of supplies had been unloaded onto the dock. But some things were now being loaded onto boats as well. What, she wondered, could those be at an hour when every Roman should have been sleeping or drunkenly celebrating victory? She saw a tall cloaked man overseeing the loading, a man as pale and hawk-nosed as most Romans. She recognized him as the man Netak had pointed out to her— the hated Roman prefect governor, Petronius. Clearly he was taking great pains to ship some things away before tomorrow, when negotiating Kushites might see them.

Then torchlight gleamed off a patch of bronze where a bundle's wrapping gaped open, and Tari knew.

The statues. These were the statues of Roman gods and emperors that the Kushites had captured in last year's victories, the ones taken to the great temple as divine offerings. The statues Kinidad had died defending. Petronius was trying to spirit them away before the fact that the Romans were stealing them back could inflame the Kushites. But in that he would fail.

Tari crouched as low and tense as a hunting lion. Slowly she and Naga inched forward. Petronius, it was said, spoke Egyptian, and as an educated Kushite she did as well. But now he spoke to the workmen in his own barbarous language. Tari didn't need a translator to understand his orders to unwrap the statue and redo the bundle.

In the torchlight, Tari saw the life-sized statue of a man. These pathetic Romans, she'd been told, had mere human forms for gods, unlike Egyptians and Kushites, whose gods shared the power of animals. This creature was a weakling compared to her own lion-headed warrior god, Apedemek.

Tari smiled, and before the workmen could move, she leaped among them. With a fierce swing of her steel sword, she sliced off the statue's hollow head. It bounced nearly to the feet of the astonished Petronius. Tari lunged for it, wrapped it in her shawl, and fled into the night.

Yelling erupted behind her, and a startled horse whinnied somewhere ahead. Tari swerved that way, hacked at a surprised guard, and, wrenching the horse's tether from a picket, leaped onto its bare back. The animal bolted off, spurred on as much by fear of the lion running beside it as by the rider's urging.

Soon Tari heard mounted pursuit. She first thought to take her trophy back to camp, but she couldn't bring angry mounted Romans down on her sleeping people. Instead, she directed her mount into the desert.

The waning half-moon had risen in the east, and in the clear, dry air its light washed the rocks and gravelly ground with liquid silver. She looked over her shoulder. Three mounted figures pursued her. Laughing joyfully, she knew she didn't care. This was her land—the desert, the abode of lions, the realm of Apedemek. She felt his closeness as she never had before. He would guide her in life and in death.

The chase wore on until Tari noticed there was only one rider behind her. Had the others fallen, or had they gone back for reinforcements? She didn't care, but rode on and on until the clouds mounded along the eastern horizon blushed with dawn. Then, as the sun god reared above the cloud bank, her horse, blinded or exhausted, stumbled and sent her rolling over the gravel to the base of a bare rock outcrop. She staggered up and limped toward the horse, but it shied and trotted off. A gust of wind whipped sand into the air as the lone rider bore down on her.

In the gold light of an oddly clouded dawn, she saw his face. Petronius.

Wearily he dismounted and, sword drawn, walked toward her. "The head," he rasped in Egyptian. "Give me the head of the divine Emperor Augustus. You have desecrated a god!"

"This is a god?" Tari laughed. "Our gods are not so easily humbled. This is their land; they draw strength from it and will not let you claim it no matter how many hollow statues you set up."

Petronius halted at the sound of her voice. "A girl?"

Clutching the bronze head, Tari backed toward the rocks. "A princess, sister of the man you killed, heir of Kush and priestess of Apedemek."

The man laughed. "Woman warriors—one weapon Rome does not have. But holding you should help our bargaining position."

Trying to keep her voice steady, Tari continued to back away. "Any treaty you make will fail if you try to hold land that is ours. Your empire is a bloated monster. Kush is one bite too many."

Petronius ran a tired hand over his face. "True, in time every empire finds limits. But I am to fight for mine until they are reached. We have not found them here."

He stepped forward, but halted at the sound of a low growl. On the rocks above Tari stood a massive lion. Advancing clouds had dimmed the light, but Tari cast a grateful glance at what she thought was Naga, then realized that her lion was beside her. The huge lion on the rocks growled so deeply that the ground seemed to shake. Other lions appeared, striding from behind rocks or out of the cloud-darkened desert.

In the ghastly light, Petronius suddenly looked as pale as sand. Tari, dark and confident in contrast, drew her own sword and advanced.

"Go back, Roman. This is not your land. Draw your empire's line where your pathetic gods can hold it, and leave us be."

The Roman stepped back a pace; then, glancing over his shoulder, he stopped and smiled in relief. "Brave words, Princess, but more Roman soldiers are nearly here, and not even your storm clouds or unnerving beasts can turn us back."

That was when the storm hit. A massive desert sandstorm crashed down, choking the air with blinding sand, windblown sand that cut through skin and clothes like merciless arrows. Tari crouched back among the rocks. She heard nothing but shrieking, the shrieking wind and human shrieks beneath it. She saw nothing but dark shapes moving in the roiling air. Shapes of lions, perhaps, or perhaps the looming shape of a man, a man with a lion's head, wielding two vengeful swords.

Three days later, representatives of Rome—their forces newly depleted, it was said, by a freak sandstorm and an attack of wild beasts—met with the queen, the heir, and the counselors of Kush. The foundations of a treaty were laid down. Rome would extend its empire only to the ancient border of Egypt. Territory to the south would remain the lands of Kush.

When, months later in Rome, the Emperor Augustus questioned his general on the treaty's lenient provisions,

Petronius was reported to have rubbed the healing claw marks on his cheek and answered, "When the gods tell men their limits, a wise man listens."

Tari returned to Meroe. In time she ruled it long and well, with Netak as king by her side. But before that, when still a young warrior and priestess, she buried the bronze head of the Roman emperor at the threshold of the temple of Apedemek. It lay there for millennia, an offering of thanks and a promise to the protector of her land.

PAMELA F. SERVICE

PAMELA F. SERVICE grew up in Berkeley, California, where she developed an early passion for science fiction, fantasy, and ancient history. Her degree from UC Berkeley was in political science with an emphasis on Africa, but that emphasis soon moved back in time. When she relocated to London, newly married to Robert Service, her field of study was ancient African history. She completed her master's degree and spent a season in Sudan on an excavation at Meroe, the ancient capital of Kush.

Returning to the United States, Pam and Bob settled in Bloomington, Indiana, where she went into museum work and politics. During seventeen years as a museum curator, twenty years on the City Council, and the raising of daughter Alexandra, Pam also channeled her many interests and her love of the unlikely into writing for young people. She has by now published twenty books and numerous short stories and articles—a mix of history, fantasy, and science fiction. Today

Pam lives in Eureka, California, where she continues her work as a museum curator, a political activist, and a writer for young people.

Her story "Lioness" combines her own experiences and studies of Sudanese archaeology with her desire to create fiction that shines light on the events, myths, and personalities of the past. Much in this story happened, much might have happened; the joy of fiction is the freedom to interweave the two.

THUNDERBOLT

Esther Friesner

HE TOOK ME TO ATHENS. I hate Athens. It sprawls like a bird-dropping over some of the meanest, least promising land in all of Greece. Just about the only things its fields can raise are olives, vases, and philosophers. He carried me up the narrow pathway to the citadel where the royal palace stands and set me down by the courtyard well, then took a step back and grinned as if he'd given me half of Mount Olympos for a birthday present. I wonder whether he wore that same self-serving grin right after he killed the Minotaur? No matter what he did, Theseus, king of Athens, was always so very proud of himself.

"Welcome home, Helen!" he declared, spreading his arms wide. He'd sent a runner ahead to announce our arrival, so there was a crowd assembled to greet us—slaves, guards, servants, and others who had no choice in the matter. They all sent up a small, dutiful cheer. Only Theseus' mother, Lady Aithra, sounded as if she meant it.

I looked around. I wasn't impressed, and I didn't mind

saying so. "What a midden. I thought you were bringing me to the royal palace of Athens."

Theseus scowled at me. "This *is* the royal palace," he said. There was something dangerous in his voice, but I was still too angry to pay attention to things like that.

"Hunh!" I snorted as loudly as my favorite mare. "In Sparta, we'd use a place like this to stable the king's third-best horses."

That was the first time he slapped me. He hit hard. I staggered back from the blow, and I think I would have tripped on the hem of my gown and taken a tumble if not for Lady Aithra. She moved with the grace and silence of shadow, suddenly there at my back to catch me. My face stung and tears tried to escape my eyes, but I reminded myself that I was Helen, princess of Sparta, and that it didn't matter if I was only fourteen years old, this man would never see me cry.

"Child, apologize." Lady Aithra's voice was soft and gentle, but I could hear the urgency behind her words. She knew her son's nature better than I did. My mother, Queen Leda, often complained I was a hasty girl, prone to act first and think afterward, but this time she would have been proud of me: I fought back my first impulse, which was to spit in Theseus' eye. Instead I bowed my head, just as if I were some spineless little slave girl.

"I'm sorry," I said, staring at my dusty feet.

He didn't respond right away. He must have imagined that I meant my apology, that I really was afraid of him. I'm sure he drew out his silence because he thought it would make me squirm. He was a fool. In Sparta we know how to deal with our enemies. If sometimes we let them believe that they've won a battle, it's only so we can study their tactics and weapons long enough for us to win the war.

We are never afraid.

At last I heard him chuckle, almost the way my father, King Tyndareus, does just before he gives me a present or a treat. When I hear that laugh from my father, it makes me smile. The same sound from my abductor was wrong, and the anger burning in my heart filled my mouth with bile.

"That's better," he said. "That's a good girl. I forgive you. You're probably tired from our journey. Girls are too weak to endure hard travel. Mother, take her to your room and help her get clean. Order food and drink—only the best for my bride—and have your slaves fetch her fresh clothing worthy of Athens's new queen."

I felt his rough hand come up under my chin, forcing me to look at him. I already knew every curve and crease and scar of that hated face. I'd had more than enough time to commit it to bitter memory during our headlong race from my beloved Sparta to this flea-fart of a kingdom. When he grinned at me, I recalled the tame baboon that a wandering Egyptian merchant dragged into my father's court, except the baboon smelled better.

"Perithos and I have some business to attend to, but when that's settled and we return, you and I will be married. Now smile for me, sweet Helen, and maybe I'll bring you back a pretty present as a wedding gift."

I couldn't smile. I tried, if only to hurry him on his way and be free of him. I had things to attend to myself, things that I wouldn't be able to accomplish if Theseus hung around. I wanted him gone, but I couldn't smile. The best I could do was to twist my lips so that they must have looked like a pair of earthworms with stomach cramps. Theseus wasn't pleased by my disobedience. He slapped me again. This time he did it harder, and so suddenly that Lady Aithra never saw it coming and couldn't catch me. I fell on my rump in the courtyard.

"Spartan barbarian," he snarled. "You should count yourself lucky I've brought you to rule a civilized land!"

I met his scowl with one of my own. The gossips claim that I am not King Tyndareus' daughter, that my royal mother took Zeus of the Thousand Thunderbolts for a mate. I love my father, Tyndareus, and hate the gossips who try to dishonor him with such stupid lies, but when I scowled at Theseus I was Zeus' daughter in truth. I put all the black ferocity of a storm cloud into my face and imagined I could make my eyes shoot flashes of heaven's own fire. It worked. The fool-king of Athens actually blanched just a bit and took a step away from me, but then he recovered his nerve and was angrier than before.

"Mother!" he shouted, even though Lady Aithra was standing right there. "If you can't teach this wildcat some manners by the time I come back, you'll wish you had." With that, he turned his back on all of us and stalked away.

Lady Aithra helped me to my feet, her eyes sad as she surveyed what her son had done to my face. Her fingertips were smooth and cool as they traced the spots where his heavy hand had fallen. I would have a bruise or two, but they'd probably heal before I could find a proper mirror anywhere in this crude excuse for a palace.

"You must forgive him," she said, her voice soft as the breath of a summer's breeze through a barley field. "He has a king's temper."

"With respect to you, Lady, my father is a greater king than your son will ever be," I said, bearing myself stiff and tall, the way I'd seen the priestess of Demeter stand before the holy altar of the goddess. "He says that if a man can't govern himself, he shouldn't govern others."

That made her gasp and dart her eyes fearfully in the direction of the doorway through which Theseus and Perithos had vanished. Did she think he had a god's heightened sense of hearing, or had he simply terrified her to the point where she could no longer think of him rationally? Had he struck his own mother? It wouldn't surprise me at all.

"Princess, please." It was painful to hear so much fear in a woman's voice. "Don't speak so rashly. If he should learn of what you say—"

"He will," I replied. "He must have spies throughout these halls—all kings do, even the stupid ones. I want him to know what I think of him. What will he do about it? Hit me again? But then he might leave a mark that won't heal. I doubt he'd risk that. Do you think he stole me from my father's house because I'm so wise, so skilled at the spindle, the loom, and the needle, such a wonderful teller of tales to pass winter nights?" I laughed. "I'm a girl! I listen to the winter stories and I haven't lived long enough to gather any wisdom worth the name. As for my handiwork, my royal mother tells everyone that I couldn't make a worse showing if I spun and wove and sewed with my feet. Lady, there's only one reason why your son made me his captive and wants to make me his queen: I am beautiful."

She stared at me as though I'd uttered blasphemy. O gods, spare me; not another woman who's been trained to scorn her own looks. How stupid! And how tiresome to have to hear such women go on and on about how their hair is too straight or too curly, their skin too dark or too light, their bodies too bony, too fat, too soft, too hard. Why do they do it? Power is a queen who carries many spears. Beauty is only one of them, but I suppose these silly women don't dare touch any weapons for fear of what their men might think.

We Spartan women have a different attitude when it comes to spears.

Lady Aithra shook her head. "Child, it's true that you are beautiful. My son heard tales of your beauty from the lips of a score of travelers. Still, a proper woman practices modesty."

I wanted to laugh. A proper woman! Then I realized that I didn't want to defy my captor's mother, not when I needed her on my side. This was war; I needed allies. The battle lines were drawn the moment Theseus snatched me from my bed and galloped away with his gang of ruffians around him.

"I'm sorry," I said, biting back my laughter, choosing my first weapon: false words. There is no dishonor in lying to a thief, and if Lady Aithra wasn't the thief himself, she was his unwilling agent. "I—I spoke without thinking. I'm so tired and hungry!" I rubbed my eyes as though I were about to cry.

Lady Aithra gave me such a look of tenderness and sympathy that for a moment I almost regretted deceiving her. "There, child, there, it's all right," she said, embracing me. Her hair smelled of sun and pine boughs and the sea. For an instant I missed my own mother dreadfully. "You'll learn. I'll help you."

That was my intention, to have her help me. She wouldn't need to know that her idea of help and mine were as different, one from the other, as my brothers. Castor and Polydeuces are twins, yet as unalike as they can be and still claim the same birth. I suppose that's why the wag-tongues claim that Polydeuces also had Zeus for a father, just like me.

Theseus' mother led me to her room. We were followed

by several slave girls, all of them meek as mice, and by six guardsmen bearing tall bronze-headed spears. The sight of them was almost comical: were they supposed to defend a palace using weapons more suited to a boar hunt? Long spears are good enough in the open, but when a king's dwelling is your battleground, you want something to hand that can be used freely between walls. No doubt Theseus gave them spears because it made a better show, to his supposed glory.

The guards did not follow us into Lady Aithra's room. I admit that I was afraid they might do just that. Theseus had made no secret of the fact that I was to be warded constantly. He put his faith solely in the number of men he had to serve him, not in their quality.

Good. I could use that, too.

The walls of Lady Aithra's room were painted with scenes exalting her son. I walked slowly around the perimeter, studying them, pretending to be interested, acting as though this were the first time I'd ever seen or heard anything of my captor's exploits.

It was all a lie, of course, though this was war—my war for my freedom—and in war, lies are often called strategy. When Theseus and his brutish friend Perithos first came to call at my royal father's house, it didn't take them long before they launched into an endless boasting session. We all had to listen politely as those two regaled us with their tiresome tales of how Theseus was really the sea-god's son; how Theseus defeated the cruel Procrustes; how Theseus overcame the wicked Sciron the Pine-Bender; how Theseus freed his mortal father, King Aegeus, from the evil spells of the Colchian sorceress Medea; how Theseus put an end to the Cretan tribute of seven youths and seven maidens by slaying the

Minotaur, King Minos' pet bull-headed monster, which devoured them.

Theseus, Theseus, Theseus! It was a miracle that the brash Athenian kinglet didn't go completely voiceless from singing his own praises. Only the rules of hospitality kept my father and the rest of us from laughing in his face. As if we were children, to believe in monsters!

Lady Aithra watched me as I made my way around the room. She was smiling. I'm sure she believed everything her son told her, even when he told her that she'd given birth to a god's child. Whether out of fear or love, she wouldn't dare to contradict him.

"Wonderful, isn't he?" she said. "My boy, my dear boy. When I first held him in my arms he was so small, such a helpless little thing. I had no idea that he would grow up to be such a great hero." I bit my tongue at that. My deliberate silence made her add: "You see now how fortunate you are to have such a husband."

"I had no idea." I looked her right in the eyes so that she couldn't doubt my sincerity, clasped her hands, and without her ever knowing it, sent my armor-bearer onto the battlefield to deliver the challenge to my enemies: "He never spoke of his accomplishments to me."

That was all she needed to start talking. If I'd ever imagined that Theseus and his friend were the greatest trumpeters of his exploits, now I learned better. The hero's mother must be the unchallenged victor in that contest. And could I blame her? Her glory days ended when her baby grew up and left her side. What else did her life hold now? Spinning, weaving, sewing, harrying her slaves? Theseus was her life.

Listening to her gabble on so worshipfully, I gave thanks to all the gods that I would never be reduced to such a state.

My life would be my own, not merely the mirror of some man's grand deeds. (I know that even thinking such things is hubris, the great crime of pride. We are taught that the gods delight in punishing mortals for this above all other offenses, but that only happens in stories.)

Make no mistake: I didn't hold Lady Aithra at fault for how she was raised or what she had to do to make the best of her life. We Spartan women are the exception to the sad rules that govern the rest of Hellas. We're given the same training as our brothers: taught to harden our bodies, to use the javelin, even to wield the sword if we show any inclination for it. My mother, Leda, still laughs when she hears the tales of how Zeus overpowered her in swan's form. God or mortal, any swan that came within sight of Leda would learn that the Spartan queen still knew how to cast a spear and bring down a fat, white-plumed contribution to our dinner table.

You don't blame the prisoner for the prison that holds her, but if someone tries to shut you up in the same cage you have a choice: settle yourself on the bench beside her willingly or pick it up and use it to batter down the door and escape.

I let Lady Aithra speak on uninterrupted until she stopped praising her son's heroics and—as I knew she would—became nostalgic. The hero Theseus faded, the child Theseus filled her heart. "I wish you could have known him then," she said, with the beautiful irrationality of doting mothers. It didn't even enter her thoughts that when her son was a child, my parents weren't even married.

"Oh, so do I!" I cried, clapping my hands together. Then I gestured at the painted walls of her chamber. "What a shame that you have nothing like these pictures that could tell me more about his childhood. My own mother keeps a chest filled with keepsakes from when my brothers were small, but that's just the custom in Sparta. You Athenians would never—"

"As if I'd part with my son's childhood!" Lady Aithra took real offense at what I'd deliberately implied. "And I will thank you to remember that I am no Athenian. I was the princess of Troezen once."

I'd stung her. I meant to do just that. When I was ten I'd escaped my nurse, stolen Castor's clothes, and sneaked out of the palace to follow my father and his men on a great boar hunt. I watched how the hounds stirred the boar to a red-eyed fury so that it lost all common sense and charged straight into the hunters' waiting spears.

Lady Aithra almost dragged me from her room into another chamber, where the dust lay lightly over many wooden boxes, some painted, some plain. One of these was almost entirely free of dust and was elaborately decorated and carved. I heard Theseus' tame guardsmen taking up their new positions in the hallway outside the storeroom just as Lady Aithra flung back that chest's lid so that I could see what it held.

I smiled. It held what I'd hoped it would: my freedom.

Poor Lady Aithra. When I crooned and fussed and prattled over her son's childhood things, she became my slave as surely as if I'd bought and paid for her. She saw nothing wrong with letting me linger in the storeroom. If only the place had boasted windows it would have suited my wishes perfectly, but you can't have everything.

I took my time over Theseus' childhood trash, waiting for what I knew must come. Since Aithra was the woman responsible for the smooth running of palace matters until the king's return, I knew it wouldn't be too long before a domestic crisis would surface, demanding her attention. I was raised in a proper palace: I knew that such things happen on a daily basis, and frequently.

I recognized the sound of running feet approaching the storeroom and rightly guessed what that meant even before one of the manservants came bursting in, begging for Lady Aithra's help with a problem in the kitchen. By the time she turned to bid me come with her, I'd already slumped myself across the open chest as though I'd fallen asleep. I made sure to smile gently, as though lost in dreams of her precious son. She murmured something about how it would be a great shame to disturb me and how pretty I looked, sleeping there. (The shortsighted fool who thinks beauty isn't a weapon will lose many battles.) Then she was gone, shutting the door after her.

She didn't leave me alone—it's a mistake to believe that a sentimental woman must also be stupid. When I opened my eyes just a hairsbreadth, I saw the slave girl she'd left behind to guard me. I sat up so suddenly that she uttered a squeak of alarm and nearly fell off the chest where she'd perched.

"Quiet," I said, even as I strode toward her and knocked her to the ground. I kept my voice low. "Another sound out of you and you're dead." I saw her mouth open, as if to shout for the guards outside the door. That wouldn't do. I seized her hair with one hand, her throat with the other, and hauled her up. How ludicrous we must have looked! She was at least three years older than me, and taller, but she'd been fed a slave's diet of scant food and plentiful fear. She couldn't even imagine a life beyond the miserable one she knew. I took her terror and made it into my second weapon.

"If you call the guards, they'll find me asleep; they'll think you're crazy. Consider this, too: spoil my plans and I'll be forced to become your queen. Do you really want a queen who's got reason to hate you?"

She shook her head violently, then managed to stammer out: "P-plans? Wh-what plans, Lady?"

"What plans do you think?" I replied. "I mean to have my freedom. Help me and I'll give you yours as well." And I explained what I had in mind.

I don't know whether she consented because she wanted to be free or simply because she was used to taking orders; I didn't much care which it was, so long as she worked with me. I stripped off my gown and threw it at her before plunging into the chest holding Theseus' things. Garments flew everywhere. We dressed ourselves in record time—I as a young man, in one of Theseus' boyish castoffs; she as me. It took longer for us to arrange our hair to suit our disguises. I wished aloud that Lady Aithra had seen fit to give her little boy a helmet and a sword.

"You can use a sword?" The slave girl stared at me in awe, as if I really were the daughter of Zeus the Thunderer. I nodded, and a strange look came into her eyes. Without another word she led me to a corner of the storeroom where someone had piled up old cloaks too damaged to be of further use as garments. A mouse took fright and scampered away when she jerked back one of the cloths.

Swords. Not many—maybe ten in all, none of them much larger than my father's hunting knife, some hiltless, all notch-bladed and battered and dull—but swords. My hands were shaking as I rummaged through them, seeking one that looked as if it wouldn't bend double if it struck something hard. I looked up at the slave girl: she was grinning.

"Lord Theseus ordered Thales the smith to use these to make new weapons. Thales argued that this batch of bronze was defective, to be so badly scarred after so little use. Our king hates being contradicted almost as much as he hates having to pay for decent weapons for his men. His own sword and spear are of the best, but as long as he has plenty of other people's sons to throw into battle, he doesn't care how poorly they're armed."

Quantity over quality again. Yes. I'd gotten the measure of the man right enough. "Thales disobeyed Theseus?" I asked. I thought I knew the answer: the evidence was in my hands.

The slave girl chuckled. "Thales is no fool. These swords are merely what's left after he secretly sold off the rest of the pile in order to get a decent grade of bronze for the king's men."

"Lucky he left us these," I said, standing. "He wouldn't have happened to keep a defective helmet around, too, would he?"

He hadn't. Ah well, I'd had more than my fair share of good luck already; no sense tempting the gods. I nosed around the storeroom until I found a discarded brazier from the winter months, the inside still thick with smut. Soon my face was no longer recognizable under the greasy ashes. I was ready for war.

The slave girl broke out of the storeroom screaming bloody murder, racing past the startled guards. I followed hot-foot on her trail, giving voice to my brother Polydeuces' most bone-shivering battle cry. The old sword in my hand would have shattered like a perfume flask under a horse's hoof if I'd used it, but I didn't have to. Not yet. The guards saw Helen running away, saw their lives on the line, their necks paying the forfeit if she escaped. All but one of them took off after her. That one turned to face me, holding his ground.

"I am Polydeuces, son of Tyndareus of Sparta, son of Zeus the Thunderer, king of the immortal gods!" I bellowed, brandishing my blade the way I'd seen my brothers do when they practiced with their trainers. "In the name of the gods, I challenge you to single combat, the combat of heroes!"

The guardsman's face was hidden by the cheek plates and nasal of his helmet, but I think he wasn't much older than the slave girl now wearing my gown. When he lowered the tip of his spear for battle, I saw it was shaking. I had no helmet, no shield, no armor to cover me, yet my shouted challenge alone had thrust fear into his heart. Thus I learned a new lesson of words and war.

Then the butt end of the haft knocked into the wall at his back; he couldn't get it level with my chest and had no room to pull it back to fling at me. I didn't wait around to see if he could puzzle out the problem at hand: I attacked.

My sword was useless as a sword, but there was no one present to judge me for using it . . . creatively. I ducked beneath the shaft of the guardsman's unwieldy spear; came up just past his line of sight, where the right-hand cheek plate of his helmet blocked his vision; and drove the pommel hard against the side of his head. He staggered, still holding tight to his spear.

That was a mistake. If he'd dropped it, he would have had his hands free to draw his own blade. Even a good knife would have been a better weapon against my sorry sword. I howled like a wolf and gave him another thump in the head before he could think of doing that. I struck him hard enough to send his helmet flying. That did make him drop the spear, but by then he was too dazed to do more than scrabble after it on the floor. I leaped over his hunched body, kicked the weapon beyond his reach, and gave him one sharp kick at the point of his chin. His teeth clattered together loudly enough for me to hear them just before my sword-turned-club slammed down right on top of his skull. He crumpled at my feet.

I don't know whether I killed the man or not. I like to think I only knocked him senseless. With his helmet gone, I could see I'd been right, that he was very young. It's a heavy thing to carry the weight of dead men, especially those whose beards have hardly sprouted before they're shipped away to war; it's a burden best left to cold-souled kings. I took his helmet and the shortsword at his belt, then ran to catch up to the other guards.

Thanks to the helmet, no one could see my face and I was able to make my voice pass for a stripling's. "To the gates! To the gates! The Spartans are upon us! The sons of Zeus have taken the palace!"

O gods, how many lies flew from my lips that day! And yet I think that words more often win wars than spears and swords. The gods witness, words begin enough foolish battles. I know I am beautiful, but if idle tongues hadn't spread tales of how my beauty was the greatest in all Hellas, would Theseus have come troubling my father's house? He might have seen me, thought I was a pretty little thing, and gone back to guzzling wine and bragging about his own accomplishments if not for the words "Helen is the fairest."

Words made me his prize; words freed me. The guards put more faith in their ears than their eyes when they heard that the god-born Spartan princes were in the palace.

The slave girl heard my shouts and seized the opportunity. She raced through the palace by routes she knew best, darting through the kitchen, finding the chance to snatch a burning brand from the cookfire and trail it over anything flammable in her wake. The other guards and I found smoke fouling our way, the palace in an uproar. She'd spread my battle cry along with the fire. There wasn't a man or woman in Theseus' halls who wasn't convinced that Castor and Polydeuces had come to carry back their stolen sister. They were all equally convinced that my brothers were Zeus' own.

Who can fight the thunderbolt? It falls from heaven and shatters all in its path. Common sense topples as easily as roof tiles, for in all the time that slave girl and I rampaged through the royal palace, not one of the guardsmen paused to ask himself why Helen would be running away from her rescuers.

Well, "Helen" didn't run away forever. While the guards and I were pounding along a smoke-wreathed passageway bordering the palace courtyard, I glimpsed the slave girl cutting across that open space.

"There she goes!" I cried, purposely gesturing with my sword so that I knocked one of those stupid boar-spears into a wide arc. It slammed into the rest, and soon the guards were enmeshed in a clattering confusion, spears knocking one against the other, feet sliding and stumbling as they strove to stay upright, curses tangling with the cries of panic all around them. They'd almost gotten themselves sorted out when I renewed my shouts of "There! There! After her! Lord Theseus will have our heads if she gets away!" I flagged them down a side passage before taking off myself in the right direction.

I caught up with my ally on the path leading down to the royal stables. (Theseus' horses lived better than his men. Then again, they were more intelligent.) I had my sword ready for any unlucky stablehand we might meet, but the slave girl's fires had smoked out every available pair of hands, drawn them all back up the hill to help put down the flames. It was a moment's work for me to pick a likely steed and mount it, though I wasted some precious time getting the girl up behind me.

We were galloping down the road from the smoking heights of the citadel when we saw them. The fading sunlight glittered from their helmets and struck sparks of red and gold from the points of their short war-spears. It was one of the gods' seldom mercies that they didn't kill us as soon as we plunged into their midst. My father's men are the greatest warriors in all Hellas, but sometimes they are . . . hasty.

And so it was that my brothers came to rescue me. They came too late to execute the rescue itself, but just in time to claim the credit. Sing, O Muse, of how great Castor and famed Polydeuces overwhelmed the Athenians' fierce defense, killing hundreds with no losses to their own troops! Sing also of how they managed to enslave my abductor's own mother, Lady Aithra, and present her to me as a gift for my troubles. (The slave girl who'd fled with me said she didn't mind her new name, nor the fact that she was forced to remain a slave. I never treated her like one, and her fellow slaves always showed her the deference due to a captive queen.)

I wonder if the Muse giggles when she sings such bosh.

It did no good for me to tell my royal parents how things had really come to pass. They sided with my brothers, insisting that my story was not in keeping with what a princess is supposed to do under the circumstances. They gravely reminded me that I was only fourteen and a fourteen-year-old girl could never save herself, even if she was a princess of Sparta. Anyone with half a brain knew that. (Yes, anyone with half a brain.) My father also pointed out that someday he would have to pick me out a worthy husband, and that there wasn't a king in all Hellas who'd want a wife with an unbecoming reputation, whether or not she was the most beautiful woman in the world.

The tales are all now too well established for a little thing like truth to unseat them. My brothers, mortal and divine, saved me from Theseus, who was driven mad by my great beauty. The suitors hear the tales and come flocking like sheep to see me. I sit between my royal parents and receive them all most graciously, as befits a princess.

But under my gown I always wear a small bronze knife, under my bed I keep a battered helmet and a stolen sword, and in my heart I hold the knowledge that I am Helen: I make my own fate, my own choices, in my own time. I hold the blood of gods, the thunderbolt's inheritance, and I alone am master of the heavenly fire that is my freedom.

* * *

ESTHER FRIESNER

NEBULA AWARD WINNER Esther M. Friesner (the "M." is optional) has published thirty novels and over one hundred short works in addition to editing seven anthologies, including the popular Chicks in Chainmail series. Her works have been published in the United States, the United Kingdom, Japan, Germany, Russia, France, and Italy. She is also a published poet and a playwright and once wrote an advice column, "Ask Auntie Esther." Besides winning two Nebula Awards for Best Short Story (in 1995 and 1996), she has been a Nebula finalist three times and a Hugo finalist once.

Esther loves looking at familiar characters in ways that are new but that actually make sense if you stop and *think* about it. For example, Helen of Troy was born a Spartan. Spartans gave both their sons *and* their daughters hard physical training. There's also evidence that Helen was the independent queen of Sparta. (This perspective also turns stereo-types and natural prejudices on their head, and who doesn't love that?)

Esther lives in Connecticut and has the regulation husband, two children, and author's cats, as well as an op-tional and fluctuating population of hamsters. Check out Esther's Web site for more hamster humor at www.sff.net/people/e.friesner.

DEVIL WIND

―◆―

India Edghill

The thorns which I have reap'd are of the tree
I planted: they have torn me, and I bleed:
I should have known what fruit
would spring from such a seed.
    —*Byron,* Childe Harold's Pilgrimage,
        Canto IV, stanza 10

OUR LIVES ARE SHADOWS flung upon the world by a careless fire; dust blown by a cruel wind. But if we deal justly, and with honor, in this life, the gods will reward us in the next. So we are told. So I believed.

My mistress believed differently. To her mind, those who lived a good life in this world gleaned eternal favor of their single god. When first I heard this, it seemed to me that the English heaven must be full of English angels.

For if one need live only one good life, how hard could that be to achieve? And if one knew one had but a single life in which to obtain salvation, would not one tread lightly, speaking only fair words and giving lavish alms, lest one spoil a Christian's only chance to win heaven?

Well, however many lives we live, in each we are all young and credulous once. I soon understood that however many English souls basked in the glory of their god's radiance in their heaven, the Christian hell claimed even more of them.

Impatient fools.

In my last life, I had been good enough to be reborn human; bad enough to be born a girl. In compensation for being reincarnated female, I was granted beauty, and a father just rich enough to give me to a good, honest man at the proper time.

As was suitable, my husband was twice my age, old enough to be settled in his trade and to know how to treat a wife well. The man himself was handsome and kind, with a good job working for a rich English family. And he was alone, for some years ago cholera had killed all his family between one sunrise and another; being away in the Hills with his employers, he had escaped the dread sickness.

So I would be the only woman in his house. When I heard that, I went to the little shrine to Parvati I kept in my room and knelt before the goddess's image to give thanks. I gave the goddess a dozen new glass bangles, too. No mother-in-law to make my wedded life misery! What joy!

"So this is your new bride, Manoj. She is very pretty—and very young." The English mem smiled at me; I ducked my head modestly, while keeping my slanted gaze fixed upon her face. This was the first time I had been close to an English-woman, and I was amazed by her skin's pallor. She looked as cool as new ivory.

But although her skin looked cold, her smile was warm as the sun that bright March day. "Welcome, my dear. I hope you will be happy with us."

"For heaven's sake, Maud, don't be an idiot; the chit can't understand a word you say." Her husband shifted, plainly restless and eager to be gone. "Very good, Manoj, and I suppose you'll expect a raise in your wages now. Well, I won't be held to ransom just because you've chosen to marry, and so I tell you. You'll get another twenty rupees a quarter and that's the limit."

My husband heard this grudging offer placidly. "You are kind, sahib." Manoj bowed; I wondered what he truly thought, but of course I could not speak now.

"That's done, then." The English sahib nodded abruptly. "Maud, I'm off—don't expect me back until late."

"Of course not, Gerald." The lady's voice was soft and low; her smile never wavered—at least not until her husband had left the verandah.

Then she sighed, softly, so that only someone listening as closely as I would hear it. "Thank you, Manoj," she said. "You may show your wife to your quarters now. And if she would like, she may act as ayah to the miss-sahiba. That will mean extra money, of course."

"The memsahib is kind," my husband said, and this time sounded as if he meant his words. Then, to my surprise, he spoke directly to me, in our own tongue. "You, too, should thank her, wife."

Amazed to be addressed directly before another, I managed to whisper, "I thank you, memsahib." Those badly spoken words used up half the English I had so painstakingly learned when I was told whom I was to marry, but my new mistress's face lit up.

"You speak English! How delightful! Well, then, you will be the perfect ayah for Estella; she chatters away like a little magpie in Hindustani and I can hardly understand a word she says. Now you can act as go-between for us."

While I understood more English than I spoke, I barely grasped half a dozen words of this—but the memsahib's tone was warm, and she smiled, so I assumed she was pleased. Daring, I smiled back.

"That's all settled, then," my new mistress said, and my husband bowed again and led me away to start my new life as his wife and as Miss Estella Humbolt's ayah.

I soon learned that Mrs. Humbolt had given me the position of ayah more to grant my husband increased income than because she thought me a suitable guardian for her daughter. For one thing, the miss-sahiba already had an ayah, a round, jolly-looking Muslim woman who had cared for Estella since the child was born.

When I met Fatima-ayah, I feared she would be jealous and torment me out of spite. But again I was favored by my goddess, for despite her affable, easygoing appearance, Fatima-ayah was a stickler for rules and for order.

Children are destroyers of both, so once she learned I knew my place and would not try to undermine her authority, Fatima-ayah was glad enough to have an assistant. For one thing, it added to her own importance. And for another, Fatima-ayah was no longer young. To have me to entertain and play with the miss-sahiba was a great relief to her.

Miss Estella was already past thirteen, and by English custom should have been sent over the black water to England itself at least half a dozen years ago. But as I learned, Gerald Humbolt spent lavishly upon himself but grew tight-pursed when it came to his womenfolk. Despite his wife's pleading, he had steadfastly refused to pay the money for Estella's passage and for her board and keep at an English school.

"*Ai*, that was a time," Fatima-ayah said. "The memsahib wept and called him child-killer, and claimed the right to use her own money to send Missy-baba away. But it came to nothing, for we were stationed far to the northwest then, in the High Hills, and what was our memsahib to do? So Missy-baba stayed—and still lives. She was born under a fortunate star."

Fortunate indeed; it was known that India's air was deadly to English children once they passed their sixth year. That was why their mothers, weeping, sent their sons and daughters into exile.

"Would the sahib have sent a son to Belait, did he have one?" I asked.

Fatima-ayah shrugged in eloquent disparagement.

"Oh, aye, perhaps. But he loves his money, that one— more than he loves even himself, I think. And his wife's money he loves better still."

I think Fatima-ayah was right. What else could explain Humbolt-sahib's anger at all the world save that he lacked all love, even of self? Why else could he not live peaceably with a good-tempered wife and a pretty daughter?

"Because he's a beast, Taravati, that's why." That was Miss-baba Estella's answer to that riddle. Estella loved her father as little as he loved her; she rarely saw him, and all her affection was bestowed upon her mother and her ayah—and upon me, in time. For we became friends the moment our eyes met—nay, more than that. Sisters.

And that was the second reason our memsahib had granted me rank and status as Fatima-ayah's assistant. Miss-baba Estella led a lonely life; she was the only English child of her age in the station. Although I was a married woman, I was not yet twelve; less than two years separated us.

In truth, my job was not servant, but companion.

This suited both Estella and me perfectly. My wifely duties were hardly arduous. Many men would have claimed me as a true wife although I was barely past childhood, but Manoj did not. "The memsahib thinks you too young yet to be a wife," my husband told me, "and so do I. We will wait."

And just as I was too young to be a wife, Estella was far too old to be under the care of a baba-ayah.

So we spent our days together. In lieu of a governess, Mrs. Humbolt taught her daughter in the mornings. When she saw me watching the lessons from the corner, she invited me to be her student as well. "A well-tended mind is as important as a well-tended body," Mrs. Humbolt said.

I begged my husband's permission for this, which he granted without even a grumble on the folly of teaching women. "Take what pleasure you can now," he said, "for your life will be a wheel of work soon enough." Yes, he was a good man, my husband; better than I deserved. Better than the fate he found.

So our mornings were given over to scholarship. During the heat of the day, we were supposed to rest within the bungalow, out of the deadly sun. The memsahib herself retreated to her own room, there to remove her clothing and lie in her chemise upon her bed. "Stay indoors, shun the sun," English wisdom ran. "It will drive you mad, kill you, if you venture forth."

Well, and so it would, had Estella and I been fool

enough to venture forth clad in corsets and crinolines and half a dozen petticoats beneath a garment that covered us like a heavy skin. But when we claimed the afternoons for our own, we dressed in Punjabi garb; in cotton shalvar-kameez, with large veils to shield our heads from the sun, and our faces from curious eyes.

So clad, we explored the bazaar and the temples, the Moghul gardens and the riverbank. We ventured into places neither Miss Estella Humbolt nor Taravati, wife of Manoj, should have set her feet.

That was how we met the *jadu*—the witch.

Estella and I first heard rumors of this *jadu* in the bazaar as we shopped for jellabies. As we nibbled the sticky sweets— we dared not carry them home, for they would be instantly confiscated as unclean—a crowd of young men wandered past, aimless and seeking amusement.

The bazaar seemed, to their bored eyes, to offer a treasure trove for mischief. One of the youths snatched an embroidered slipper up from a row of footwear and brandished it. "What is this made of? I vow it's leather"—a terrible accusation to fling at a good Hindu merchant, and besides, the shoe was clearly velvet sewn with gold thread. The youth was trying only to start a quarrel, for excitement's sake.

But the merchants had no desire to lose a day's business for idle young men's pleasure. "Set that down, lout." The slipper-*wallah*'s neighbor, who offered cotton cloth goods, came to his fellow merchant's defense. "Off with you, or I shall summon a constable."

"Summon—summon away—some day you'll summon in vain!" chanted the slipper-snatcher. "Some day a wind will rise and blow you all away, you and the English—some day soon—"

One of his fellows grabbed him and hauled him away before he could finish. Another yanked the embroidered slipper out of his hand and tossed it back to the slipper-merchant.

"Some day," the sweet-maker mumbled, stirring boiling fat and preparing to drop another length of dough into the seething golden liquid. "Some day, some day—them and their some days. That old witch should watch what she says, or some day the English will come and blow *her* away!"

"What witch?" Estella asked.

"The old *jadu*—you don't want to see her, Miss-sahiba." Although Estella liked to pretend she passed as an Indian girl, all the station-folk knew better. Except the English, of course.

"Why not?" The Miss-sahiba was nothing if not persistent.

"Because she's a *jadu*." The sweet-man dropped dough into the sizzling fat and we watched as it turned into a jellaby before our eyes. *"Hai,* mind your fingers, *chota-mem.* They will burn." He plucked the jellaby out of the fat and laid it atop the pile he had already cooked.

"Where does the *jadu* live? If I'm to avoid her, I must know where to not go." Estella smiled; a charm which always worked.

"Then do not walk down by the bend of the river, by the old burning-ghat." He folded a handful of jellabies into a length of brown paper and handed it to me. "Six *pice*," he said.

"Two," I said instantly.

"You willful girls will bankrupt me. I am a poor man. Five."

In the end, I gave him three, and left him satisfied. Estella and I walked along slowly, nibbling jellabies, knowing we must wash carefully before either Mrs. Humbolt or Fatima-ayah spotted us. Jellabies are not a tidy food.

At the end of the bazaar street, I began to turn left, toward the bungalows, only to realize Estella had turned right. "Oh no," I said.

"Oh yes," Estella responded. "Don't you want to see a real *jadu?*"

"No," I said promptly.

"Well, I do. She can tell our fortunes."

"So can I, if we're found out!"

But it never did me any good to argue with Estella. Sometimes I wonder what would have happened had we gone straight home, that afternoon in early May. Most things would have fallen out just as they did, of course. But some would have died who lived, and some would have lived who died.

And some of those who died would not have rested easy, for there would have been no avenger to free their mourning ghosts.

When Estella and I approached the *jadu's* hut, the sun was high overhead and all about us was silence, save for the endless murmur of the muddy river. I had ample time on the walk there to think of all the punishments both Mrs. Humbolt and my husband might mete out if this escapade were discovered.

"She's not here." My relief was plain in my voice.

"Don't be silly, Tara—where else would she be?"

"Getting water from the river," said a voice like a silver bell, and Estella and I gasped in guilt and fear as we whirled to face the witch.

She stood no taller than we did ourselves, although she was plainly a woman grown. She wore only a length of worn silk tucked around her hips as a skirt; her head and arms and breasts were bare. A necklace of little skulls hung about her neck, and iron bangles adorned each wrist. Her hair fell down her back in long cords and knots to her knees. Her hands were stained crimson to the wrist.

And she carried a bright brass *lota*, just as if she were any woman returning from the well or from the river with the day's water. "Welcome, seekers of wisdom. What would you know?"

Estella stared at her. "You're the *jadu*?" she said, sounding disbelieving. I could have pinched her. It's folly to quarrel with magic—just as it's folly to seek it.

"If you like." She didn't seem to care whether we were there or not. "What do you want of *jadu, chota-mem*? Go home, seek shelter. The wind blows."

Her words seemed oddly familiar. *"Some day a wind will rise and blow you all away, you and the English—"*

So the youthful lout had chanted in the bazaar. *It means nothing,* I told myself. Yet a chill slid over my skin, like a cold invisible serpent.

"What wind?" Estella demanded.

"The Devil's Wind. It blows. It brings death and destruction. Go home, baba. You are needed there." The *jadu's* eyes stared past us, into some future only she could see. We waited, but the witch neither moved nor spoke again.

At last Estella and I looked at each other. "Come on," I said, and took her hand. We backed carefully away before turning and walking swiftly toward home. We did not run— what good would running do, from a *jadu* who could fly through the air or send a cobra after you to strike like lightning? But we walked as fast as we could; the effort took all our breath. At the bend in the road we stopped and looked back. All we saw upon the old burning-ghat was the round reed hut. The witch had vanished.

"What kind of skulls do you think those were? Do you think she *shrank* human skulls? Was that blood on her hands?"

"Birds," I said. "Birds, and perhaps monkeys. And henna on her hands."

"A wind—what do you think she meant? A storm?"

"I don't know. But we must go home, Estella. We must go home *now*."

But even had we known what the witch meant, it was already too late for us to carry a warning. For the Devil's Wind had already broken free and even now blew fire and death across the land.

Halfway from the crossroads to the lines of bungalows, we smelled the smoke. Then we heard the screams.

A party of sepoys ran past us, and at first we thought they hurried to aid at whatever disaster had struck. Then we saw that their swords were drawn, and that red liquid dripped from the glinting blades. *"Maro! Maro!"* some shouted, "Strike and kill! Strike and kill!"—and others *"Din, din!* For the Faith!"

They ran past without seeing us, blinded by bloodlust. A horseman followed, galloped past on a lathered horse. A woman's head bounced at the horse's side, tied to the saddle by long light-brown hair.

Stunned to silence, Estella and I stared at each other. Then, wordless, we began to run.

By the time we reached the bottom of the garden, the Humbolt bungalow was burning. As we ran towards the house, we tasted smoke upon our tongues. We saw no flames as yet. But once inside the darkened house we heard them, a fierce crackling growl that raised the hairs upon my nape in deep, instinctive fear.

Nor was that all. A body lay sprawled across the hallway, a huddle of pale cotton cloth streaked with red. Fatima-ayah. And beyond her a larger form. Manoj.

As Estella stood still as salt, I sidled around Fatima-ayah's body and sank to my knees beside my husband. He was still alive; I do not know why, for blood wept from a wound in his breast, a red hole the size of my hand. There was blood on his hair as well. I touched his head gently and the bone sank, soft beneath my hand.

"Husband," I whispered, and Manoj opened his eyes. It seemed hard for him to see, but he knew me. His hand moved, slowly, to touch mine.

"Wife." The word was a mere sigh. "Run. You and Miss-sahiba. Run. The sahib—"

The last word faded out on a long breath; life dulled from his eyes. He was gone.

I rocked back on my heels and stood. *Run,* Manoj had said; his last order to me in this life. I must obey.

I turned to Estella, who had not moved from the doorway. Her eyes stared past Fatima-ayah, past Manoj—past me, to something beyond that turned her eyes to stone. I looked and saw Humbolt-sahib coming toward us. He carried a sword in one hand and a pistol in the other, and when he saw us standing there he stopped.

"Estella." His voice slapped flat upon the air. He looked at his daughter as if she were a stranger. His eyes passed over me unseeing. At the two bodies on the floor, he did not look at all.

"Papa. Papa, where is Mama? Where is my mother?" When her father made no answer, Estella ran forward, past Fatima-ayah's body, past Manoj. I tried to grasp her arm as she pushed by me, but she twisted away like a mongoose to flee to the back of the house. Not knowing what else to do, I followed her. I glanced back to see if Humbolt-sahib would come after, and saw him bent over my husband's body.

And I saw him bring up the sword he carried, and swing the blade down across my husband's throat. If Manoj had not lain already dead, the blow would have slain him.

I found Estella in her mother's bedroom, clinging to her mother. Like my husband, the memsahib lay—not dead; her attacker had been too hurried to grant her swift death. But she was dying; dying as her life flowed away in a slow crimson tide. As I came up beside them, I saw the memsahib's lips move; she wished to speak, but had no more breath for words.

"Mama," Estella whispered. "Mama." I stared down at Mrs. Humbolt and said nothing; I did not yet know the full horror of what had befallen today.

Again the dying woman's lips moved soundlessly. Too stunned to weep, Estella bent close. "What is it, Mama? Tell me."

"The sepoys. The bloody damned sepoys." It was Humbolt-sahib; he stood in the bedroom doorway, swaying as if drunk. "They've mutinied. Run amok. Killing everyone. Everyone."

His voice was slow, his words slurred. His eyes were flat as a cobra's. "The sepoys killed them," he said again, and as he spoke I felt a cool touch upon my hand, light as a dragonfly skimming water.

Memsahib Maud had lifted her fingers enough to brush the back of my hand; I looked, and saw a fearful light flicker in her dying eyes. Her lips formed words, and this time I understood what she wished to say.

No, he has done this.

The knowledge flowed through my veins, cold as venom. The memsahib saw that I knew, I am certain of it. For the spark faded from her eyes and she let herself go, now that she had passed on the truth to another.

Shocked as I was, I knew Estella and I must flee this house and Humbolt-sahib both. I laced my fingers tight through Estella's and backed away from the bed and its accusing burden.

Once we had stepped through the windows, I pinched Estella sharply. "Wake! We must run!"

That roused her. She began to struggle and cry out; I grabbed her and pressed my hand hard over her mouth. "Silence—and run. Now come!"

I had to half-drag Estella across the verandah, but once we were down the steps she came more willingly. We fled across the back garden into the jungle beyond. There we stopped and looked back.

Fire had caught the Humbolt bungalow in hot red teeth; flames began to gnaw through the thatch. Soon the roof would burn, and then crash into the rooms below, burying the bodies lying there in rubble and ash.

As we watched, a figure emerged from the smoke. Humbolt-sahib. "Estella!" he called. His head turned from side to side, his eyes seeking. "Estella! Come back!"

Clinging to Estella's hand so hard I could not feel my fingers, I dragged her on, into the jungle brush with me, away from the burning bungalow and her father's mad eyes.

* * *

Later I learned that the Devil's Wind blew indeed, just as the witch had said it would. The sepoy regiments had risen in rebellion, slaying and burning and looting their way across the land. And in that horror, that disaster for English and Indian alike, Humbolt-sahib had seen only one thing: his own chance to strike.

That day the air itself burned hot, too hot even for May; too hot for anyone of any race to venture safely under the sun. Heat slammed down upon us like a tiger's paw, raging and deadly. Even I suffered, and I was not a pale English miss. Estella could not bear it; by the time we reached the ancient deserted temple, fever glazed her eyes. Once I had half-dragged her into the darkness beneath the rocks and vines, I laid my hand upon Estella's forehead.

Her skin scorched my hand as if she were made of fire.

Sunstroke. The word etched itself in the white-hot air. Sunstroke, and no water within a mile of us. All I could do for Estella was lay her down upon the hard stones of the broken temple, and fan her with a bunch of leaves that wilted as soon as they were plucked, and pray.

No god heard. At last I was desperate enough to risk slinking off through the jungle to the river; if Estella did not have water, she would die. As I shifted, readying myself to leave her, I felt a touch on my hand, soft as owl-wings at twilight.

"Estella." I bent over her; her eyes opened, gazed into mine. Sun-madness burned within her; her eyes blazed like twin pyres. "Estella, I go for water. I will return soon."

"No. We both go, Taravati. And I will not return."

"The heat speaks, not you, Estella. Wait; I will bring water, yes, and ice. Ice, Estella." She did not even hear my pathetic attempt to comfort her.

"Oh, do be quiet, Tara. Listen to me." Estella breathed the words, low whispers in the noonday shadows. "He killed them. Father. You saw."

"Yes," I said. "I saw."

"They will blame the sepoys." Estella's eyes glittered like a tiger's. "That's not fair. The sepoys didn't kill Fatima-ayah and Manoj. And Mother." She lifted her hand, clutched mine hard enough to press the small bones together. "Not fair, Tara. Tell them. Father." I could hardly hear the last word. I bent forward so that I might whisper beside her ear, hoping she could still hear me.

"Justice," I said. "Our dead will have justice. I swear it."

I do not know if Estella heard; her feet were set already upon the road to Lord Yama's kingdom. With her last breath, the word "Mother" hung upon the air, ghost-word for a ghost. I kissed my friend's forehead.

The air about us still burned, but under my lips Estella's skin was cool at last.

By the time I reached the *jadu*'s hut beside the river it was past moonrise; moonlight flooded the land, laying down shadows like black velvet. In all that dead landscape nothing moved save the river rippling past, slow and sullen, its water glinting hard as iron. As the moon climbed higher, I knew I could wait no longer or my own fears would trap me here when the sun rose, when the hunters once more would roam, seeking prey. I could not risk that. I was prey. A girl, a widow, a memsahib's servant—any of these creatures was fair game for cruel men.

I was all three—and one thing more. I was witness to Humbolt-sahib's murders. That alone condemned me to hide, and to flee.

No, I would wait no longer. I stepped forward, out of the hot shadows, and walked boldly up to the *jadu*'s door.

She awaited me there, sitting cross-legged upon a tiger-skin, letting the little skulls upon her necklace slip through her fingers like a monk's rosary. "So she comes." The witch spoke as if she had expected my return; perhaps she had. "Comes begging favors. Beg, little sacrifice. Beg."

I knew better than that. Beg, and play her game, and lose. I drew a deep breath and began.

"I do not beg, great one. I bargain."

Her eyes flickered at that, little flames dancing in the night. "What would you offer?"

"A life," I said.

"Whose?"

My next word would either lose the game or win it. "Mine," I said.

I had known that was all I had to offer up—my life. Nothing, and everything. Now I waited to learn if a bargain would be struck. It must be; I had nothing else to sacrifice.

The witch stared at me with her god-mad eyes. She did not speak again until I had counted one hundred beats of my own heart.

"And do you think your life worth such a favor as you would ask?"

"It is not I who set a worth upon my life." My voice was low but steady; I took a small pride in that achievement. "It is you, great one."

"True. True." The *jadu* nodded; the little skulls strung upon her necklace seemed to blink and grin at me. A trick of moonshadow, I told myself.

For a long time after that, neither of us spoke. I waited, patient as a serpent on a rock.

"And your desire, small one?" The *jadu*'s words slid into the air like a well-honed dagger into flesh. "Think well."

But I did not need to think; my desire had been burned into my bones as the sun had burned death into Estella.

"Vengeance. Justice. Life to repay life stolen."

"You ask a great deal, child." Now little skulls slipped through her fingers, as gently as if she counted pearls.

"I ask what is owed. No more."

"If what you ask is granted, your own life is forfeit."

"If that is the price," I said, "then I will pay it."

The witch bowed her head; the long knots and coils of her hair veiled her face. Her fingers stilled, the bones of small creatures long dead cradled silent and motionless in her crimson hands. When she raised her eyes again, I seemed to look into them as into a dark mirror.

"Pay, then," she said, and rose to her feet, the long coils of her hair weaving like serpents in the moonlight. Beckoning, she retreated into the darkness behind her, and I followed the witch into her shabby reed hut.

Never afterward could I truly remember what befell me within the witch's sanctuary. Sometimes a certain flicker of candlelight will flare into an image of burning bone, or a cat's cry become a low song of pain and loss. And sometimes I dream, hot black visions; smoke rising from endless pyres that I myself have set ablaze.

The reed hut reeks of smoke and of ash. And it is dark within its woven walls—at first.

The jadu *sits cross-legged on one side of a cold firepit, and I on the other. Between us lies a bed of ashes, gray and lifeless; not even an ember remains alive to kindle a spark.*

"Light it." The jadu's *voice slithers through the hut like a cobra questing for prey.*

I stare at the bed of ashes. How can I light a fire that has already burned to ash? I stare, and feel the weight of the witch's eyes upon me.

"You promised me justice," I say, and the jadu *laughs.*

"I know what I promised, little sacrifice. Light the fire, if you would obtain what you seek."

Again I stare at the bed of ashes before me. "How?" I ask at last.

For a time there is silence in the witch's reed hut, silence thick and hot as velvet. The jadu *counts the beads upon her grim necklace; I hear the faint click of bone against bone as the little skulls fall through her fingers. At last she speaks.*

"Fire is life. Why were you born a woman, if not to kindle new life?"

I do not understand; I expect her to chant an incantation, to perform a spell, to summon demons to my aid. The witch does none of these things. She sits and counts her skull-beads. I stare at the heap of ash between us.

Fire is life—but this fire has burnt out. To rekindle it, I would need food for its flames to feed upon. Wood, or dried cow dung—or flesh and bone. I close my eyes, and behind my lids see hot red teeth eating the Humbolt bungalow, devouring the bodies that lie within its dying walls.

I open my eyes; the heap of ashes has not changed. I look up at the jadu, *whose staring eyes are black as moonless midnights. "Fire is death," I say, and hear another faint click as another skull passes through the witch's fingers.*

"*So are you.*" *Click, and again click, a small steady sound of time passing.* "*Light the fire.*"

"*I cannot.*" *Tears burn my eyes, spill down my cheeks; tears of anger, and of loss.*

"*And I can give you nothing you do not already possess. You are like me, little sacrifice; all women are alike in the dark. Light the fire.*"

Her endless serenity before my passion angers me; rage sinks its fangs into my heart. I reach out and scoop up cold ash from the firepit—and the ash glows. A spark—

Fire. I hold fire in my bare hands.

"*You are a woman. You are life and death.*" *In the new firelight, the* jadu's *hands shine wetly red against pale bone as she counts her little skulls.* "*Go now, and remember what you have promised me.*"

Flames swirl between us, the fire in my hands leaping up to catch in the woven reeds, turning the witch's hut into a funeral pyre. Flames light up the night, and even in a dream, I know the pyre I have kindled is my own . . .

And when I dream such dreams, I know the *jadu* reminds me of what I was, and what I am, and what I will become. All I know is that I offered up my life to her magic, and endured what passed that night; endured and survived until the moon set and the sun rose, and its light upon my eyelids burned me awake.

It was morning, and I was alone. Save for myself, the reed hut was empty—truly empty—and I knew the witch was gone and would not return. I crawled out of the hut and down the bank to the sullen river, and in the sun-bright water I saw what the *jadu* had created from my craving for vengeance and my vow of payment.

A face pale as the moon; eyes bright as the sky. I looked upon myself in the river's uncertain mirror and saw what others would see, when they looked upon me now. A miss-baba. An English girl.

Estella.

That was how I became Estella—or rather, the semblance of Estella, the Estella that English men and women would expect to see. To achieve that was not hard, for Estella and I had been close as twin sisters. What was hard was to survive long enough to reach Humbolt-sahib again. For the Devil's Wind still blew across the land, devouring all in its mad path.

I walked first back to our station, only to find its dwellings burned and death still lingering in the hot dry air. Standing before the heap of smoking ash that had once been the Humbolt bungalow, I weighed what I knew of the English settlements, trying to decide where to seek Humbolt-sahib.

No. No more would I call him sahib. For I was no longer Taravati, wife of Manoj the *khitmagar*, but Miss Estella Humbolt, daughter of Gerald Humbolt, Englishman. And murderer.

Our station was—had been—small, of little importance in the grand scheme of English rule. But downriver lay Agra and Cawnpore, great cities with large cantonments. Surely Mr. Humbolt would travel to one of those strongholds?

I turned away from the ruined bungalow and began to walk toward the main road, the highway that ran past our station and led to the greater world beyond. As I set my feet upon its sun-hardened dirt, I knew my journey would be arduous and long. But I did not care; I was strong, and time did not matter. Only justice for the dead would end my journey.

*   *   *

But my journey was easier than I had feared, made so by the very conflict that had set my feet upon the path to death. For all that season the Devil's Wind blew across the burning land—and carried me with it. Carried me implacably to my prey.

No one took any notice of me as I walked the road. It seemed that the *jadu*'s magic veiled me from the savage life around me; I walked inviolate as a *purdah-nishin* behind her curtain. I might have been a shadow falling across the hard-packed earth. A shadow, or a ghost.

Only when I came at last to an English cantonment far up Sher Shah's Road, far from the blood and fire and death, did I become tangible once more, my reality reflected in alien eyes.

"Good God, I don't know how she did it. To walk all the way from Kalipur to Guljore—a mere child—safely through those devils—" The colonel's voice caught as if upon a sob; I had not known an Englishman could weep.

"Hush, my dear; you'll wake her. She needs her rest, poor thing." The colonel's lady spoke low and soft, yet with a firmness that commanded obedience even from her husband. "To-morrow will be time enough to ask questions."

I listened, and smiled, and knew I had no more to fear from them than I had from the dangers of the road. *Men see what they wish to see.* The *jadu*'s voice seemed to whisper through the dim room like a serpent. The English wished to see a miracle, and so when I walked into the colonel's bungalow and proclaimed myself Estella Humbolt, that was who I became in English eyes.

I looked deeply into those wondering, grateful eyes and saw no doubt there. No doubt at all.

The English could not treat Estella Humbolt too well; all the ladies vied to care for me, to give me dresses and bonnets, stockings and hair-ribbons. The men regarded me as a portent of victory, a banner to flaunt before mutinous India as proof of English courage. Estella's survival granted them hope.

And the English needed hope during those hot black days, for little news reached them, and all of it was bad until I walked into their lives. Too many lay dead, too many still remained in peril. So to see young Estella Humbolt walk untouched out of the hell India had become lifted English hearts; restored English faith in themselves, and in their English god.

Nothing was too good for Estella Humbolt. I was the darling of the station, as if I were their one and only daughter.

I found their care touching, their defiant calm admirable. Their concern for me was useful as well; I had only to ask to have my wishes granted. I had the sense to express only moderate desires, suitable to a young English girl.

What could be more suitable, after all, than a daughter's ardent longing to see her father again?

Information was hard to come by, but I heard something of Gerald Humbolt's new life when a messenger slipped into the cantonment upon the summer's hottest day. He had traveled all the long road from Calcutta, bringing orders for the colonel: Stay and hold, forbid passage to any mutineers who sought to ravage westward. The colonel frowned and muttered low and fierce, like an angry tiger, "Stay and hold our position? Bah! Nonsense! A child could hold this fort—why, Estella here could hold it!"

He patted my shoulder and I reached up and clasped his hand, like a trusting child. "Could and shall, if you order it, sir." I sounded more like a plucky English girl than Estella herself would have.

The colonel's scowl eased. "You see? *That's* the stuff England's made of!" Then he introduced me to the messenger from Calcutta, proudly displaying me as if I were the regiment's luck-stone.

Upon hearing the name Estella Humbolt, the messenger said, "Humbolt—not Gerald Humbolt's daughter?" His voice rose with an odd excitement, an emotion explained by his next words. "Estella Humbolt, alive—what news to take back. Your father thinks you dead."

"I know," I said. "All the others are." I glanced down, veiling my eyes, feigning a struggle against tears. I knew what they would say now—*brave little girl; how you have suffered!* Just as I knew what they would say if I told the whole truth, that Gerald Humbolt had murdered his family and his servants—*poor thing; suffering has addled her wits.*

"Is—is my father well?" I asked, and was assured that Gerald Humbolt was not only alive, but very well indeed, having reached Calcutta unscathed. Of course he mourned the vile slaying of his wife and his daughter by mutineers—*but the fact that he now controls his daughter's fortune consoles him,* I finished silently.

"But the news that his daughter is alive will console him."

After a moment, I lifted my head and saw the colonel and his lady and the man from Calcutta all smiling wistfully at me. "Have you a message you would like me to take to your father?" the courier asked.

"Yes," I said. "Tell him that I am here. Tell him that his daughter awaits him."

And I waited all through the long, hot span of time the Wind blew red death down the plains. Meerut, Delhi; Agra and Lucknow. Jhansi. Cawnpore. Doomed cities; skulls strung upon the Dark Goddess's necklace. But no wind blows forever, and She Who Dances Death is a harsh mistress. Those who offer life to her must do so with a pure heart. Hatred and bloodlust have no place in her service.

Her favor withdrawn, the Devil's Wind blew itself out, leaving behind only silence and death, and the seeds of vengeance. And when that Wind no longer blew, Gerald Humbolt traveled the length of India as if the Devil drove him, drawn by the news that Estella lived as a moth is drawn to lamp-flame.

He rode up the drive when the sun soared high and few others were abroad; only the mad or the desperate ventured forth under the deadly noonday sun. Gerald Humbolt could not afford to wait for the reunion with his daughter. He would wish to know at once what she had seen and heard last May—and what she had said, and to whom.

I watched him ride up, and smiled and rose to my feet. I had prepared for our meeting with great care. I wore a white muslin frock, its skirt billowing over three petticoats; half-boots of bronze leather clad my feet, and blue ribbons tied back my hair. A vision of the perfect English girl, wide-eyed, innocent, trusting; a girl who lovingly awaited her loving father.

I could feel his eyes upon me as he stared, trying to decide whether he faced danger. I smiled upon him, my eyes clear as rain-water, and called out to him.

"Father—oh, it is you, it really is!" Behind me I sensed the presence of the colonel's lady, coming to greet her guest, to watch his reunion with his daughter.

Before me, Gerald Humbolt had dismounted; now he walked towards me, forcing himself to smile. A poor effort, showing his teeth in what might as well have been a snarl.

"Estella." He stopped in front of me; he looked ill, his face a sickly, pallid mask. "No. It can't be. You—"

"Did you think your daughter dead?" Since I stood upon the verandah steps, I could look him in the face, deep into his angry, frightened eyes. "Aren't you glad to see me, Father?" Then, as I leaned forward, I suddenly knew what to do; understood the power granted me by the *jadu*'s magic. The power to create justice for my dead.

Smiling, I kissed him upon the cheek—and as I straightened, I let Estella's shadow slip away. Let him see me.

His eyes widened and his breath seemed to choke him; he forced words past his lips. "You—you cannot be Estella. It's a trick. She—"

"Is not dead, while I live. And I am here."

On the verandah behind us, I knew the colonel's lady waited, granting us privacy for the reunion of father and the daughter so miraculously restored to him. And I knew Gerald Humbolt would not reveal my masquerade, lest he betray himself as well. So when he spoke again, it was in a harsh low voice that carried to my ears alone.

"Who are you? What do you want?"

"Why, I stand in place of your daughter. And what

should a dutiful daughter want of a good father?" I moved closer. "I want what you owe your daughter. I want what you owe your daughter's mother. And, Humbolt-sahib—I want what you owe me."

As I spoke those last words, I set my hand upon his chest, where his heart beat hard beneath muscle and bone. "This is what you owe us, Humbolt-sahib. Life."

As he stared at me, I summoned the lives he had stolen, drew them from his own beating heart. At first I felt the pounding of his blood as a constant rhythm, like a wild drum. And I felt that rhythm falter, and fade. And then, with a final shudder, cease altogether.

By the time the colonel's lady ran down the steps, crying out for the servants to come help, Gerald Humbolt was dead.

I looked upon what I had done, and felt only a kind of flat, weary gratitude. My task was completed; the dead had been released to rejoin the Wheel. They were no longer trapped, no longer ghosts forced to haunt the places of the dead.

I knelt beside the body that once had held the soul of Humbolt-sahib. In his last desperate struggle against the power that drained his life, the veins in his throat had opened; blood had poured from his mouth, flooded the front of his coat and shirt. The blood was warm and stained my fingertips.

This was my power, to summon life. What else does a woman do, after all, but rule life, and death, and all that lies between? The *jadu* had given me no power I did not already possess. Her magic had only granted me the wisdom to know my own.

The colonel's lady put her arms around me, telling me I

must be brave. I did not answer; I looked at my bloody hands, and knew what I now must do. The life I had borrowed was not mine to live. That I had known when I bartered upon the riverbank for my past and the *jadu's* future.

The witch had kept her side of the bargain; now I must keep mine.

That night I waited until the moon rose high and the night lay silent. And when all slept and the house dreamed, I slipped out of the English bed and pulled off the English nightgown—and with the English nightgown, I shed Estella from me as a snake sheds its dead skin. She had no further need of me, nor I of her. It was time to let her go.

I unbound my hair from its two braids and shook it loose until its strands rippled like a veil about my naked body. Then I looked into the mirror and saw what others would see, when they looked upon me now. A native. A wild woman.

A *jadu.*

I blew out the night-candle upon the dressing table. And then I walked out of the bungalow, across the verandah and through the faded garden, to find a road that would lead me to a riverbank where a little reed hut waited.

Waited for the *jadu* and her blood-red hands.

<hr />

INDIA EDGHILL

A WRITER OF historical novels (*Queenmaker* and *Wisdom's Daughter*), murder mysteries (*File M for Murder*), and fantasy short stories, India Edghill has been interested in books since childhood, as everyone in the family for the past three generations has been an avid reader. Her father was a history buff and passed on his love of history to her. The natural result is that she owns far too many books on way too many subjects, including nearly a thousand on her favorite topic, the history of India. Her day job—librarian—doesn't help cut down on the books any. India lives in the mid–Hudson Valley in New York.

THE BOY WHO CRIED "DRAGON!"

Mike Resnick

You've all heard the story about the boy who cried "Wolf!"

Teachers and parents have been using it to teach children a lesson for centuries now. It's become a part of our culture. *Everybody* knows about the boy who cried "Wolf!", just as everyone knows about the Three Blind Mice, and the little Dutch boy who put his finger in the dike, and the night Michael Jordan burned the Celtics for 63 points in a playoff game.

But would you like to know the *real* story?

It began a long, long time ago, in a mythical land to the north and west which, for lack of a better term, we shall call The Mythical Land To The North And West. Now, this Land was the home of exceptionally brave warriors and beautiful damsels (and occasionally they were the same person, since beautiful damsels were pretty assertive back then). Each young boy and girl was taught all the arts of warfare, and was soon adept with sword, mace, lance, bow and arrow, dagger, and the off-putting snide remark. They were schooled in horsemanship, camouflage, and military strategy. They learned eye-gouging, ear-biting, kidney-punching, and—since they were destined to become knights and ladies—gentility.

So successful was their training that before long enemy armies were afraid to attack them. Within the borders of the Land justice was so swift that there was not a single criminal left. It would have been a very peaceful and idyllic kingdom indeed—except for the dragons.

You see, the Land was surrounded by hundreds of huge, red-eyed, razor-toothed, fire-breathing dragons, covered with thick scaly skin and armed with vicious-looking claws, and just as fifty years ago a Maasai warrior became a man by slaying a lion with his spear, and today you are hailed as an adult when you can break through Microsoft's firewall, back in the days we are talking about, a boy or girl would be recognized as a young man or woman only after slaying a dragon.

Okay, you've got enough background now, so it's time to introduce Sir Meldrake of the Shining Armor. Well, that's the way he envisioned himself, and that's the name he planned to take once he had slain a dragon and found someone who could actually make a suit of shining armor, but for the moment he was just plain Melvin—tall, gangly, a little underweight, shy around damsels, and more worried about pimples than mortal wounds received in glorious battle. His number had come up in the draft, and it was his turn to sally forth and slay a dragon.

He climbed into his older brother's hand-me-down armor, took out the garbage, kissed his mother good-bye (but only after he made sure none of his friends were watching and snickering), climbed aboard the family horse, and—armed with lance, sword, mace, and a desire to show Mary Lu Penworthy that he was everything she said he wasn't—he set off to slay a dragon, bring back both ears and the tail (or whatever it was one brought back to prove he had been victorious), and become a knight rather than a skinny teenaged boy who couldn't get a date for the prom.

Soon the city was far behind him, and before long he had crossed the border of the Land itself, and was now in unknown territory. He hummed a little song of battle to keep his spirits up, but he was tone-deaf and his humming annoyed his horse, so finally he fell silent, scanning the harsh, rocky landscape for dragons. He found himself wishing he had paid a little more attention in biology class, so he would know what dragons ate when they weren't eating people, and where they slept (if indeed they slept at all), and especially what kind of terrain they liked to hide in when preparing to ambush young men who suddenly wished they were back home in bed, looking at naughty illuminated manuscripts beneath the covers.

At night he found a cozy cave and, lighting a fire to keep warm and ward off anything that might want to annoy him— like, for example, a pride of dragons (or did they come in flocks, or perhaps gaggles?)—he sang himself to sleep, which kept his spirits up but almost drove his horse to distraction.

When morning came he peeked out of the cave, just to be certain that nothing lay in wait for him. Then he peeked again, to be doubly certain. Then he thought about Mary Lu Penworthy and decided that the mole on her chin that had seemed charming only two days ago was really rather ugly in the cold light of day, and hardly worth slaying a dragon for. The same could be said for her eyes (not blue enough), her lips (not rosy-red enough), and her nose (which seemed to exist solely to keep her eyes from bumping into each other).

One by one he considered every young lady of his acquaintance. This one was too tall, that one too short, this one too loud, that one too quiet, and to his surprise he decided that none of them was really worth risking his life in mortal combat with a dragon. In fact, the more he thought about it, the more he couldn't come up with a single reason to seek out a dragon. It was a silly custom, and when he returned to the Land, which he planned to do the moment his horse calmed down and stopped looking at him as if he might burst into song again, he would seek out the Council of Elders and suggest that in the future the rite of passage to adulthood should consist of slaying a chipmunk. They were certainly more numerous, and what purpose was served by slaying a dragon anyway?

His mind made up, Melvin climbed atop his steed and turned him for home—and found his way barred by a huge dragon, twenty feet high at the shoulder, with little beady eyes, thin streams of smoke flowing out of his nostrils, claws the size of butcher knives, and a serious case of halitosis.

"Why have you come to my kingdom?" demanded the dragon.

"I didn't know dragons could talk," said Melvin, surprised.

"I don't mean to be impertinent," said the dragon, "but I could probably fill a very thick book with what you don't know about dragons."

"Yes, I suppose you could," admitted Melvin. He didn't quite know what to say next, so he finally blurted, "By the way, my name is Sir Meldrake of the Shining Armor."

"Are you quite sure?" asked the dragon. "No offense, but you look rather rusty to me."

"My own armor's in the shop getting dry-cleaned," said Melvin, starting to feel rather silly.

"Oh. Well, that explains it," said the dragon charitably. "And since we're doing introductions, my name is Horace. Spelled H-O-R-A-C-E, and not to be mistaken for Horus the Egyptian god."

"That's a strange name for a dragon," said Melvin.

"Just how many dragons do you know on a first-name basis?" asked Horace.

"Counting you, one," admitted Melvin. "Just out of curiosity, how many men have you encountered?"

"The downstate returns aren't all in yet, but so far, rounded off, it comes to one." Horace paused uneasily. "What do we do now?"

"I don't know," said Melvin. "I suppose we battle to the death."

"We do?" said the dragon, surprised. "Why?"

"Those are the ground rules. You meet a dragon, you slay him."

"That's the silliest thing I ever heard!" protested Horace. "I meet dragons all the time, and I've never slain one. In fact, I plan to marry one when I'm an adult and sire twenty or thirty thousand little hatchlings."

"Had you someone in mind?" asked Melvin, interested in spite of himself.

"Nancy Jo Billingsworth," said the dragon with a sigh. "The most beautiful seventeen tons of wings and scales I've ever seen." He looked at Melvin. "How about you? Have you picked out your lady yet—always assuming you survive our battle to the death?"

"I'm playing the field at the moment," said Melvin.

"So you can't get a date either," said Horace knowingly.

"It's these darned zits," said Melvin, trying not to whine.

"Take off your helmet and let me get a good look at you," said Horace.

"You'll be disgusted," said Melvin. "Everyone is."

"Try me," said the dragon.

Melvin removed his helmet.

"God, I would *kill* for zits like those!" said Horace fervently.

"You would?" said Melvin. "Why?"

"Look at this hideous smooth skin on my face," said Horace, holding back a little whimper of self-loathing. "Let's be honest. Nancy Jo Billingsworth winces every time she looks at me. She'd die before she'd go out with me."

"I know exactly how you feel," said Melvin sympathetically.

"It's not just my face," said Horace, a tear rolling down his smooth green cheek. "It's *me*. Whenever we choose up sides for basketball, I'm always the last one picked. When it's Girls' Choice at the dance, I'm the only one who's never asked."

"They won't even let me in the locker room," Melvin chimed in. "They say I'm just wasting space. And the girls draw straws in the cafeteria, and the loser has to sit next to me."

Before long the young man and the young dragon were pouring out their hearts to each other, and because no one had ever listened to them before, they continued until twilight.

"Well, we might as well get on with it," said Horace when they had finished their litany of misery.

"Yeah, I suppose so," said Melvin unenthusiastically.

"I want you to know that if you win, I won't hold it against you," said the dragon. "No one will miss me anyway. I haven't got a friend in the world."

"That's not true," protested Melvin. "*I* like you."

Horace's homely green face lit up. "You do?"

Melvin nodded. "Yes, I do." He paused thoughtfully. "You know, I've never had a real friend before. It seems a shame that one of us has to kill the other."

"I know," said the dragon. "Still, rules are rules."

Suddenly Melvin stood up decisively. "Who says so?"

Horace looked around, confused. "I think *I* just did."

"Well, I'm going to break the rules. You're my only friend, and I'm not going to kill you."

"You're *my* only friend, and I'm not going to kill you either." Horace paused, as if considering what to do next. "Let's kill the horse. At least we'll have something to eat."

Melvin shook his head. "I need him to get home."

"I kind of thought we'd stay out here and be friends forever," said Horace in hurt tones.

"Oh, we'll be friends forever," promised Melvin. "And as my first act of friendship, I'm going to save your life."

"That's very thoughtful of you," said Horace. "But don't be so sure I wouldn't have killed you instead."

"I'm not talking about me," said Melvin. "But every week a new candidate is chosen to go forth and slay a dragon, and next week it's Spike Armstrong's turn."

"Who is Spike Armstrong?" asked Horace.

"He's everything I'm not," said Melvin bitterly. "He's the captain of every sports team, he's the most handsome boy in the Land, and even though he has the brains of a newt all the cheerleaders fight to sit near him in the cafeteria."

"I dislike him already," said Horace.

"Anyway, if he finds you, he'll kill you," concluded Melvin.

"So you're going to fight him in my place?" asked Horace. "I call that exceptionally decent of you, Melvin. I'll always honor your memory and put flowers on your grave."

"No, I'm not going to fight him," replied Melvin. "I wouldn't fare any better against him than you would. But any time I know he's sallying forth in your direction, I'll go to the far side of the city and tell everybody that a dragon is approaching, and Spike will immediately head off in that direction and you'll be safe."

"That's a splendid idea!" enthused Horace. "And whenever Thunderfire goes out hunting for a man to eat, I'll do the same thing to him."

"Thunderfire?" repeated Melvin.

Horace grimaced. "Females swoon over him. He's got lumps the size of baseballs all over his face, and his flame shoots out ten feet, and he just struts around like he owns the place. But I'll see to it that he never finds you."

"You know," said Melvin, "I *like* having a friend."

"Me too," said Horace. "My mother says one should always seek out new experiences."

Their ruses worked. Spike Armstrong never did slay Horace, and Thunderfire never did eat Melvin. As for Melvin and Horace, they continued to sneak away and meet every Saturday afternoon except when it was raining, and although neither of them ever did become king or marry the damsel of their dreams, they each had a friend they could trust and confide in, which in many ways is better than being a king or marrying a dream.

And that is the story of the boy who cried "Dragon!"

Of course, when dragons sit around the campfire at

night or tuck their children into bed, they tell the story of the dragon who cried "Boy!"

MIKE RESNICK

MIKE RESNICK is the author of forty-eight science fiction and fantasy novels, twelve collections, more than 180 short stories, and two screenplays, and has edited forty anthologies. He has won four Hugos (science fiction's Oscar) and has been nominated a near-record twenty-five times. He has won other major awards in the U.S.A., France, Japan, Croatia, Spain, and Poland, and has been nominated for awards in England and Italy. His work has been translated into twenty-two languages. He lives in Cincinnati, Ohio, and his Web site is www.mikeresnick.com.

Mike confesses that he has never quite understood why men rode forth to slay dragons, and he thought it might be fun to write about a man (a young one) and a dragon (also a young one) who didn't understand it either. Also, everyone has heard the fable about the boy who cried "Wolf!"—and wouldn't it be nice if he had a *reason* for doing so?

STUDENT OF OSTRICHES

———◆◆◆———

Tamora Pierce

MY STORY BEGAN as my mother carried me in her belly to the great Nawolu trade fair. Because she was pregnant, our tribe let Mama ride high on the back of our finest camel, which meant she was also lookout for our caravan. It was she who spotted the lion and gave the warning. Our warriors closed in tight around our people to keep them safe, but our people were in no danger from the lion.

He was a young male, with no lionesses to guard him as he stalked a young ostrich that had strayed from its parents. He drew closer to his intended prey. Its mama and papa raced toward the lion, faster than horses, their large eyes fixed on the threat. The lion was young and ignorant. He snarled as one ostrich kicked him. Then the other did the same. On and on, the ostriches kicked the lion, until he was a fur sack of bones.

As the ostriches led their children away, my mama said she felt me kick in her belly for the first time.

If the kicking ostriches were a good omen for our

family, they were not for my papa. Two months later he was wounded in the leg during a battle with an enemy tribe. The leg never healed completely, forcing him to leave the ranks of the warriors and join the wood-carvers, though he never complained of that. Not long after my papa began to walk with a cane, I was born. Papa was sad for a little while, because I was yet another girl. He would have liked just one son to take his place as a warrior, but he always said that when I first smiled at him, he could not be sad anymore.

When I was six years old, I asked my parents if I could go outside the village wall with the herds. Who could be happy inside the walls when the world lay outside? My parents spoke to our chief. He agreed that I could learn to watch goats on the rocky edges of the great plains on which the world was born.

Of course, I did not begin alone. My ten-year-old cousin Ogin was appointed to teach me. On that first morning I followed him and his dogs to a grazing place. Once the goats were settled, I asked him, "What must I know?"

"First, you learn to use the herder's weapon, the sling," Ogin said. He was very tall and lean, like a stick with muscles. "You must be able to help the dogs drive off enemies." He held up a strip of leather.

I practiced the twirl and release of the stone in the sling until my shoulders were sore. For a change of pace, Ogin would teach me the names of the goats' markings and body parts until I knew them by heart. Once my muscles had relaxed again, I would take up the sling once more.

When it was time to eat our noon food, my cousin took the goats, the dogs, and me up onto a stone outcropping. From there we could see the plain stretch out under its veil of dusty air. This was my reward, this long view of the first step to the world. I almost forgot how to eat. Lonely trees fanned their branches out in flat-topped sprays. Vultures roosted in their branches. Veils of tall grass separated the herds of zebra, wildebeest, and gazelle in the distance. Lions waited near a watering hole close to our rocks as giraffes nibbled the leaves of thorny trees on the other side.

Watching it all, I saw movement. I gasped. "Ogin— there! Are those—are they ostriches?"

"You think, because your mama saw them, they are cousins to you?" he teased me. "What is it, Kylaia? Will you grow tail feathers and race them?"

The ostriches *were* running. They had long, powerful legs. When they ran, they opened their legs up and stretched. They were not delicate like the gazelles, like my older sisters. They ran in long, loping strides. Watching them, I thought, I want to run like *that*.

For a year I was Ogin's apprentice. He taught me to keep the goats shifting in the fields around the stone lookout place so there would be grass throughout the year. He was patient, and he did not laugh at me as I struggled to learn to be a dead shot with a sling, to be a careful tracker, and to understand the ways of the dogs, the goats, and the wild creatures of the plains.

Ogin taught me to run, too, as he and my sisters did— like gazelles, on the balls of their feet. After our noon meals, as Ogin slept, I would practice my own ostrich running. I opened up my strides, dug in my feet, and thrust out my chest, imagining myself to be a great bird, eating the ground with my big feet. Each day I ran a little farther and a little faster as Ogin and the dogs slept, and the goats and the songbirds looked on.

When I had followed Ogin for a year, my uncle, the

herd-chief, came out with us. Ogin made me show off my skills with the goats and the dogs.

"Tomorrow morning, come to me," said my uncle. "You shall have a herd and dogs of your own."

It was my seventh birthday. I was so proud! I was now a true member of the village, with proper work to do. Papa gave me a wooden ball painted with colored stripes. Mama and my sisters had woven me new clothes and a cape for the cold. I ran through the village to show off my ball and to tell my friends that I was now a true worker.

Five older boys caught me on my way home. They knocked me down and they took my ball.

When I reached our hut, my family noticed my bruises. Papa limped through the village until he found my ball and brought it back to me.

My pride lay in the dust. I pretended to ignore my family's conversation as my sisters demanded that the boys be punished, and my father said he would appeal to our chief. Whatever punishment the boys got would have nothing to do with me, only with the peace of the tribe. Their penalty would not make me any taller, or less ashamed.

In the morning, I took my new herd to graze in the tall stones. While the goats found grasses tucked into rocky hollows, I stared at the plain. The village would deal with the boys, but later they would take their vengeance out on me. What would I do then?

I don't know why a wild dog decided to be a fool that morning, or why he left the protection of his pack. I only know that he was alone when he found the old ostrich nesting-ground. It was not breeding season. There were no eggs or young to protect. The king ostrich, his queen, and his other wives were nibbling grass seed as a shift of wind brought them the scent of wild dog. My thigh muscles twitched as the pair ran to catch the intruder, their great legs eating up the yards between them. The dog tried to flee too late. The ostriches were upon him. The queen's first kick sent the wild dog flying into the air. He lurched to his feet, but the ostriches had already caught up. A few more kicks finished the dog.

He must have taken their ball, I thought, impressed with ostrich vengeance. If *I* had been an ostrich, those boys would have returned my ball to *me*.

An idea flowered in my mind. It was said that Shang warriors, masters of unarmed combat, could kill by kicking alone, but I had never seen a Shang. Our young men wrestled for the honor of our tribe. The only time they used their feet was to hook a foot behind an opponent's leg to pull him off-balance. But surely a person with strong legs could fight by kicking, as ostriches did. One kick would knock an opponent—an enemy—onto his back. Onto his thieving, mocking back . . .

So I tried to kick like an ostrich, and fell on my behind.

I was a stubborn girl. As the dogs and goats watched, I kicked. And kicked. I learned that I had to stand a certain way in order not to fall. Then I learned to stand in a better way, so I would not fall or wobble as I kicked. My legs cramped, so I ran like an ostrich to stretch them. But I did not let go of my ostrich-kick fighting. I chased the idea through my days as I took my goats out to graze, then I practiced my sling and kicking—with attention for both legs—as well as ostrich-running, all before the noon meal. When I finally ate, I watched the thousand stories of the plain. Afterward, I continued my many practices though they made me sweat, and sometimes made me sick in the dry season's heat.

At day's end I went home, too weary to do more than play catch with my ball and my little cousins.

I was not yet eight when the bullies caught me alone again. "*We* could be playing kick-the-ball and building the muscles of our legs, while *you* only play with children," their leader told me. "The ball is wasted with you. You will give it to us and tell your papa that you are tired of it. If you do, maybe we will leave you teeth to chew with."

His friends laughed. The boy behind me wrapped his arms around my chest, pinning my arms. He was going to help me, though he did not mean to, by keeping me balanced and free to use both legs. I watched their leader come closer to take the ball from my hands.

They were wild dogs. I was an ostrich. I kicked their leader in the belly so hard that he bent over and vomited. One of the others tried to punch me. I kicked to the side and rammed his upper thigh. He fell. Another boy rushed me. Twisting in my captor's hold, I drove my heels into the rushing boy's leg, knocking him down. Then I used my elbows to make the boy who held me let go.

I learned many things from this, like what will make a boy yell and what will leave him unable to chase me. And I kept my ball. The bullies did not dare complain of me to the chief, either. They were older than I. Everyone would laugh to know they feared a girl.

The next morning I scrambled up onto the rocks to watch for my next lesson. The zebras, who are mean and tricky, had come to the watering hole, where a family of giraffes were already drinking. Giraffes take time to drink, spreading their legs to lower their bodies, then dipping their heads at the ends of their very long necks. They took up half the water hole. Some zebras got impatient waiting for their zebra chiefs to drink. I could see it in their wicked black eyes. If the zebras made the giraffes go, then all of the zebras would have room to drink.

One of the young zebras pretended to be idling along as he circled the giraffes. It was a male giraffe who saw him. He watched as the zebra drew near.

Then the male giraffe did a strange thing. He pulled his head back. The zebra took two more steps toward the giraffes. The male giraffe swung his head like a mallet and clubbed the zebra with his heavy skull. The zebra went tumbling in the dust. With a snort, as if to say he had only been playing, the zebra struggled to his feet and went back to his herd to wait.

I had discovered the secret of punching.

I began to practice. Soon I learned the best way to punch was to make a giant fist of both clasped hands, fingers locked together. The flesh of my hands, though, was tender. A few blows against the nearby rocks and trees taught me that. I ground my teeth and began to toughen my hands as the warriors did, a little at a time, striking bark and stone day after day. Young antelopes toughened their horns, after all. I had toughened my feet on the rock-and-briar-strewn ground outside the village wall. I could toughen my hands to hit like a giraffe.

Two years passed as I practiced my new skill with the goats and the dogs for company. I built calluses on my hands, feet, and elbows. I hit, I kicked, and I ran. I drove off wild dogs with my sling. I began to hunt, bringing extra meat to my family at the day's end.

When I was ten, I was eligible for the harvest games we held with neighboring villages. I entered the girls' races. I was too slow to win the short races; my gazelle sisters overtook me easily there. Then came the long race, three times around a neighboring village's wall. I ran across the finish line while my gazelle sisters limped in after me. I was not surprised; after all, I ran greater distances than that every day, with the goats.

Five months later, before the spring planting celebration, Ogin and my sisters took me aside. "We want you to do something that will put coins in our purses," Ogin said. "We want you to run in the boys' races. We will bet on you, and everyone will think we have gone mad."

"Or let our pride in our village fool us," Iyaka added. "They will bet against you, and we will win."

My sisters' eyes were bright and shining. Ogin—now fourteen and chief herdboy—grinned wickedly. I turned to my sisters, who were runners. "You think I can beat them?" I asked.

They giggled. "We know you can," said Iyaka.

And so at the spring festival I lingered on the sidelines of the boys' first short race until Ogin, according to our plan, dragged me over to the starting line. Everyone hurried to bet against me as the boys who were to race protested. The judge said that there was no rule against girls; only custom. The boys had to give in.

I was third in the first short race of sixty yards, second in the second short race of seventy-five yards, and first in the ninety-yard race, as my sisters had planned for me. I won the boys' long race, too. That night there were honey cakes with supper and coins in the family purse.

Our lives marched on, through festivals and races. My sisters grew older and more beautiful. I simply grew. "She is turning into a giraffe!" boys would tease me. I ignored them.

Thanks to my height and strength, my boy-less family had meat in the pot and coins for my sisters' dowries.

Besides, I liked giraffes. They looked silly, but wise creatures let them be, and they feasted among thorns.

My goats were exchanged for Ogin's old cattle herd when I turned eleven, while Ogin was made a hunter. As I learned the ways of the cows, I studied the plains and the rocks. In the tall grasses and wiry trees of the plains, I was free to join nature in its blood and power. There I practiced running, hitting, and kicking, using the blows to break fallen branches for firewood or to give a wounded animal a quick death. I learned more kicks from zebras, a double-hand strike from lions, and a back-of-the-fist blow from elephants.

Sometimes I dreamed about the world beyond the plains, trying to imagine its shape. My first taste of it would come when I was thirteen, when I would be allowed to attend the Nawolu trade fair for the first time. It was a week's journey from our village, a gathering where tribes came from hundreds of miles to sell and to buy, to marry off daughters and sons, and to hold games of strength and speed. Daughters were presented when they were thirteen, though they were not actually married until they were sixteen or seventeen. During my twelfth year, my next-oldest sister went with the others to the fair. She came back talking of nothing but boys.

Iyaka, who was then seventeen, returned quietly. Mama told us the good news. A chief's son, a wealthy young man named Awochu, had seen Iyaka race. He had fallen in love with her. It was odd for young people to choose their own mates, but Awochu's father could not deny his only son. It did not matter that Iyaka's dowry was tiny. For a bride-price Awochu would give us thirty cattle, and he would accept

Papa's blessing in return. Awochu would marry Iyaka at the next trade fair.

"What can I say? I am so honored by my family-to-be," Iyaka said when we begged for details. "Thirty cattle will make Papa rich and honored. I could not have refused even if I had wanted to."

When she put it that way, she made me ask myself what I would say if a man's family offered for me. I thought about it as I watched over my cows the next day. Did I want to be married? I would have to leave my days on my beloved plains, and never see the world beyond. I would retire behind a wall like the one around our village to weave, cook, sew, and bear children. No more watching for game at the watering hole. No more entertainment from zebras and giraffes. No more gazelle and cheetah races.

I could wait to marry.

Still, every girl must turn thirteen, and so did I. The time of the trade fair came around. Our whole family went to Nawolu for Iyaka's wedding and my first fair. Nawolu was a walled city on a deep river, so different from anything I had seen on the plains. In the distance towered a lone mountain, capped in white. Everywhere there were travelers, animals, bright cloths and flawless animal skins. I thought my eyes would burst from all the new sights.

Our village had a place by the fairgrounds outside the walls. Before we had pitched our tents, friends from other tribes came to visit and stayed for supper. Our chief finally sent them away so we could sleep. In the morning we would dress in our finest to meet Chief Rusom, who governed Nawolu and the lands around it.

I was close to sleep when Mama whispered, "I did not see Awochu."

After a very long silence, Iyaka said, "He did not come."

The next morning we girls fixed our hair, put on our best dresses, and decked ourselves out in our few pieces of jewelry. Then, with our mothers to guard us, we went to the fair. There was so much that was new. I saw the wonders of the world beyond my plains and felt a tug on my heart, a call to see where everything had come from. What exotic creatures wove the wispy cloth called "silk"? Who made fine jewelry from countless tiny gold beads? What ingredients went into the strange new perfumes and filled small stone pots with cosmetics? I wanted to know all of these things. The people who sold the goods would only point and name a country or a city I had never heard of.

Mama, Iyaka, and I moved ahead of the others. We were admiring exotic feathers for sale when Iyaka suddenly fell silent. Mama and I looked up. Here came a handsome young man, well-muscled, with the scars of a warrior on his cheeks and chest. A girl clung to his arm like a vine. She wore a blue-silk dress, and so much gold jewelry that it was impossible to tell if she was truly beautiful or simply dressed in money. She looked at him with passion in her eyes.

The young man, who also wore gold, halted. The blue-silk girl had to halt with him, and stared, as he did, at Iyaka. The girl looked at Iyaka, who had gone pale, and she *smirked.* At *my* sister, who was more beautiful than she without jewelry or silk!

"Awochu," Iyaka whispered. The young man in gold licked his lips as if they were dry.

Mama stood in front of Iyaka. "Is this how you act before the family of the girl you are to marry in a week?" she asked sharply. "You parade this fair with a strumpet on your arm, mocking my daughter's good name?"

The girl with the gold scowled. She will have wrinkles before she is thirty, I thought as I put an arm around my sister.

"She is no strumpet!" said my sister's betrothed. "*She* is my bride-to-be. I will not honor a contract with a witch and the family of a witch."

Mama put her hands on her hips. "My daughter is no witch, you pompous hyena! You slander her name and ours to speak so!"

"She put a spell on me last year," said Awochu. "My father's shaman cured me of it. Now I will have nothing to do with a witch!"

A crowd was gathering. People are jackals, always willing to feed off someone else's kill.

"You signed a marriage contract in blood," Mama said. "You did it with your eyes open and your mama bleating like a sheep, telling you there were girls more worthy of you. 'More worthy,' with Iyaka and her family and chief standing right there! The only witchcraft was in you knowing she wouldn't lie down for you without marriage, and you being like a spoiled baby who won't hear 'no'!"

"She put a spell on me!" Awochu cried. "She put it in the stain she used on her lips, so I was half mad."

"Witch," someone whispered behind me. I whirled to glare and saw people crowded all around us.

"Unlawful to spell a man into marriage," a woman said.

"Oh, no," Iyaka said. She shook out of my hold and walked up to Awochu, her muscles tight with anger. "You courted me with flowers and sweets and promises until I barely knew my name. You pursued me because I said no to you that first day, when you kissed me like a barbarian. And now you sully my name and the name of my family?" She spat in the dust at his feet and looked at the blue-silk girl. "You want to be watching now," Iyaka told the other girl. "This is what you want to marry. He will blame *you* when things go wrong between you." Iyaka turned her attention back to Awochu. "You want your freedom? You may have it—*after* you pay half my bride-price for breaking the contract and lying about me."

Awochu had looked arrogant, then petty, then furious. Now he looked smug. "I pay you *nothing*," he told Iyaka. "Not to one who uses magic for love. Nawolu chief Rusom judges all trade fair disagreements. *He* will know what to do."

He marched off to the chief's pavilion. We had no choice but to follow, to stop him from lying to Chief Rusom. The witnesses followed, eager for more of someone else's quarrel and the chief's judgment.

Luckily, friends heard Awochu's claim and ran to fetch our tribe. By the time we could see the chief's bright red pavilion, Papa, our shaman, and our own chief had come, with the rest of my kinfolk. Now Chief Rusom would see that my sister was a girl of good family, the kind who would never use magic in a foul way. He would order Awochu to admit to his lie before everyone, so my sister's name would go untainted.

In order for the chief to hear the many people who came to speak with him during the day, his men had built the pavilion with the floor raised up a foot from the ground. Chief Rusom and his companions could then sit at the edge, under the shelter of the canopy, and talk with those who stood on the beaten dirt before them. We moved to the front of the crowd, passed along by people who knew why we were there. Iyaka clutched my hand and Mama's and would not let go. I had to stand right behind her as she stood in a line with Mama, Papa, our shaman, and our chief.

Awochu bowed to the man who had to be Chief Rusom. I glanced at the man on the chief's right and almost gasped like an ignorant country girl. I had never seen a man so pale-skinned. Everyone in my life was dark brown or black. Some of the fair's visitors were a lighter brown than I had ever seen before, but their skin was still brown. This man was bronze on his face, hands, and forearms, while his jacket, open at the collar, showed a chest that was *white.*

He had brown-black hair, straighter than the hair of anyone I knew. His eyes were brown-black, almost the color of normal eyes. He didn't dress like a normal man, though. He wore a loose cloth jacket and, instead of a long skirt, a garment made of two cloth tubes that covered each of his legs. Instead of sandals he wore leather shoes that covered his feet and legs all the way to his knees. Only his hands looked right. They were hard, broad, and scarred, the hands of a warrior. His neck was muscled like a bull's.

"Do you know who that is?" Ogin had worked his way up behind me. I looked at him. His eyes gleamed as he looked at the pale man. He shifted his weight from foot to foot, unable to stand still.

"No, but he looks very sick," I whispered.

"Pf," Ogin said, pushing me a little. "You know the stories of the Shang warriors, who fight and kill with bare hands? That man is the Shang Falcon. He is a great warrior!"

The pale visitor looked like a man, not a legend, to me. "He is a horse who will burn and bloat and explode in the sun," I replied. "Put him back in the oven and let him cook until he is done."

I looked at the platform and got a very bad feeling. Awochu had left his blue-silk girl to wait and climbed onto the platform to go to the other man, who sat on Chief

Rusom's left. This man wore gold on his arms and fingers. Awochu kissed him on both scarred cheeks. He looked enough like Awochu to be his father. Worse, there was a table placed between the man dripping in gold and Rusom. He and the chief shared food and drink like allies, or friends.

"Awochu, why have you brought these people?" asked the man with the gold, his voice filling the air. "Why do you disturb the chief?"

Awochu bowed to Chief Rusom. "Great chief," he said with respect, "I come to you as a wronged guest. Last year at this fair I was overtaken by a madness that made me want that girl as my bride." He pointed at Iyaka. "After I stole a kiss from her, I could not sleep or eat unless I was with her. I offered her my name and the wealth of my family. I begged my father and mother to accept this match with an ordinary plains girl." He shook his head in sorrow. "When we returned to our own great village, our shaman saw the traces of magic on me. He kept me in his hut for nine days and nine nights to cleanse me of the evil spell. He told me—he will tell you, if you ask it—that the girl had painted charm color on her lips. When I stole that kiss, magic made me hers. It made me desire her to the point that I had signed a marriage contract with her family.

"Great Chief Rusom, is it not the law that no contract a man enters into while under the influence of magic is binding? For so my honored father explained the law to me. I owe this girl nothing. She cannot have me, so she binds me to a false claim, in order to steal my father's cattle."

"I do not steal!" cried Iyaka. "I happily release him from the contract. I do not want a man who is so fickle or so easily swayed." She glared at Awochu's father and the elegant woman who stood behind him, who had to be Awochu's mother. "But he has sullied my name and the name of my family with his accusation of love-magic. He must pay half the bride-price for his lies. He should be grateful I do not ask for it all. You see?" She took the delicate skin on which the contract was written from her sash, unfolded it, and offered it to Chief Rusom. "It is written there. If I release him, he must pay half the bride-price to me. If he lies about me, he must pay it all and apologize for his evil, and admit he lied."

"It is she who lies!" cried Awochu. "It is also written that if I am forced to this or lied to about her honor or her maidenhood, I am free of the contract!"

Chief Rusom read the document carefully, his eyes flicking to Awochu, to Iyaka, to my parents, to our shaman, and to our chief. He did not look at Awochu's father. But when he reached down to that table for his teacup, Awochu's father picked it up, filled it, and gave it to Chief Rusom. It was as plain as a baboon's red behind: Awochu's father would find a way to fill the chief's cup if the chief could help his son.

Chief Rusom let the contract fall. "When there is such disagreement, and good names are at stake, there are several ways to resolve the matter," he said in a voice like oil. "But involving magic . . ." He stroked his chin. "No, I think it must be trial by combat. The gods will allow the innocent side to win. Awochu?"

"I fight my own battles," Awochu said, thrusting his chest out. His eyes held the same gleam as the eyes of the chief and his father. He knew the way was prepared.

"Me," Ogin said, thrusting his way past Papa and me. The Shang Falcon was also getting to his feet, as if a pale man could know anything of us.

The chief was already shaking his head. "It must be a

member of the girl's direct family," he said, proving he knew quite well who we were.

Papa took a limping step forward. The gleam in Awochu's eyes brightened.

Without thinking, I pushed ahead, suddenly noticing that I was as tall as my papa. "I will fight," I said, though my voice cracked when I said "fight." I ignored people's laughter and made myself say, "She is my sister. It is my name, too."

"No!" cried Mama. "I forbid it! She is a girl! She is no warrior!"

But Chief Rusom already was shaking his head. "Do you believe the gods will help you, girl? This is no time to thrust yourself into serious business if *you* are not serious."

I trembled as I answered, "I believe in the gods." What I believed in was the ostrich gods, the giraffe gods, the lion gods. This dishonorable chief knew nothing of them.

"If the gods decide, then surely it only matters that she is of the girl's blood," said Chief Rusom. "I call for the combat when the sun leaves no shadows."

All was noise then. Mama and Papa scolded me. Iyaka hit me with her fists. My own chief told me I was a fool and had cost my sister *and* my papa their honor. The gleeful crowd followed us to the enclosure set aside for trial by combat. Servants came to take away Awochu's golden ornaments as his girl poured a cup of wine for him. His mama set a stool in the shade for him to rest upon while he waited for the proper time.

Ogin and the pale man brought a stool for me. They made me sit and drink some water. Gently the pale man, the Shang Falcon, placed hands like iron on the muscles between my neck and shoulders. I felt him hesitate. Then he raised my hands, examining my callused knuckles. He probed my back muscles with those hard fingers, then bent down to look at my legs and feet.

"Well," he said. His voice was deep and smooth, like dark honey. "Perhaps this is not the folly it looks to be." His Dikurri accent was thick, but I could understand him.

Of course, peahen, I told myself. He sat with the chief. They must be able to talk.

He was asking me something. I turned to look up at him. "What?" I asked. My lips felt stiff.

"What do you wear under your dress?" he asked slowly, as if he knew I could only understand slow speech, just then.

"How dare you!" cried Mama.

He put a hand on her shoulder. "Your daughter cannot fight in a dress," he said kindly. "The women warriors of the Chelogu tribes fight entirely naked, in tribute to the Great Mother Goddess. I think your daughter may wear a *little* more than that, but a skirt will hobble her like ropes hobble a donkey."

"She *is* a donkey," my mother whispered, her lips trembling. "A stupid donkey who does not understand what she has done here."

"She wears a breast band and a loincloth," Iyaka said.

"If they are snug, that is enough," said the Falcon. He asked me, "Can you remove the dress on your own?"

I plucked at my sash until it came apart. Someone pulled it away; then Iyaka took the dress from where it had fallen. I did not know why Mama was so upset. I raced in no more than this at every festival.

The Falcon crouched behind me and began to work the muscles around my collarbone with those iron fingers. They spread warmth and relaxation down into my arms. "What is your name, girl?" he asked me, his voice coming from behind me like a ghost's.

Ogin answered for me. "Kylaia," he said, his eyes as over-bright as Mama's. "She is Kylaia al Jmaa."

The Falcon picked up one of my hands and began to work on it. Across the arena, servants rubbed oil onto Awochu's shoulders. "Kylaia," the Falcon said for my ears only, "who taught you to fight?"

I blinked at him like a simpleton. "The ostriches," I said. "The killers of the plains."

"She is mad," Papa said abruptly. "I will make them stop it. *I* will fight him."

The Falcon said, "It is in the gods' hands now, sir. But I do not think they have chosen badly."

"Why do you help her?" asked my papa suddenly. "You sat with Chief Rusom."

"I help her because we of Shang help those who defend the unjustly accused," the Falcon replied. "A blind man could see who lied back there, and who told the truth. And I sat with Chief Rusom because I had just arrived in his lands, and it is polite for a warrior to meet his host."

By the time the sun left no shadows, the Falcon had loosened the muscles in my arms, back, legs, and feet. I was as relaxed as if I had just finished a quick sprint to get my blood warm.

Someone struck a gong. It was time. I walked out to the center of the arena, ignoring the comments of the crowd. If they were properly bred, like the people of our village, they would no more laugh at a maiden dressed to show her body's skills than they would laugh at a woman giving birth.

Awochu met me at the center. Chief Rusom's shaman prayed. I ignored him. My eyes watched Awochu. He would want to hit me hard and fast, to get it over with, so he could enjoy my sister's defeat. I had said my prayers. Now it was time for me to take down this hunter who had come into my territory. He was stronger on his right side, the muscles of that arm clearer than the muscles of his left. He would try to grapple with me, as the young men did in unarmed combat. If he actually took hold of me, I would be in trouble. He was taller, stronger, heavier. He had fought in battle to earn his scars. He had fought with his hands.

Now Chief Rusom had something to say.

Awochu shifted on his feet for balance.

Someone struck the gong again. Awochu lunged for me. I pivoted to one side and ostrich-kicked him. The ball of my foot slammed him just under his ribs with all the speed and strength I had built up. He gasped and turned to grab my kicking leg, but I was already behind him. He was so *slow*. I did not understand that all those years of repetition had not just made me a fast runner. All that practice on wood and stone, as I pretended they were living lions and wild dogs, had made me a fast kicker, a fast mover, a fast hitter. With that speed, each blow and kick had also gained power.

I drove the ball of my other foot into Awochu's back, above his right kidney. He staggered away from me and fell to his knees. I lunged forward and hammered my linked fists giraffe-style into the side of his neck. Wheezing from pain, he grabbed my hands. I bounced up and swung down to drive my knee into his spine. He straightened with a strangled cry, letting me go. Then I wrapped my arm around his neck from behind, gripping my fist with my free hand. I pulled back, resting my knee against his spine for leverage. Choking, he clawed my arm, ripping my flesh with his nails.

"Confess," I told him. "Tell the truth. Swear it on your

mother's name, or I will cripple you." I did not think I could do it, but it sounded like the right thing to say to a bully who had shamed my family before all the trade fair.

He tried to speak and could not. I eased my grip just a little.

"The gods have humbled me!" he shrieked. "They sent a demon into this girl child to shame me! Iyaka al Jmaa is an honorable girl!"

"Mention the magic," I whispered. If he wanted to believe a demon had beaten him, I did not care. I only wanted my sister to get what was owed.

"I won't," he said. I tightened my hold briefly, then relaxed it. When he could breathe again, he confessed to everything and begged his father for the fifteen cattle for my sister.

We did not trust Awochu's family to arrange things honorably. Instead my chief made Awochu and his father sign new words on the old marriage contract, saying that the agreement was ended and that the right price would be paid for the slight to my sister. Then the men of my village went with Awochu and his father to collect the fifteen cattle.

This I was told of later. As soon as I let Awochu up, my sisters came, wrapped me in my dress, and took me back to our tent, to clean up and sleep.

When I awoke, only a small lamp was burning in our tent. Light was also flickering through the cracks around the door flap. It was night, and the campfires were lit. I could hear the low murmur of voices outside.

I could also smell food. I got up, every muscle of my body aching. In my rage I had done more than I was used to, and my body was unhappy. Like an old woman, I crept outside.

The Shang Falcon sat at our fire with my parents, Iyaka, and Ogin, eating from the pot with one hand, as if he had eaten that way all his life. He nodded to me and said, "I have been talking with your parents about your future," as though continuing a conversation we had already begun.

"I have no future," I told him as I accepted a round of bread from Iyaka. I scooped food onto it and crouched between my parents. "Boys won't want a girl who gets possessed by demons."

"You were no more possessed than I am," said the Falcon. "Ogin told us about the way you watched animals, and the way you practiced fighting as they did."

I glared at Ogin, who grinned at me and shrugged. "I am a hunter as well as a herder," he said cheerfully. "If I cannot be quiet, I catch only grubs."

The Falcon smiled. "And so I was saying to your parents, while the Shang school for warriors normally does not take a new student of your advanced age—"

"Advanced age!" I protested.

"Shang students begin training between their fourth and sixth years," Papa said. "Let the man say what he must. Stop interrupting."

"I believe they would take an old woman if she had your unusual skills," the Falcon said to me. "In fact, I am so sure of it that I am willing to pay a proper bride-price for you. But you will not be my bride on our journey to Shang, you will be my student. You would be as safe with me as you would with your father."

I scowled at him. "Are you buying me? I am no slave."

He chuckled. "No," he said, laughter still in his eyes. "This is an offering of thanks I give to your family, for the honor of being allowed to teach so inventive a young lady."

"We believe him," Mama said quietly. "We trust him. But you must choose."

"He says you may visit, when you have finished the studies." Iyaka smiled at me, but tears rolled down her cheeks.

Papa took my hand and kissed it. "I think you saved our family's honor today at high cost to your future," he said, his voice as soft as Mama's. "Even less than a bride possessed by a demon will a young man like a wife who can kick his ribs in."

I looked at the Falcon. "Why should I want to study the ways of warriors out of grandmother tales?" I asked him, feeling my heart beat a little faster.

He got to his knees and rolled a stone half the size of my head over in front of him. His eyes half-closed, he seemed to go away for a moment. I did not even see him cock his fist and punch the stone.

The stone broke in half.

For the first time since we had met Awochu in the street, I felt like myself again. "How did you do that?" I asked. "Will you teach me that? And what is your idea of a fair bride-price? If I am to be a Shang warrior, I must not dishonor my family with a few coppers."

TAMORA PIERCE

TAMORA PIERCE is the *New York Times* and *Wall Street Journal* bestselling writer of twenty-two books of fantasy for teenagers, almost half of which (The Song of the Lioness quartet, the Protector of the Small quartet, and her most recent books, *Trickster's Choice* and *Trickster's Queen*) are set in the same universe as "Student of Ostriches." The idea for the story came from her fans, who have requested more stories about the Shang warriors of that universe, and from a character mentioned in her book *Lioness Rampant*—Kylaia al Jmaa, the fabled Shang Unicorn. Tammy thought it would be fun to see how the Unicorn first set out on the warrior's path. She has long been fascinated by wildlife, as fans of her Immortals quartet know, and it occurred to her that it would not be unusual for an observant and imaginative girl to turn the animal behavior she saw into ways to defend herself. Once Tammy understood that, it was as if Kylaia stood beside her and dictated her story. "It's not an experience I have often," Tammy says, "but it really rocked while it lasted!"

Tammy lives in New York City with her own wildlife: four cats, two parakeets, and her beloved Spouse-Creature, Web designer Tim Liebe.

Her Web site is www.tamorapierce.com.

SERPENT'S ROCK

Laura Anne Gilman

GULPILIL STOOD IN THE *middle of the red-rock canyon and wondered how long it would take him to die.*

"I stand against you, my brother, not because I wish you harm, but because you and I cannot be in the same place at this same time. I stand against you, my brother, not because I wish you to be no more, but because I wish to continue.

"In the Long-Ago Time you knew your place and I knew mine. But you walk across your place and into mine, and therefore, my brother, I must stand against you."

He was repeating himself. Knowing you were going to die might do that, he supposed, but it made his telling weaker, and that was no good. The shaft of his spear was slick and useless in his hands. He almost dropped it, but what then would he hold?

Not that weapons would matter, in the end.

Across the rocks, the shadows crept closer. When the shadows overtook him, it would be time.

* * *

Four days earlier, the Great Serpent had shifted deep underground, and the earth had moved. Busy with fishing, the people thought little of it for three days after.

"Marwai!" Jinabu collapsed to his knees at the outskirts of the fish camp. "Marwai!" His skin was shiny-dark with sweat, and his thick black hair was matted against his neck.

Gulpilil was the first to reach him. Jinabu had taken Gulpilil's sister Malle back with him, last Gathering Time. Gulpilil had not seen them since then. But Jinabu had no time for the teenager, his gaze restlessly searching the growing crowd until the elder came forward, the others parting to give him room.

Marwai was ancient—some said as ancient as the sand— and there was nothing he did not know, no story he could not recite. Whatever had so driven Jinabu to a frenzy, Marwai would set right. Gulpilil knew that this was so.

The others began to drift away, back to bringing in the heavy stone traps, rebaiting them, and casting them into the shallow waters. Redshell did not keep well, but it was good in season. The dingoes would eat whatever the people did not, and make their coats glossy and their bellies firm until it was time to hunt the quick-leapers again.

Gulpilil's skill lay not in setting traps or in hunting the quick-leapers, but in fixing the traps and honing the spearheads. Stone moved under his hands as it had for the All-Father, they said. But Jinabu's anguish drew him, and so instead he followed the men to the stone overhang where Marwai built his fire, and spoke to those who came to him.

"You, boy, go back to your work." Dundalli blocked his way. Dundalli was tall and strong, and his skin was covered in clay dust, making him look like a First Man only just carved from the red river-rock.

"I need—" Gulpilil did not know what he needed, only that he needed.

"You have other work to do. Someday you too will sit by the fire and listen to the stories others will tell. But that day is not now." Dundalli was not unkind. But it burned bitterly to be sent away. His sister's man was there. What had happened to Malle?

"Sssst!"

Gulpilil didn't need to look up to see who was hissing at him. He joined Idimi where the other boy waited, on the hill that created Marwai's shelter.

"Someday they will catch you at this," Gulpilil said, feeling his heart beat too fast inside his chest.

Idimi grinned, his teeth crooked from where the canoe paddle had hit him in the mouth five seasons before. "But not today. Come!"

The two boys crawled on their hands and knees up the hill. It was covered with tall grass, which was excellent for concealment, but the ground was studded with rocks, which weren't so good for crawling. Gulpilil's knees were bruised and torn by the time they got to where Idimi was leading him.

"Shhh," his friend said, his grin even wider. "Here. You go first."

"Here" was a rock that jutted out of the ground a full handspan. It was two handspans across, rounded, and hollow like a reed. It, and three or four others, went all the way down into the overhang, bringing air—and carrying sound.

At first all they could hear was silence. Then a muttering, like the water in the middle of the night. Gawul, and his brother Bunjil. They had been born muttering, his mother once said; then her eyes got all round and bright, and they both had to smother their giggles over the stone chips they were smoothing for spearheads.

But their muttering sounded angry now. And scared. Gulpilil smoothed the ground by the stone-pipe and leaned his elbow on that spot, putting his ear closer to the stone's opening.

Jinabu was speaking, of shadows that moved on their own. Of the people—trusting the mountain to keep them safe, under siege from something they could not see. Of a monster, something terrible that came from the rock itself to attack them.

"What're they saying?" Idimi hissed, and Gulpilil batted his hand backwards blindly to shut his friend up.

"When the sun rose and the shadows fell, we went higher in the rocks, thinking that it would not follow. But it did. I was . . ." Jinabu took a sip of something and cleared his throat. "I heard the screaming. We—there were two others with me, and we saw it. Or saw what it left. And the remains . . . we could not identify who it had been. It follows us. It may have followed me even here—"

"You brought it among us!"

"It will come for us all! Don't you understand that? We have done nothing to offend, and yet it kills and consumes. Not the meat we had been bringing back, not the dogs—only the people. But Marwai is the eldest of us all, and we thought he might know some way to stop it. Before it takes us all down into the shadows, and the people are no more."

There was silence, the only sound the crackling of the fire. Then Marwai spoke, and his words were dry and thin. And no one spoke against him. Not even Jinabu, his breathing harsh and blood-laced.

Gulpilil pushed himself away from the stone-pipe and stared at it in disbelief.

"What is it?" Idimi asked. "What did they say?"

The boats were drawn up on shore, the children sleeping. Normally there was only one watch-fire at either end of camp, to mark the way. But tonight five fires glowed under the dark sky. Men walked from one fire to another, nervous in a way they weren't before a hunt. More like when wind-storms came up in the dry seasons, or rain lashed down and set everything to mud in the growing time. Gulpilil sat by the water and listened to the men talk. They knew even less than he did. Only that something terrible had happened, something they had no defense against.

"Marwai will tell us how to protect ourselves," they said. "There's a story for everything in that one."

Gulpilil knew what they did not—that Marwai had no stories, no answers. That Marwai could not keep his own camp safe, much less save others.

His sister Malle, who sang like the night-bird while she worked. Who had been so happy when Jinabu's gaze fell on her, and who danced like grass-seed in the wind when their mother said she might go with him.

And now Jinabu was here, unable to take another step unaided, and no aid would be coming.

Marwai could do nothing for Malle. Nothing for the child she carried, whom Jinabu wept for as dead.

Gulpilil looked down at the spearhead he held in his hand. It was still rough, the edge unsharpened. As a weapon, it had all the dull spirit of the rock it came from.

But even a dull rock, if thrown hard enough, could hurt an enemy.

Gulpilil rubbed the spearhead between his fingers. He wasn't much of a thinker, but his mother was clever and his father had been a fine hunter. And he knew what he knew when he knew it. And what he knew was that Marwai would move the camp soon, abandoning the fish traps and the canoes far too early, moving his people up the coast, circling around the red rocks.

Something had opened somewhere when the Great Serpent twitched its tail. And something had come through that opening.

Gulpilil wasn't very good at thinking. You didn't have to be a good thinker to know that one boy could not stand against a creature the All-Father had let loose.

But Gulpilil loved his sister very much.

The sun emerged from the waters and began its climb back into the sky. Nobody noticed when one slight boy slipped away from the camp, too busy looking for something coming in to wonder what might be creeping out.

Gulpilil had taken with him one of the better red-rock knives and strapped it to his thigh with fish-gut cord. A spear, its shaft cut down for his arm's length, was in his hand, and two extra heads were in a gray quick-leaper pouch tied around his waist.

Once past the reach of the fires and the quiet sounds of men talking and water splashing on the shore, Gulpilil stood up straight, tied his thick black hair away from his face with the quick-leaper headband Malle had given him for his tenth birthday, and waited to let his eyes adjust.

Stretching out to his left were the hunting-plains. If he went across them, after a handful of days he would come to the black sands, where other tribes hunted and lived. When he was a man, perhaps he would trade his work for theirs; perhaps bring home a wife from their people.

He turned his face away and looked to his right, to where the red rocks rose from the edges of the plains, their jagged edges hiding paths, trails, and camps where the hunters and the stone-gatherers lived. He had gone there once with his father.

The thing that threatened his sister was there.

He was only a boy; he had no cause to go chasing after it when the elders would not.

But his sister was there.

Gulpilil went.

The time he traveled with his father, they carried water with them, and rolls of dried fish and wetweed. This time he had taken a skin of water, but it was only half full. There had been no food left out where he could take it; everyone was putting things away, packing up for when Marwai gave the word that they should leave.

He tried not to think that they might not be there when he returned.

He tried not to think that he likely would not return.

I am Gulpilil, son of the Woman Who Thinks and the Man Who Went Away. I am the shaper of stone for my people, and because of me they bring down the quick-leaper, the sharp-toothed lizard, the fast-running dingo.

His people were much for stories. He had none—yet. But this might be the way they would speak of him later. After it all was done.

Despite the grass he walked on, the air was thin and

dusty. His mouth became dry, and he left off the storytelling. Later, perhaps. When there was something to tell, then he would begin again.

The sun rose farther into the sky and sweat began to form under his headband, running down his face. He took a sip of water and wished that the rocks were not so far away.

It occurred to him then that it might have been wise to learn more before he left. Jinabu would have told him what this thing was. Did it have claws? Teeth? Or was it magical, able to take the life from a man without needing to touch him?

In truth, Jinabu would have done what the other did—send him back to the women and children, telling him that he was not yet old enough to take counsel with the men.

The sun rose still higher, and Gulpilil thought for certain that the rocks were closer, rising into the sky in a jumble of red-and-gray striations . . . Yes, they must be closer if he could tell the colors one from the other. But they were still so far away, and his legs were sore and tired. He lifted the waterskin to his mouth and let just a bit of water trickle into his mouth, swishing it around so that every part of his mouth was wet. Only then did he let it slide down his throat.

"I am Gulpilil, son of the Woman Who Thinks and the Man Who Went Away. I am the shaper of stone for my people, and because of me they bring down the quick-leaper, the sharp-toothed lizard, the fast-running dingo. I am Gulpilil, Malle's brother, who will take her from the shadow for the love of our mother, the Woman Who Thinks."

That was the proper opening of a story, yes. The who and the what and the reason for doing.

A noise behind him made him tighten his grasp on the skin, thinking there was someone who would try to take it from him. It happened, although not often.

"I am Gulpilil, the shaper of stone . . . ," he whispered for courage, turning around only to be knocked off his feet. The skin went flying, landing just out of reach.

A quick-leaper passed him, then came back again in lazy jumps that took Gulpilil's breath away. Only one, a red-furred male without his group, far on the edges of the grasslands.

"You're lost, my brother." Polite was easier than fighting, his mother said. And one kick from this buck's leg could break him in two. Gulpilil reached for the knife on his thigh, then stopped. One knife, no matter how well made, was no match for a full-grown quick-leaper. Maybe in the hands of a grown man. Not wielded by a boy.

"I am no threat to you, brother."

The buck paused, barely arm's reach away. Its sides were heaving, as though it had run far too quickly, even for it. Gulpilil rolled slowly onto his side, his gaze never leaving the long-muzzled face of the creature beside him. Its brown eyes looked at him curiously.

Fumbling blindly, Gulpilil's fingers closed on the water-skin, and he brought it forward slowly. The fur around the quick-leaper's mouth was stained with spittle, and the creature looked as parched as Gulpilil felt.

"Have some water, brother. Come, take some water . . ." Gulpilil squeezed some out into his palm, forming a cup as best he could and offering it forward.

The quick-leaper hesitated, rocking back on its huge feet, its tail—almost as long and heavy as Gulpilil himself—twitching nervously. Then it bent forward, and a heavy red tongue took up the water out of Gulpilil's palm. Its front paws, oddly frail-looking compared to the rest of it, twitched as it drank, and Gulpilil watched the sharp black claws carefully. Not that he had ever heard of a quick-leaper attacking unprovoked, but stories were told of the unusual far more often than of the usual.

The quick-leaper hopped away, awkward in slow motion, and stared at Gulpilil some more. Its eyes were very large, he noted. And very brown, with lashes like a young girl's.

"I would share more, brother, but I need it myself to reach where I am going."

The quick-leaper nodded its head as though it understood. And then it departed in long, graceful bounds, like a rainbow arching over the land.

Once it was gone, Gulpilil got to his feet, slinging the waterskin over his shoulder. There was less in it now, and that was not good, but he could not regret having shared it.

The soles of his feet were beginning to burn and the sweat was drying on his lips when the sun rose fully overhead, and he stopped to rest. His destination was much closer now; he could see the stripes running across the stones where the All-Father had run his fingers through the different-colored sands, building mountains out of the ocean.

A wild yam pulled from the ground and a mouthful of water refreshed him, and the sun warmed him from his skin down into his bones until Gulpilil could almost forget that he was on a terrible journey; that danger and killing death waited for him. Only the spear by his side and the knife against his thigh reminded him.

It was tempting to stay here in the sun, where shadows and fears and terrible noises in the darkness couldn't reach him. But the sun would go over the mountains and leave even this earth-warm spot in the shadows. So he rolled to his feet and bent down to pick up his spear, increasing his pace until he was trotting through the grass. It was lower now, and easier to move through.

"I am Gulpilil, who carried the spear with the head he himself shaped and the knife with the blade he himself made. I share water with the quick-leaper, and I go to the aid of my sister and her people, against the thing which rises from the shadow."

The story fit his movement so easily that it was some time before he realized that his shadow had doubled. He glanced to his left and stumbled over his own toes. Catching himself before he fell, Gulpilil kept striding along, his eyes fixed firmly ahead on the red-rock hills.

And beside him, bushy red tail held high, the dingo ran.

There were dingoes who hunted with his people, but they were smaller, sleeker creatures than this. And their red fur was brushed with white around the eyes and muzzle. This beast rose to Gulpilil's thigh, and its fur was dark red, the color of the sun before a storm. But it seemed content merely to pace Gulpilil as they moved from the grasslands into the scrublands where the hills' toes dug into the dirt. Gulpilil was thankful that the quick-leaper had left long before, although a dingo battling a full-grown quick-leaper was something he might have wished to see in another place and time.

When the ground changed entirely from firm brown earth to dry, dusty red-gray soil, the dingo fell back, sitting on its haunches. Gulpilil looked back and saw its open-jawed grin as it watched the human go.

"Thank you, little brother, for accompanying me."

The dingo yipped once, muzzle pointed toward the sky, and loped off, back toward the grasslands.

Gulpilil's stomach rumbled a wish to be going hunting with the dingo. In the fishing camp, if his people were still there, the smell of fresh-caught fish would be rising from the fires, and the rest of the catch would be going into the smoke. He should have risked taking food for the journey.

But he hadn't, and so he didn't, and now there was no choice but to go on. But he still wished he had something to eat.

The red-plumed tail gone from sight, Gulpilil cast his glance to the sky. The sun was still overhead, but the shadow behind him was lengthening. Dusk would fall soon. He needed to be in the rocks before then.

"I am Gulpilil, who was late to the fight, late to the shadows, late to his death . . ."

Sometimes a bad story could be a good retelling. The problem was, who would tell it for him?

He had gotten to the encounter with the quick-leaper when something made him look up. The sun blinded him until he lifted his arm to block its rays. A dark shadow in the sky was circling overhead.

"Go away, feathered brother," he told it. "I'm breathing yet."

But as the bird swung lower, Gulpilil saw that he was mistaken. It was not the great-winged carrion-eater waiting on him. The sun flashed on one down-stretched wing, and colors glinted in the brightness.

"Good flying, brother!" he called to it. The rough singer was far from its wooded home, but seeing it reminded Gulpilil of time spent underneath the branches of those trees, and the green shadows that promised rest, not danger.

The bird sang out once, its usual harsh cry, and dipped again. As it pulled back up into the sky, an object fell downward, not fluttering but dropping straight like a stone.

Gulpilil reached up instinctively and caught the feather

between two fingers. It looked blue at first, then green, then golden in the sunlight, and the beauty of it made him laugh.

"Thank you, brother! Now I am Gulpilil the stone-worker, who wears the colors of the sky." Tucking the feather into his headband, Gulpilil felt as though wings had been placed on his feet as he continued toward his destination.

The entrance to the mountain's path was smaller than Gulpilil remembered, but the handprint was the same, white clay pressed against the left-hand rock. The thumb pointed up to where the trail cut through the rock and wound into the hillside.

Walking into the cooler air should have been a relief. But when the air touched his sun-heated skin he shuddered; it was a reminder of how short time was getting. The beast had struck at sundown. Jinabu must have left at sunrise, and still it had taken him a full day to reach the fish camp. Gulpilil was younger and he moved more swiftly, but still, too much time had gone by.

The path led up, into the hills. Here and there boulders had rolled into the cleared area, shaken loose when the Great Serpent had twitched five days earlier. One boulder blocked the entire path, and Gulpilil found purchase with his hands and toes in order to climb over it, picking up the trail on the other side. He had just jumped down to the ground again when he saw something move out of the corner of his eye.

Snakes were elder brothers, short of temper and long on venom. You walked carefully when on their ground.

"Forgive me, I meant no harm," he said, watching the creature as it coiled around itself, head raised to scent the air. If you were polite, if you were well-meaning, they let you pass. He tried to remember that, especially when the muscular brown-scaled snake slid out of the rocks and into the middle of the path, directly between Gulpilil and his destination, pulling back its head as though considering whether or not to attack his interloper.

"Elder brother, I must pass," he tried explaining. "I have a reason and a cause and a need . . ."

The snake stared at him, tiny black eyes unblinking, and Gulpilil felt the sweat run down his skin.

"Eldest brother, please." He was begging, but the snake was unappeased. Something brushed the side of his face and Gulpilil resisted the urge to jump, which would have made the snake bite for certain. The something brushed his face again, and the snake's attention shifted from Gulpilil's torso to higher up.

Gulpilil blinked and reached up with a slow, cautious hand to touch the feather he had tucked into the hide headband.

"This, eldest brother? You wish this? It is yours."

He pulled the feather free with the hand not holding the spear and held it off to the side, watching as the snake's eyes followed it away from him. He dropped it, letting it drift back and forth as it slowly settled to the ground.

The instant the blue tip touched the dirt, the snake lunged, its narrow head touching the feather. In the next instant, in the space of an eyelid's closing and reopening, both the snake and the feather were gone.

Gulpilil stood for a long moment, staring at the space where both had been, and then—carefully—stepped forward again.

No other snake crawled out to interrupt him, and he climbed farther and farther up the trail until he came to a plateau where another hand-marker pointed down into the valley Jinabu's people had called home.

The sun was trailing over the far side of the rocks now. On the side he had come from, the blue shadows would cover the grasslands and the watch-fires would be lit near the water. Here, the shadows crept in the undersides of boulders and lingered just out of reach. Gulpilil felt the skin between his shoulder blades crawl, as though someone were staring at him with evil thoughts. His hand clenched the spear more tightly. The desire to fling it into the deepest pile of shadows almost overwhelmed him, but he stayed the need. There might come a time for the spear and the knife. That time was not now.

The path led him to a ledge of rock where he could look down into the valley. Small stone-roofed shelters met his gaze. Normally there would be people about. Children, women, men. A dingo or two. Activity.

Perhaps they were already inside, the doors drawn shut against shadows, waiting for dawn to come again.

Perhaps . . .

THE DINGO KNOWS.

Gulpilil almost fell off the cliff at the dry, amused-sounding voice behind him. Had someone else come to fight the shadow-beast? He turned, and saw . . .

No one.

He looked to the side. Nothing. To the other side. Empty air and untrodden path.

THE DINGO KNOWS IF THE HAND WILL FEED OR SLAP.

Gulpilil looked down at his feet. And let out a yelp that echoed in the still air.

The serpent chuckled, moving its coils slowly so that

each feather shifted against each other just so. Two larger feathers, shading from red to gold to green to blue at the tip, grew from over its small black eyes like plumed eyebrows.

THE DINGO KNOWS WHEN IT'S TIME TO RUN . . . AND WHICH WAY TO GO.

"I'm not a dingo," Gulpilil managed to say.

THE QUICK-LEAPER KNOWS WHICH WAY THE RAIN WILL FALL.

"You're being no help at all!"

Gulpilil wasn't wise like Marwai. He wasn't brave like Jinabu. He was only a boy, and he was tired and alone, and he wanted to have something he could hit so it would all be over and he could lie down and not have to walk anymore.

ALL ARE OF THE SAME SUBSTANCE. THE ANSWER LIES NOT WITH COMFORT BUT WITH FEAR . . .

Gulpilil looked at the feathered serpent, then back over his shoulder at the seemingly deserted camp. When he looked back, the serpent was gone. But a faint trail in the dust showed where it had gone.

Down the other path. Farther into the stone.

Farther into the shadows.

The quick-leaper trusted me to share water, he thought. And he followed the serpent into the shadows.

Gulpilil stood in the middle of the narrow red-rock canyon and wondered how long it would take him to die. Die like the bones scattered on the hard rock-floor. Die like those in the camp below him, in the valley. And they were dead, because everything died—because nothing could stand against this.

He turned, noticing the fissures in the rocks from which something might slither, the overhangs where larger beasts might lurk. And as he watched, something moved in the depths of those shadows, as though hiding . . . or gathering itself to leap. He could feel the hatred oozing from it like mud underfoot. Hatred directed at him, because he could walk in the sunlight.

Gulpilil did not question how he knew this, he only understood that it was true. This thing would kill him, as it had killed all the others who came within its reach.

"I stand against you, my brother, not because I wish you harm, but because you and I cannot be in the same place at this same time. I stand against you, my brother, not because I wish you to be no more, but because I wish to continue."

The dingo ran the earth. The bird flew the sky. The people walked the sunlight. This creature had no place here.

"In the Long-Ago Time you knew your place and I knew mine. But you walk across your place and into mine, and therefore, my brother, I must stand against you."

He was repeating himself. Knowing you were going to die might do that, he supposed, but it made his telling weaker, and that was no good. The shaft of his spear was slick and useless in his hands. He almost dropped it, but what then would he hold?

Not that weapons would matter, in the end.

Across the rocks, the shadows crept closer. Gulpilil could feel those eyes on him again, even stronger, with ill will that should have knocked him over already. The elders were right: whatever the earth's shaking had released *would* be coming down from the rocks as soon as the nights got longer and the shadows deeper.

But first there was this night to face. In very little time the sun would disappear behind the stone walls that rose high above his head. And at that moment the beast under the rock would spring, wrapped safe in the darkness. When the shadows overtook him, it would be time.

"Serpent-guide, were you sent to aid me or to lead me to death?" he wondered aloud, then threw the question away. It did not matter. In the end, none of it mattered. Save that he tried.

He hoped that somehow the quick-leaper and the dingo and the snake would tell their own people his story; that it not fade forever from the knowing.

And with that thought, the killer came at him in a rush of motion, a shadow taken form. The spear, so long his companion on this trip, was almost forgotten as he dodged the first rush, coming up hard against the rock wall and spinning on the soles of his feet to avoid the second rush.

Gulpilil paused, and they both gathered themselves. He blinked, but the beast refused to come into focus. It was long and lean, built like a serpent upright, but with an oversized head that tapered into a point. And yet there was something else within its outline, a mass of broken shards and molten red rock. It did not seem as though it could move as fast as it did, and yet it did.

Gulpilil grasped the spear and held it the way he'd been taught when they were practicing for quick-leaper hunts. But as much as he had practiced, there was no way to be ready for the beast he faced now. It came at him again, and its breath on his face stank of old piss and bad water and the rankness of dead fish. His arm came up, gripping the spear, and the impact staggered him back a full pace, causing him to hit the stone wall again with a painful slap.

The spear caught on the beast's hide, and Gulpilil hung on to the shaft, pushing as best he could to penetrate the creature's flesh. The beast snarled, making a sound of rocks grinding against each other, and the two stared into each other's eyes for a heartbeat before the creature twisted and broke away, leaving Gulpilil with half the shaft in his hand, the other half embedded in that strange, rough-textured hide.

Gulpilil had not even heard the snap of the shaft; the hardwood had broken without warning. He stared at the spear in disbelief, then used it to block the next attack; the jagged end was almost as good as the stone head had been. It didn't penetrate the hide, but a jab toward the face made the beast retreat long enough for Gulpilil to grab the knife from its sheath.

But he was no hunter, no fighter. He was a builder, a mender. And the knife—his fine work, his strong work—shattered between the beast's dark red eyes. Its breath, as hot as the heated water of the sacred pool where initiation ceremonies were held, touched his skin, and Gulpilil pulled away, tripping backwards, falling onto his backside, and rolling away as the beast leapt for him. A blast of flames came from that endless maw of a mouth and licked at Gulpilil's skin, making him cry out in pain even as he rolled again.

Out of the corner of his eye he saw a flicker, a flash of color in the shadow-heavy darkness. Red and blue and gold—the serpent!

BRING HIM HERE, the serpent commanded.

Gulpilil rolled in that direction, giving himself over to hope where there was none, and rolled again under a heavy rock overhang. An instant of panic—a pit, yawning and fetid. This was where the beast had come from! But then the serpent flicked over him, scales warm and heavy and dry, and there was light on the other side. Gulpilil kept rolling, feeling the sand scrape against his skin, the rock rough on his burns—and then he was out the other side. The beast was sliding in after him, slipping faster than the serpent could move, but there was a flash of color and Gulpilil could hear the story in his mind—how the serpent fluttered its wings and blinded the beast, and how its head turned toward Gulpilil even as its serpent-fangs went for the darkness's throat, and how one of the serpent's small eyes was suddenly the color of the sky and winked at Gulpilil, a wise and knowing and grateful look.

And then the ground shook, and Gulpilil covered his head with his arms and cowered until the earth was still once again.

When he opened his eyes once more, the overhang was gone, the entire wall fallen forward, a slab of rock sheared off from its source.

And gone too were the serpent, the beast, and the shadowed pit from where it had come.

Gulpilil crawled around in the rubble, coughing a bit from the red dust that hung heavy in the air. The shards of his knife lay on the stone, along with the shaft of his spear.

He bent down, wincing as his body protested, and picked up the shaft. The wood crumbled into ash as he touched it, leaving the stone head heavy and cool in his palm. His fingers clenched it, then opened slowly. It too had melted in the blast of flame, the stone melting and running until the point now looked . . . like a feather.

Gulpilil's fingers closed around it once again, and he followed the path out of that canyon and back to where the path had split. The stone feather still in his palm, he watched the sun make its final dip before disappearing. The air, so silent before, was filled now with tiny sounds of things moving and living. And in the last ray of sunlight reaching out over the distance, he saw a faint, sinuous shape twisting in the sky, the red light glinting off its feathers as it swooped, curled up, and disappeared into the darkness.

"My thanks, Galeru," he said softly, finally naming the guardian spirit that had helped him. "My thanks for saving our lives, as you have done for my people before."

Tucking the stone feather into his pouch, Gulpilil went to find his sister's village, and do what could be done.

LAURA ANNE GILMAN

LAURA ANNE GILMAN is a professional writer and editor with more than twenty short story credits to her name, in magazines such as *Realms of Fantasy, Mars Dust, Flesh & Blood,* and *Oceans of the Mind* and anthologies such as *Spooks!, Murder by Magic, Powers of Detection,* and *ReVisions.* Her first fantasy novels have been published recently: *Staying Dead* and *Curse the Dark,* with a new young adult trilogy, Grail Quest, to come in 2006.

Laura Anne runs d.y.m.k. productions, an editorial services company. A native New Jerseyan, she loves to travel (although she has not yet been to Australia, the setting of her story) but always comes home to the East Coast. For more information, go to www.sff.net/people/lauraanne.gilman.

HIDDEN WARRIORS

—◆—

Margaret Mahy

1.

THERE IN THE ROOM of Reception and Debate—there before the King himself—light flared along the blade of a knife. One of the men who, only a moment ago, had been standing meekly behind one of the Dannorad envoys was darting across the room, making for the King's Magician—Heriot, the Magician of Hoad. A knife! A knife flourished where, it was understood, the only weapons were to be artful words and the cunning with which diplomatic men wielded them. For a moment Heriot was terrified, yet in that exact moment of terror, quicker even than the light skimming the surface of the blade, he made an inner connection—something that came and went before he could quite grasp it—and drew, from within himself, a weapon of his own strange kind.

"*Freeze!*" he found himself ordering.

Halfway across the room, the man locked in midstride, shaking and crying out as he strained forward, then toppled, unable to lower that threatening arm but still able to cry out:

"I felt you in my head, twisting . . . twisting like a worm in an apple."

Heriot looked toward the knife, still locked into the man's trembling hand, then away to one side. He felt sorry for the man, but a magician must survive as best he can.

"I *have* to be a worm," he muttered softly as the King's guards burst in, bending to lift the man, to unlock the knife from those shivering fingers, then hustling him, still shouting, out of the room. "It's what I am!" Heriot told himself, though he was not sure just what he was. He had been uncertain of this for years.

"You might even be the Hidden Warrior," said Lord Glass in a soft voice, lips close to his ear. "Perhaps you really are that legend." No one but Heriot heard him. The Dannorad envoys, looking every bit as horrified as the men of Hoad at the gross violation that had just taken place, were clustered around the King, apologizing. But one envoy had something to add to his apology.

"Of course there is no excuse for such an event," the envoy said. "But surely in civilized debate, men's heads should be inviolable territories." He shot a glance of severe dislike at Heriot. "Worms should have no place in the presence of a king."

"He is not a worm—he is my Magician," said the King. "After all, we authorities do our best to read each other's thoughts, do we not? My Magician is just better at thought-reading than most people. And those who tell the truth have nothing to fear."

"Well, Magician," the King said a little later, when the Dannorad envoys had retreated, bowing and still apologizing. "It seems you can make a formidable weapon of yourself. But first things first! Why did the Dannorad servant make for you like that? What do you have to tell us?"

The Hidden Warrior, thought Heriot, hearing Lord Glass's words all over again. That magical figure, that haunting possibility, promised in so many Hoadish stories and legends. *They can call me a warrior over and over again because they like the idea of warriors, but it is not what I am.* He cleared his throat.

"I didn't read much, Lord King," he replied. "These days the Dannorad keep their deep plotters at home and send us men who carry single messages and not much else. But there was one thing."

The King leaned back in his chair. "So?" he said.

"That man at the envoy's elbow had heard some whisper of a plan to assassinate someone close to Your Majesty. He did not know who was to be killed, but the rumor of it was running around in his head. Not so much like a worm in an apple—more like a rat in a cage."

"A plot against one of my sons, perhaps?" asked the King.

"I couldn't tell," Heriot said. "The thought was smudged. He'd just picked up a whisper of it, and here in this room he remembered what he had heard." He looked over at the table where the princes and the Lords of Consultation sat. "You lot should be careful. That's all."

Later he was dismissed and stepped out and away, leaving the Council behind him. As he entered the first courtyard, the guards who always escorted him through the castle dropped back a few steps, and Heriot felt himself free to tremble. *What am I?* he thought again, gripping his shaking hands behind his back. *What am I? And what was that connection?* And then: *The Hidden Warrior . . . that hero of children's stories! Perhaps after all . . .*

And as he played with the idea, he felt as if the city— the city of Diamond, jewel of the land of Hoad—had opened its great mouth and swallowed him. All in a moment he was devoured—digested. All in a moment he became the city ... became its braided streets, gardens, marketplaces, and stalls, its changing maze; became an ancient question being asked over and over again. He stood still, eyes closed, until the thought that possessed him fell away, as he had known it would, and he became once more a country boy with inexplicable powers, misplaced in a city whose rich heart was walled away from its own savage edges—edges that might assail it, yet also make it strong. *I've lived in this city for years now,* he thought. *I still don't know it. But I don't know myself. How did I freeze that man? The command came and went too quickly to be understood.* He took a step; stopped once more, so suddenly that he stumbled in midstride; and then straightened, to stand staring blankly into the air inches in front of his nose. *How do I stop you from eating me?* he asked the city—a silent question. *Must I be the one to do the eating? Eat you? All right! Tonight I'll test myself against the edge—with any luck, someone else will try to kill me. And either they will kill me or I'll make that connection again—solve that part of my own puzzle, at least!*

2.

Heriot passed through the castle gate, automatically showing his medallion of passage. Guards fell back, watching him go. The great castle became a stony garment he was shrugging away.

They call me a warrior because "warrior" is one of their compliments, he thought. *They're trying to reassure me with a compliment. But what am I, really?* He came to a standstill for a third time, this time on the edge of the King's garden. And as he stood there, frowning, he heard his name called, turned, and saw the young Lord Roth striding along the narrow path that curved around the edge of the garden, waving and laughing as he came.

Heriot greeted his friend with huge relief, glad to escape into lightheartedness. Roth laughed at his expression, flinging an arm around his shoulder.

"Let you out on your own, have they?" he asked. "And who did you betray today?"

Heriot's initial relief faded. He looked down the road, his gaze leaping along the retreating line of ancient metal lampions in which flares would be lighted that evening.

"No one!" he said.

"What? No reading the secret thoughts of our adversaries?" Roth asked, somewhat mockingly. Heriot shrugged.

"Look! I can't automatically read everyone," he said vaguely. "Some people are closed in. I can't tell a thing about them. Others—well, it's as if they open up wide to me . . . and their secrets are set out like lines of a poem. And yes, I sometimes do read those poems to the King. It's what I was brought here to do." Then he saw Roth was laughing at him, and he sighed and laughed too. "Luckily for you, I don't read friends," he said. "Weren't you born a Dannorad man?"

"Born, not bred. I've lived in Hoad so long I count myself totally Hoadish," Roth replied rather defensively. Then he asked, "Wasn't it Dannorad men the King was talking to today?"

"Yes," said Heriot. "And—no harm in telling you; there won't be any secret about it because they'll set guards around the princes, I think—I did read something. There's a threat against someone close to the King. I don't know who."

Roth looked at him incredulously. "Did you tell them?" he asked.

"I told what I could," Heriot replied. "But before I did

my telling, one of them came at me with a knife. I stopped him . . . froze him . . . and I don't know how I did it. And it's thrown me—saving myself all in the heart of a second, without knowing how."

They had come to the edge of the grove of trees—part orchard, part forest—that history had flung around the King's castle like a careless cloak. Heriot's cottage, an old gardener's hut, stood in a curve of apple trees. Under the branches, something was dancing and spinning in the dappled light.

"Your servant boy, the street rat!" exclaimed Roth. "He's growing up, isn't he? Nearly as tall as I am now. Hey! He's holding a sword."

"He dances, and that sword's his partner," Heriot said. "Has to be. He dreams of being a warrior—a true warrior, not one like me—and plays warrior games."

"Every street rat in the city plays warrior games," said Roth, losing interest.

"Now then," Heriot said. "Come to the cottage. We can sit on the bench beside the door, drink cider, and talk about books."

"I'll walk on by this time," Roth said. "I've got things to do. You know how it is. I'll call in later, maybe." He hesitated, looking at Heriot with a troubled expression. "You will stay here—here in your special place, where you'll be safe, won't you?" Heriot nodded, not really listening. Cayley was coming to meet them in a series of somersaults and cartwheels.

"Hey! What's wrong?" Roth asked.

"Nothing's wrong!" said Heriot. "Why should anything be wrong?"

"You looked—I don't know—startled, as if you were seeing your street rat for the first time."

"Everything astonishes a magician," Heriot muttered. "Especially the things he already knows."

He and Roth hugged one another. Then Roth walked away, past the green fringes of the King's orchard toward the houses and marketplaces of the inner ring of the city. As Heriot watched him go, Cayley sprang up beside him.

"So he's not coming to the cottage," Cayley said, adding, with a sudden change of tone, "Hey! Does he *know*?"

Heriot smiled. "Are you asking me if he knows you're a girl?"

"Did you tell?" Cayley asked.

Heriot shook his head. "Though I did tell him that you dreamed of being a warrior."

"He'd have laughed at that one," said Cayley, "him being a lord and me a street rat, like. But me—I'm going to be the warrior of warriors."

"Dream away!" said Heriot derisively.

Cayley was jiggling from one foot to the other, still staring after Roth.

"Have you ever read him?" she asked curiously.

"I don't read friends," Heriot replied severely. "You know that. He knows it too. Anyhow, I'm glad he's got business in the city." He looked at her sideways. "I fancy going out to the edge tonight. Coming with me?"

Cayley looked into the orchard. The air was glowing with late sunlight. As the wind blew, shadows shifted under the trees, melting into one another, then drifting apart.

"Why?" she cried. "Why go there? Me—I struggled to get away from the edge. When you picked me up out of the gutter, back when I was small, and brought me back to life— that was wonderful luck for me. Look! It's safe here. It smells sweet. No one wants to hurt you. Why go off into dark places where every second man would kill you for your shoes alone? Because it's deadly to be an unarmed man with good shoes, walking in a place where most people go barefoot on mud and broken stones."

Heriot smiled. "Something happened a little bit earlier . . . something that I don't understand," he said. "I need to test myself against a bit of danger, and the easiest place to find danger is out on the edge."

"Right, then! Who am I to argue?" said Cayley. "Walk on, Magician. I'll follow!"

3.

So they walked through the late afternoon, past houses, gardens, and marketplaces, then through the door in the wall around the city's heart to where crazy old buildings, erected during the childhood of the city, hunched together, leaning over the streets. Ragged people squinted at them through gathering twilight, sometimes shouting with a mixture of derision and anger, for Heriot and Cayley so obviously belonged to another place. "Like what you see?" one old woman yelled. The stink of the edge rose up around them, sifting into their hair and clothes.

"Everyone who lives here is a sort of warrior fighting doom," Heriot said. "Not recognized, though!"

"I know it better than most people," Cayley answered. "Coming here—it's like coming home to me."

Evening deepened and darkened. Heriot and Cayley strode around the rare, reluctant flares lighted at street corners, then dove into the darkness that dominated streets mushy with mud and filth. Ancient doorways gaped at them; narrow chinks that served as windows stared down at them.

I'm being a fool, I know, thought Heriot. *Winking at Death for the second time today. Beckoning him on this time. But he's playing hard to get.* He looked ahead, down an empty street, then flung his arms wide. "Hey, Death! Here I am!" he cried. "Give me a hug!"

And suddenly, as if Death were responding, there was movement in a narrow alley to their right—a quick padding sound as something came rushing toward them.

"Trouble!" yelled Cayley.

"I know," Heriot replied. *Now! Now!* He desperately reached back into himself, feeling for that hidden connection, that source of the power he had drawn on so automatically earlier in the day. *Yes! Ah, yes!* Relief! *So that was how! There!* Power! *I have you. . . .*

Suddenly men burst out of that black slot, while the buildings on either side leaned forward as if eager to inhale the scent of spilled blood. Two against five! He heard the metallic hiss as Cayley drew her sword from its sheath. A sword! What was a sword? He was the Magician of Hoad. *Now!* He felt rather than said the word (though his lips shaped it), sending it out like an arrow of power to strike and dissolve into the leaders. *Ignite!* he ordered silently, with an energy as immediate as thought. And even as, for the second time that day, a blade was raised to strike him, the lead assailant screamed and flung himself to the ground, rolling and lashing at his baggy clothes as they burst into active flame. The man beside him fell too. One of the remaining three shrank back, then tumbled forward onto his knees, crying out, but with dismay, not pain—beating at the flames with his bare hands, trying to help his friends. The other two men yelled and fled back into the alley.

"Put that silly sword away and walk," Heriot said to

Cayley. "Stroll on." So they strolled on, away from the screaming and confusion, into the tangling embrace of the edge. *My
child!* the city seemed to say, devouring Heriot once more. *My
deathly child, more murderous than the murderers! The Hidden
Warrior! Yes!* What was the sword or the spear compared to a
wish, a command, a single impulse with the substance of a
weapon? Around a corner . . . around another corner . . . and
he was released. The city's tormented arms suddenly flung
themselves wide, as if the edge had become a street conjurer,
gesturing in a moment of revelation: *See what I was holding,
hidden under my cloak! Your grove is waiting for you! Go home!*
Heriot and Cayley had regained the wall that enclosed the
noble heart of the inner city. The leaning buildings shrank
back. Now, above the wall, Heriot and Cayley could make
out the highest towers of the King's castle, distant but dom-
inating the other buildings—opaque, flat black shapes against
a clear, dark sky salted with stars. As they passed through
the gate, Heriot showed his medallion of passage to the
watchmen, but they knew him and merely nodded as he and
Cayley went by. It was night in the heart of the city, just as
it had been night at the edge, but here it was a safe darkness. Roads were clearly marked out with regular flares and
torches—with moonlight too, for the moon was rising beyond
the castle towers.

"How did you *do* that—what you did back there?" Cayley asked.

"I'm the Magician, remember?" Heriot said, somewhat
boastfully. He felt he was entitled to boast. "It seems the
world's elements are my well-trained dogs. Come when I
whistle. Do what I tell them to."

"I'm your dog," Cayley said indignantly. "You should

have turned me loose on them . . . me with my warrior sword. It would have been practice for me."

"Forget that warrior business," Heriot said. "Be what you really are and I'll look after you."

"You tell me to forget it because I'm a girl. Which you didn't know, in spite of your powers! I had to tell you!" said Cayley.

"There have to be a few surprises in the world, even for magicians," said Heriot. "And you're a friend, and I don't read friends."

"You say you don't read friends, but I've felt you beat against me, every now and then, like a bee against glass," said Cayley complacently. "Friend or not, I'm the one you can't read."

"Oh well, that's true," Heriot answered. "And it's true that at times I've been too curious about you to resist temptation. But you're more closed in than anyone I've ever met."

Now he and Cayley were walking through open courtyards, past houses that stood apart from one another. The scent of gardens mixed with the city smells.

"Diamond!" Heriot spoke the name of the city aloud, and as his voice edged back into his ears, he heard not only defiance (for he did not want the city to consume him) but his fascination with the city as well.

"Diamond!" said the echo at his side. But Cayley was laughing, deriding the city, using laughter to ward off its power. She skipped ahead and spun like a dancer.

"Your war dance," Heriot said. "But we have to be what we're born to be. You're a girl, and in the end men are just stronger. You might make a good defense with that sword of yours, but a strong man will still strike you down."

"I work at keeping my arm strong," Cayley protested. "Work at it! Work at it! Do chin-ups on branches. You! You think you'll gentle me down and make a woman of me, don't you? You think I'll wear skirts and have children."

Heriot stared at her and shook his head. "I have considered the idea," he admitted. "But so far, you and skirts and children—well, that idea just doesn't work. But the warrior idea doesn't work either. How can it?"

Cayley laughed. "Girl or not, I've got that warrior dance bred in my bones. Maybe I'll never be strong in the way of most heroes, but my arm can be strong *enough*. And in my head I'm nothing but strong."

"Well," said Heriot, "it doesn't matter right now what we are or what we might be. We'll slump down on the bench by the cabin, just being easy at last and listening to the wind in the trees. And then we'll go to our beds."

4.

At last they were walking through the King's grove once more. Light from the flares set along the paths crept under the trees. Moonlight struggled in from above. Home! Their cottage was ahead of them, and a dark figure was pacing up and down by the door. But they were in a safe place. The darkness was friendly, and the figure was that of a friend. Roth clapped his hands high above his head in greeting.

"Him again!" said Cayley, moving away from Heriot a little, dancing and spinning from one patch of light to another. She knew this small landscape by heart.

"I called in on my way back," said Roth. "You weren't here. I wondered . . ."

"Have they asked for me?" Heriot asked, looking suddenly anxious. "The King . . . ?"

"No! I just thought about that cider you promised me," said Roth. Heriot relaxed again, watching Cayley off to his right, gesturing at the air, then whirling away under the apple trees according to some inward music, striking out at the empty space around her as she leaped from shadow to shadow.

"What's he *doing* that for?" asked Roth, sounding irritated.

"It's his private game," Heriot said. "He fills the air with enemies and fights them off. He's a child of the edge, remember—more a true man of Hoad than any of you lords—so he's always on his guard."

"The edge!" exclaimed Roth accusingly, suddenly solving a puzzle. "You've been wandering around on the edge. I can smell it on you."

"You're just jealous," said Heriot. "Walking around out there is too much for lords and princes. Too much for you! But me—I've just tested myself. It isn't too much for me. I've won through twice in the same day."

But as he was boasting, there, in the very heart of his safe place, someone stepped out of the shadows behind him and struck him down.

The blow was like a flash of harsh light. There was not even a fraction of a moment of confrontation in which he might have made a magical connection. Orchard grass folded over him. Just for a moment, he smelled it and the earth it sprang from, and then he lost sight and sound and smell— lost everything.

5.

Was it a day . . . an hour . . . a moment later? First there was the smell of the earth, then the touch of the grass, and then a voice calling his name—his own voice, summoning him back into the world. Ordinary sounds came back. Voices— other voices—broke in, cursing and crying out. That thud-ding! That clashing! Lying on his back, Heriot rolled his head right, then left, making a little cradle for it in the long grass as he stared up into the branches of the apple trees, thickly black against the moonlit sky. Someone screamed out. Feet kicked against his sprawling legs, and somewhere above him someone stumbled and cursed. And the world, coming back to him, brought a sudden realization. Hours earlier he had become aware of a threat against someone close to the King. Now he knew. *He* had been the target. He, the King's Magi-cian, had been the threatened one. Heriot propped himself up, first on one elbow and then on the other. A theater opened up before him.

For there, between curtains of shadow and shafts of sil-ver, Cayley leaped and fought, not one but two men, holding Death away from him. A third man was lying a little to his left, dead already, perhaps—certainly no longer interested in any sort of battle. The two men charged in on Cayley from either side, but she spun away from them and they found themselves raising their daggers at one another, while Cayley, having slipped from their threat, became a threat of her own.

For the third time that day, Heriot saw light run a quick finger along a thrusting blade. *Three blades! Three! The fairy-tale number. I'm living in a fairy tale. Things happen three times in fairy tales and change on the third time.* One of the men dropped his knife, yelping and clapping his hands to his belly, while the other lunged at Cayley with a graceful certainty. But the street rat was already spinning away. The lunge missed. The man leaped back, then charged once more, shouting.

Heriot recognized the voice, though he had never heard it raised in quite this way before.

"Roth!" he said aloud. "Hey, you! You're my friend!" But his voice was confused, and it cracked. Weary grief, with fear as a partner, filled him. Roth! A Dannorad man after all. First and last, a Dannorad man. Urging him to stay in a safe place so he could be found . . . to stand trustingly still so that he could be easily killed.

Roth's long dagger clashed against Cayley's sword. He tried to strike while she was off guard, but in the very act of countering the blow, Cayley slanted her sword blade so that Roth's blade slipped downward into the grass. Then she leaped away, moving, with a pure certainty, not backward but sideways.

The dance! thought Heriot. *The dance!* And amazingly, for less than a second, the image of a bright, sunlit orchard imposed itself over the dark one as Cayley danced and spun. Something that felt like a beetle ran down Heriot's temple and curved toward his chin as he sat up. Blood. This place he had believed to be home—that friend he had believed to be a comfortable companion—both were as treacherous as anything out on the edge of the city. Worse, for he had trusted both the place and the man. Now the second injured man tried to lift himself, cursing and groaning. Roth swung at Cayley again. Reaching into himself, Heriot tried to lock into that connection he had used twice already that day: once without meaning to, the second time to determine just what he was able to do with it.

"Stagger!" he commanded. "Stagger and fall!" The point of connection was there, but dazed as he was, he could not quite connect.

Roth, however, must have felt the worm turn in his head, for he shot a sideways glance at Heriot, sitting under the apple trees, and then made for him, blade raised.

"Magician!" he screamed, as if it were a term of abuse.

But Cayley leaped beside him. Her sword-thrust slid under Roth's ribs—sank beyond his ribs. Heriot flung himself to one side as Roth tumbled forward, thrashing wildly. There, in the long orchard grass that only that afternoon had seemed so pure and innocent, Roth kicked and twitched, drummed the ground with his feet, and at last grew still.

How long had it taken? It felt like forever. It felt instantaneous. Another beetle of blood ran down the side of Heriot's face as he and Cayley faced one another.

"Are you all right?" she asked.

But Heriot did not answer her—at least he did not answer her question. "You *are* a warrior," he said. His voice had the curious astonished resignation of someone confronting inevitability. "Cayley. Yes! You really are a warrior. A hidden warrior. *The* Hidden Warrior, perhaps. The one that springs from the very stuff of Hoad."

It was a truth that seemed at that moment like an ultimate truth—like the truth that binds the earth to the sun and holds the sun to its place among the stars. Then Heriot looked down at Roth and understood that a sort of friendship had truly existed between them, but it had not been strong enough to resist the assertion of another, deeper identity. Heriot saw that Roth's wish to be the hero of his own first country, set out like a poem in Roth's fading self, had overcome everything else. Heriot's own death would have been Roth's ultimate assertion that he was a Dannorad man. Staring down at his friend, all Heriot could feel was anguish.

"He was my friend!" he exclaimed. "My friend! But perhaps, in the end, magicians just don't have friends."

"Hey! Look at me," said Cayley, falling on her knees beside him. Heriot stared at her.

"My sword," she said. "I take it in my hand and I feel I'm dancing with a true partner. I've told you that. I feel the blow of it and the flow of it. But hey! You're melted into that very blade. You dance with me—strike with me, true as the ring of steel."

Heriot sighed. "I'm coming back into myself," he said. He even smiled a little. He struggled to his feet. "Roth! He seemed like a friend. But—never mind! Not right now! Let me lean on you."

"Lean as heavily as you like," said Cayley. "I can be strong for you. Hey! Magician! Warrior! Two-edged! None of them will be able to stand against us."

"Side by side, back to back against the world—that's us," Heriot agreed. "Two warriors! We'll take them by surprise, one day soon. But you're the hidden one! I'm the one out there, gesturing and saying, 'Look at me.'"

"You do run on," said Cayley. "Someone comes at you to kill you and you keep on talking."

Heriot nodded. "I'm propped up by words. Now let's get the guards. I'll weep a bit later on—think it all through. And then I'll sit down and have a drink of cider, perhaps." And, Heriot's hand on Cayley's shoulder, they set off through the moonlit midnight orchard, moving deeper and deeper into their overlapping fairy tales, vigilant and wary, for there were no safe places for the Magician and the Warrior.

MARGARET MAHY

MARGARET MAHY has been writing since the age of seven and is one of New Zealand's best-known writers of children's books. When she was a child, she envied boys for the adventurous roles they were allowed to play: cowboys and soldiers (for she grew up during World War II). She loved reading adventure stories, especially *King Solomon's Mines,* and wanted to live a daring life. The boys down the road were not supposed to play with her, as their father thought it would turn them into "sissies." (Margaret thinks that she actually played tougher games than they did!) As to the characters Heriot and Cayley in "Hidden Warriors," they come from a longer story that very well may become a book someday.

Margaret writes in a range of styles for differing age groups, including picture books, broadly comic stories for younger readers, and complex novels for older readers. She has won the Carnegie Medal of the British Library Association twice, the IBBY Honour Book Award, and the *Observer* Teenage Fiction Award, as well as many more prizes in her native New Zealand, including the Esther Glen Award four times and the AIM Book Award (Junior). In February 1993 she was awarded New Zealand's highest honor, the Order of New Zealand, which is only ever held by twenty people alive at any one time!

Margaret lives on the South Island of New Zealand. When she is at home, she spends lots of time writing, ordering the cats and dogs around (not very successfully), and fussing over her granddaughters.

EMERGING LEGACY

Doranna Durgin

KELYN KNEW SHE WAS the clumsy one.

Even if she hadn't noticed it herself—with all the tripping, stumbling, dropping things, and running into overhangs and low branches she'd done—the others in her hunting pack weren't about to let her forget. How unfortunate that the words "Clumsy Kelyn" rolled off their tongues so easily.

All the same, she was still alive. They couldn't say that about Sigre, whose favorite craggy perch Kelyn now occupied, her feet dangling comfortably over the edge of a drop so deep that she found herself looking down on the distant treetops below. She took a generous bite of the dried plum she'd brought with her to this quiet moment and spat the pit out into the misty morning air.

She lost sight of it long before it reached the trees—though last week, she'd had no problem watching Sigre all the way down. Or hearing her, a fading scream that turned to echoes before Sigre disappeared into the pines below.

There were some who said it should have been Kelyn.

Sigre had always been light of foot, always graceful on the ledges and narrow, dangerous trails of these high, craggy mountains. She'd always been their trailblazer, taking them to new places in the thin air, finding them new hunting grounds.

Kelyn missed her—but the scattered community at the base of the mountain range would miss Kelyn even more. Kelyn's was the pack that had brought in the most meat from their summer hunting, providing the old and the young with plenty. This pack—young adults in training under the harshest of teachers, the high Keturan wilderness—provided for their own families and more, and at the end of each summer they descended to the harsh rolling terrain a little more seasoned, a little more capable. A little more prepared to survive this difficult climate with its lushly coated rock cats and other predatory dangers.

Or crumbling rock edges. Kelyn stood, as careful as she ever was, intensely aware of her awkward nature and her need to compensate. When she kept her wits about her, she seldom had trouble. It was only when she let her mind wander . . .

She stepped back from the edge to join the others. Even so, had she not heard her pack-mate Mungo's approach, his "Kelyn! Be careful!" might just have startled her into a scary step or two. She turned on him with a glare, but wiry Iden came up from behind to put himself between them. Behind Iden came the others. Trailing Gwawl—as usual—was little Frykla, still uncertain in her first year with the pack.

Though not so uncertain that she didn't give Mungo a good hard glare. "Kelyn saw nightfox sign this morning," she told Mungo, who scowled under the scrutiny, tugging his rough-edged leather vest as though it had twisted out of place. "It would make me proud to bring down nightfox pelts for trading in my first year. But I don't suppose it'll happen if you make her so mad she doesn't show us the spot!"

"I can find my own nightfox dens." Mungo tried for dignity, but it was hard to carry off. He looked to be growing into a stout frame, but for now he was the only one of them left with the precious fat of a well-fed child and it made him appear even younger than Frykla. "You all fuss over nothing. Kelyn's father is the great Thainn, remember? Surely with such a mighty hunter's blood in her veins, she heard me coming."

"I did hear you coming," Kelyn said coldly, picking up her staff—Reman ironwood, bound with leather and weighted on both ends. It had come from her mother and served her well as a defensive weapon, especially as she was not allowed a long blade. "I begin to understand why my father always hunted alone. And maybe even why he left."

He'd left Ketura *before* she was born—before she was even conceived. Kelyn's mother had met him in Rema, and never expected him to stay with her. Shortly after Kelyn's conception, her mother had traveled to Ketura to raise her child in her father's lands.

Any child of Thainn's, her mother had reasoned, was bound to get into more than her fair share of trouble. She wanted Kelyn hardened by this harsh land . . . trained by it. Challenged by it.

Of course, her mother had never had any reason to expect Thainn's child to be a clumsy one. Or an awkward one, with features that fought each other for attention. Or the one whose opinion faced casual dismissal, as the pack often equated clumsiness with inability.

Because she didn't like the direction her thoughts had taken, Kelyn gave the pack a good hard glare. And then, with some assurance, she stepped off in the direction of the night-fox den.

Whereupon she stumbled over nothing, twisted around her own leg, and hit the rocky ground hard.

Stupid! she chided herself, wrapping her arms around the wrenched leg. If there was one thing she'd learned, it was that she among them all could never *not pay attention.* Never be distracted by emotions or events or daydreams.

"Kelyn!" Frykla crouched by her side. "That looked bad."

"I'm not sure I've ever seen anyone fly in so many directions at once," Iden observed, but unlike Mungo he spoke kindly.

Kelyn untangled herself, pushed herself to her feet with help from the staff, and tested the leg. She'd given it a good twist, all right—but she thought she could walk out of it in a few days. And besides, she had the staff. "It'll heal," she told Frykla, who still hesitated by her side. "I don't know if I can get up to the den . . . but I can take you close enough." More than once Kelyn had admired the nightfoxes' ability to nimbly ascend the sheer rock faces to their precariously placed dens. Today she wouldn't even try to emulate them.

Not that it mattered. This one was for Frykla.

Kelyn waited at the bottom of the abruptly thrusting rock face, pulling her fur-lined vest more closely around herself and applying herself to scraping the generous layer of edible lichen from the base of the rock. *Soup tonight!* Perfect to ward off the year-round chill of the high air. Her leg pained her, but not as much as it might have; she favored it only because she knew better than to overstrain it. She'd likely find it bruised and battered beneath the loose leather of her leggings and snug loincloth, and looked forward to the hot spring in their favorite camp spot.

When the sun reached overhead, she heard the faint echoes of victorious shouting, and she smiled to herself. They might mock her lack of grace, they might ignore her concerns on the trail, but not one among them had a better eye for nightfox sign. Not long afterward, the members of the little hunting pack made their way down the back side of the thrusting rock and surrounded Kelyn with their ebullience and slightly breathless victory. They'd also discovered valuable choi buttons, which they could leave to cure for another month and then harvest for sale to outsiders.

In quick order, they skinned the two nightfoxes they'd snagged and left the bodies arranged on the flattest rock they could find in tribute to the rock cat that lived in this area. Kelyn joined them as they started down, a descent of several hours to their closest established camp. They chattered about their success as Frykla, flushed and happy, recounted the harrowing climb to the den several times over. Satisfied enough with her part in the valuable acquisition, Kelyn concentrated on navigating the rough terrain.

Perhaps that's why she was the first to hesitate—the first to think something wasn't quite right. She held up a hand and the others instantly stopped—but a moment of group inspection revealed no sound or sight out of place. Mungo was the first to shift impatiently, and Kelyn knew why—just around this stand of stunted trees, through the narrow opening in two looming sentry rocks, their favorite camp waited. The hot springs inside their low scoop of a cave called to Kelyn and her aching leg, and her stomach hungered for the gnarled tubers waiting to supplement the lichen. The others were no less tired, no less ready to settle in for the evening.

So even though she didn't yet know what little *wrongness* in their surroundings had caught her attention, the others gave a shrug and moved onward. Their habitual dismissiveness of her skills took over, and one by one they slipped through the gap in the sentry rocks to throw themselves to the ground around the banked coals of the fire.

Or so Kelyn thought, hearing the sounds within. Until she actually took her turn through the sentry rocks and discovered her pack mates sprawled on the hard-packed dirt and stone of the area, dazed and surrounded and some of them even pinned down—all by rough, dark men in unfamiliar clothing. The discovery startled her so much that she stumbled and fell, saving the men the effort of taking her down.

Men, here? After us? Shock and fear coursed along her spine; her heart hammered in her chest, lending her a burst of energy that came too late to do her any good.

One of the four men gave a short laugh at Kelyn's fall, and said something to the others in a harsh, unfamiliar language. They all relaxed slightly. *They know we're all here.* And that they'd accomplished this capture without a fight.

But why come here at all? The small band had nothing of value but the recently acquired nightfox pelts and the small collection of less significant pelts and dried meat. They had nothing but . . .

Themselves.

Kelyn lifted her head to look at them with revulsion, and the man who'd spoken gave her a nasty-toothed grin. "Figuring it out, are you?" he asked in her own language, sitting on Mungo's rump as though it were a pillowed throne. Mungo himself was still dazed, or the man's impudent self-confidence would have been ill rewarded. "*You're* our prize. All of you."

Frykla gave him a startled look. "What?"

"Slavers?" Gwawl twisted beneath the man who had his

knee on the small of his back, trying to see how the rest of them fared.

"Here?" Iden pulled against the rough ropes that already bound his wrists and ankles together.

In the lowlands, yes. Slavers and reivers both—people who preyed on the misfortune and weakness of others. But here in the craggy reaches of the Keturan mountains, surrounded by the unfamiliar dangers of climate and predator? Neither was forgiving—the very reason they forged the young hunting packs into strong, capable warriors, independent but respectful of community.

Strong, capable . . .

"You came here just for us," Kelyn said, her voice low with the horror of it. The man who'd tied Iden moved on to another, whipping another short length of coarse rope from his belt with the speed of long practice.

The man rubbed his nose. It didn't help; the nose remained dirty and ugly. "Not you in particular. Just whichever of you was up here this year." He pointed at her, then gestured at the fire circle. "Come in here."

Kelyn thought about running. If she flung herself back through the narrow aisle between the sentry rocks, they'd never catch her—and they probably wouldn't leave the others behind to even try. She could make it to safety, but their village community would feel the loss of the others for years, if it even survived. Life here was too precarious, too close to the edge.

She couldn't face it. Say good-bye to her friends, never to know how they fared? Break the news to their families?

With care, Kelyn got to her feet, closing her hand around the staff to bring it up with her. The men instantly came to alert, and the one who sat on Mungo's rump gave the barely conscious boy a severe cuff and sprang to his feet, a short spear to hand. "Leave that!"

She gave her staff a surprised glance. She'd reached for it out of entrenched habit; she rarely went anywhere without it. It served her on the rocky paths and it served her as a weapon. She wielded it with more grace than anything else in her life. She depended on it. And now she gave the man a deeply puzzled look. "It's just my mother's old walking stick. I hurt my leg."

Frykla lifted her head and gave Kelyn a startled look. *Just a walking stick?* And then she glanced quickly away, trying to hide her reaction, to cover it with scorn. "She's a clumsy oaf, that's what."

Just as startled, Gwawl opened his mouth—but Frykla widened her eyes at him, the best unspoken warning she could give him.

The dirty-faced slaver frowned. "What?"

Iden gave a sudden curse and began fighting his ropes, flipping around like a snared rabbit. *Distraction.* The man who'd tied him grinned, exposing just how few teeth he had, and moved on to tie Frykla. One man still sat on Gwawl, his fingers twisted in Gwawl's dreadlocked hair and a thick-bladed knife at the back of his neck. Another stood by with his arms crossed, watching Iden's futile struggles in dark amusement.

Kelyn took advantage of the moment to move to the center of the rock-enclosed site, limping heavily, using the staff for support as obviously as she could without overdoing it.

Perhaps she overdid it after all, for as Iden's timely struggles ceased, the man who seemed to be their leader said, "You don't look like you can keep up with us."

The man standing by Iden said something short and sharp in whatever harsh language they called their own, and the leader raised an eyebrow at Kelyn—though it was hard to see it through his brushy hair. "He wants to kill you. He thinks you'll slow us down and die along the way."

Kelyn's hand tightened around the staff just as her skin prickled all the way down her spine. She hadn't considered—

"She's not badly hurt," Frykla said in a low voice, one that already had a cringe in it. "She can keep up. And she'll heal fast."

The man snorted. "One would almost think you wanted to be slaves."

"I'm not ready to die," Kelyn told him, blunt . . . and preparing herself to run. The skin between her shoulder blades twitched, anticipating the impact of that short spear.

"Your kind, preferring slavery to death?" The man snorted again. "You're just foolish enough to think you can escape." At Kelyn's sullen glare, he shrugged. "It serves me well enough if you choose to think so. Just don't be so foolish to think you can escape from *me*. It's never happened. It never will. Now sit down." He pointed, choosing a spot where Kelyn could reach none of her friends, or even so much as exchange a discreet word. Then he gestured at one of the men, who dug into the satchel at his side and produced a folded packet. Kelyn eyed it warily as she took her seat, making sure she leaned heavily on the staff.

The man took up the cook pot left by the side of the hearth and dipped it into the hot spring. Into the water went a careful sprinkle of the powder that had been contained in the packet—and Kelyn understood then that they'd be drugged. At least for the night . . . possibly for the days. But as the rope-wielding man tied up her ankles and wrists, binding them just freely enough that she might use the staff, she felt a surge of determination overcome her fear.

We'll escape.
We'll be the first.

The next morning, the aftermath of the bitter herb still gripped them even in the bracing chill of the morning air. It was all Kelyn could do to lift her muzzy head and keep an eye on their progress along the steep, rocky trail. She limped and lurched without having to play-act the injury to her leg, and her natural tendency to stumble reasserted itself at every inconvenient opportunity.

But she knew where they were going and so did the others; at every rare chance they caught one another's eyes, and Kelyn saw the knowledge there. And while the slavers spat vicious words at the first sign of the huge rockfall that had destroyed the entire slope stretching before them, neither she nor her pack mates found it a surprise. Kelyn caught everyone's gaze with her own, holding it long enough to give it significance, until within moments they all stood a little taller, waiting.

I have an idea.

She might be clumsy, she might regularly deal herself bruises and stumbles, she might never truly be her father's daughter, but Kelyn had no shortage of ideas.

The leader looked at the captives. He found them passive and unsurprised by the avalanche damage, and it enraged him. "You knew of this!"

They said nothing. They might have inched a little closer to one another.

The leader stalked up on them in two long strides and snatched Frykla, hauling her to the edge of the trail. "You knew of this!" he repeated. "You know of other ways out, too—and you'll show us!" He gave Frykla a little shake and she froze in terror, her eyes pleading. Pebbles dislodged by her scrambling feet rolled over the sharp drop and pinged their way down the slope for a very long time.

Fight him! Kelyn thought at the younger girl. *Bite, kick, scratch—anything!*

Except she quickly realized the man had Frykla so close to the edge—*over* the edge—that along with threatening her, he was also the only thing keeping her alive. She hesitated, fuzzy-brained, and felt the others draw closer around her.

"You'll help or she dies," the leader told Kelyn, sneering the words. "And then another of you, and another. You're of no use to us if we can't get back to the marketplace."

One of the other men spoke up, a short phrase accompanied by an expression Kelyn hadn't seen before and didn't like. The leader laughed. "Grolph reminds me that we will, of course, use each of you most thoroughly before you go over the edge. We've been a long time away from home, and the only reason you haven't entertained us before now is that it would reduce your value. Doesn't matter if you're about to go over the edge, does it?"

Iden muttered something, horrified, and the group tightened into a little defensive knot—a hunt pack, expert partners in defense against animals and elements . . . and with no experience with this human enemy. Trussed and drugged and entrenched in the belief that each human life was precious and crucial to the survival of the whole—and still not used to thinking of any human life in terms of a threat.

"We'll help!" Gwawl blurted.

"Don't drop her!" Mungo added.

"Please!" Iden said, the most heartfelt of them all.

And Kelyn said, "I know another way."

*   *   *

Kelyn took them back along the trail, then cut away from it to head upward. By then her leg ached heartily; she didn't have to feign her reliance on the staff. Her wrists and ankles chafed and bled under the rough ropes. Clarity returned to her thoughts—and to judge from the puzzled glances her pack mates gave her, to theirs as well. For they were starting to wonder—and worry—what she was up to. She made it a point to catch Iden's eye, to stumble forward long enough to mutter a reassurance in Mungo's ear. To give Gwawl an assertive nod, and to smile at Frykla—who still knew very well that she would be first to die should the slavers grow impatient. She was the youngest, and she'd already caught their eye.

Kelyn didn't blame the others for wondering, not even for worrying. For she led them right back up to the nightfox den—back to where, not a day earlier, they'd left offerings for the rock cat.

But we know about the offerings, and about the cat.

The slavers had not the faintest idea.

"We *have* to go *up*," Kelyn said in desperation as Frykla was being dangled over another edge. "It's the only way around! We have only to crest this peak and then we'll start back down again. But—"

"You *arguing* with me?" the leader said, incredulous expression evident even beneath his raggedy beard. Frykla froze in his hand, waiting to fall.

Kelyn shook her head most emphatically, her hands white-knuckled around the staff as she watched Frykla. "I was only going to tell you that this is the best camp we'll see before dark. It doesn't matter to *us*, we're used to sleeping on the edge of things. I just thought—"

The leader shut her up with a sharp gesture, but he also reeled Frykla in and shoved her off in the direction of the pack. Then he hooked his thumbs over his wide, stained leather belt and stared at them. Stared at Kelyn. Suspicious. "Aren't you just the cooperative one."

Kelyn couldn't help the anger in her voice. "I don't want to be used unto death and tossed over a cliff. What would *you* do in my place?" And then she hoped he was dull enough— or overconfident enough—so that he didn't come up with the right answer: *Lead you into trouble and leave you there.*

For she'd already done the first part. Just above this spot, they'd made their offering to the rock cat. There'd be one in the area now—not taking kindly to intruders, either. Rock cats, proficient hunters that they were, didn't need human prey. But they didn't tolerate human presence, either. Perhaps one human . . . perhaps two. Perhaps someone who was quiet and didn't intrude on the night.

Kelyn wouldn't leave things to chance. She pointed up the steep slope and said, "If you're any good at climbing, you can find choi buttons up there. A whole bush full of them. We've been letting them mature for harvest, but if you like such things—"

Gwawl shoved her. "Those are ours!"

"What's it matter now?" Kelyn said, glad to have one of the others finally, finally catching on and lending a hand— for the hallucinogenic seedpods were nothing the pack ever touched. Stupid, to rob your own wits in Ketura's mountains. "If the buttons make them happier, our lives will be easier." She nudged Gwawl, nodding at the tight space beneath a granite overhang sparkling in the rays of the setting sun.

The rock cats attack from above.

Gwawl wasn't the only one catching on; Iden looked at

the granite retreat with sudden understanding, and as the slavers carried on a loud discussion in their harsh native tongue, the pack moved close to the overhang. When the leader turned to them with a peremptory gesture, it was of no matter at all to sit just where they'd wanted to be. For the first time they were close enough to exchange words freely, but for the first time it was unnecessary. They knew the stakes. Ignoring the pain of her bloodied wrists, Kelyn subtly tested the ropes, checking to see if they'd loosened from the day's activity—they had—and if she could slip her hands free.

She couldn't.

But she still had slightly more freedom than the rest of them . . . and she could work at it. They all worked at it, watching as the slavers quickly set up camp and put the sleep-powder packet on the rock for later use. The men split up, and one took on the task of climbing the steep rock, a gleam in his eye. A man who knew and liked the effects of the choi button and was willing to make the climb even with dusk coming on.

Kelyn hoped he didn't make it back down alive . . . but if he did, then while the slavers crushed, burned, and inhaled the powerful choi, the pack would still have a chance to escape.

The leader started a fire, grumbling at Kelyn in the process. "It's getting cold up here. You shouldn't have brought us so high."

"I'm sorry," she said, as ingratiating as she could be without sounding false. Mungo rolled his eyes. "It's the only way I know."

The sunlight traveled up the rock, leaving the little clearing in shadow. The other men brought more wood, gnarled dead pine that would burn hot and fast. The leader poured a small amount of precious water into a battered travel cup and added a pinch of the drug, heating the mixture over the fire until steam wafted into the air. Then he brought it to them, preoccupied with watching the rocky slope for signs of his companion. "Drink," he commanded them. "One swallow each." He took his eyes from the slope to glare at them. "Don't spit it out."

He didn't have to add threats. Unspoken, they hung loudly enough in the air between captives and captor.

They each took a swallow, making terrible faces. Kelyn took her turn last and siphoned the concentrated, intensely bitter liquid under her tongue, scrunching her face in an uncontrollable reaction to the taste.

A trickle of small stones came from above. The slaver glanced overhead, and Kelyn soundlessly pushed the liquid out between her lips, letting it dribble silently down her chin. By the time the man looked down again, she'd scrubbed her chin against her shoulder, removing all traces of the drink. Behind her, the pack held its collective breath, facing the slaver's suspicious glare.

But if he saw anything amiss, he never had the chance to say so. The trickle of stones gave way to a thump and a thud, and the slaver jumped back just in time to avoid the falling body of his companion.

The limp, falling body.

The leader shouted in surprise and anger, dropping to his knees to roll the man over, shaking his shoulders.

Almost dusk now. Hunt time for the big cats. Kelyn glanced anxiously back at her pack mates, her eyes full of question. As one they shook their heads—all but Gwawl, who mimed wiping his chin. He, too, had spat out the drug.

And the others were already drooping, quickly taken by

the warm liquid in their empty stomachs no matter how they struggled against it. Kelyn closed her eyes in resignation. *Only two of us.* And with Gwawl tied more restrictively than she.

Clumsy Kelyn.

"He's dead!"

Kelyn turned back to the slaver's leader, unable to dredge up surprise. So she didn't try to fake it. She said nothing, just watched warily, knowing the leader might well take his ire out on her. Her hands tightened on her staff. When the moment hung in the air, she gathered her courage and her most practical manner and said, "Only three of you to split the profit, then."

The leader glared, crouched over his friend's body and taking no apparent notice of the four deep, bloodless puncture wounds on the man's neck—the marks of a rock cat so irate it hadn't even bothered to play. This man's neck had been broken long before he hit the ground. Kelyn glanced back at her friends.

They'd seen the wounds. Of course they'd seen them, even through the drugs. Their tension filled the little overhang. But the slaver didn't pick up on that, either. Instead, he patted the dead man's sides, hunting for—and finding—the seedpods the man had gone to acquire. To Kelyn's surprise, he left the dead man where he lay and went to the fire. The other two men waited, wary and tight-lipped; the three of them huddled together to exchange terse words, glancing frequently at their prisoners. Then they seemed to come to some conclusion, for the leader settled beside the fire and, though the slavers had dried meat and a handful of dried tubers already set aside for a meal, the three turned their attention to the choi buttons.

Within moments they'd crushed the seedpods to a fine,

precious dust that they cupped in their palms, applying glowing sticks pulled from the fire. Pungent smoke drifted briefly
toward the overhang, but most of it ended up inside the slavers'
lungs. After a few moments, they didn't seem to notice when
their aim grew less precise and the odor of burned skin mingled with that of the choi. And a few moments after that, they
stood, staggering against one another, raucous and jovial.

Gwawl muttered, "I'm not sure . . ."

He didn't have to finish his words. Kelyn, too, had hoped
the potent choi of this altitude would hit the slavers hard, but
they were apparently well accustomed to the effects of the
herb. They didn't lose their sense of purpose as they headed
for their prisoners, three swaggering slavers standing before a
sorry group of drugged, huddled youngsters.

The leader announced, "Now that Grolph is dead, we've
decided we can spare one of you."

Spare one of us . . . ?

Suddenly Kelyn understood. *Spare the profit,* leaving the
slavers free to use and discard one unlucky youngster. She
gave the others a panicked glance, seeing her friends drugged,
seeing Gwawl still tightly tied, knowing herself to be no
closer to freedom.

But she had her staff. The staff that supported her on
the trail, that saved her from bruises when her pack mates
picked up their own casually acquired quarterstaffs and set
about causing trouble, that protected her from the attack of
everything from unexpected rockfall to irate predator. And if
her clumsy feet were tied, at least she wasn't drugged.

The leader reached for Frykla.

Clumsy Kelyn.

Their only chance.

Their *last* chance.

Kelyn cast her self-doubts aside and exploded upward in front of her friend, staff whirling deftly in spite of her tied hands—and when the men laughed, she planted one end of the staff in the ground and cast herself around it, slamming her feet into one barrel chest, knocking the man into his buddy. She landed in a crouch, lifting the weighted end of the staff to sweep it against the leader's shins. Down he went with a cry of surprise, turning the slavers into a tangle of stinking, choi-besotted men. The surprise only lasted a moment, but it was long enough for Gwawl to launch himself into the fray, loop his arms over one man's head to jam the tight ropes against his throat, and pull the man down on top of him.

Gwawl might have been smaller than the slaver, and he might well have trouble breathing beneath the man, but the slaver was now his shield, and both of the other men immediately turned to Kelyn.

She grinned at them, a fierce grin, and unleashed the ululating hunt cry that until now had only echoed through the mountains in practice—the cry that declared her prowess and confidence and intent. She didn't wait for their moves—she leaped at them, her stance as wide as she could manage in the ropes, and she turned the staff into her shield, whirling it so quickly that it became nothing more than a blur. "*I've* decided," she snarled. "We can't spare any of us—but we can spare all of *you*."

He snarled right back at her. "You bi—"

That's when Kelyn heard it. Another snarl altogether, deep and throaty and full of menace. She glanced at Gwawl, protected under his choking human shield, and dove for the overhang, miscalculating enough to land right on top of her befuddled pack mates. "Down!" she cried to them as they tried to heave her off. "Down, down, *down*!"

They stayed down. Kelyn twisted to look back to the clearing as a huge shadow passed before the overhang. A great webbed paw slapped one man, a hind paw scraped across the man on top of Gwawl, and the immense dappled white rock cat snatched the leader up in his jaws and bounded right out of the clearing.

Silence.

Kelyn sat up; the others disentangled themselves. Gwawl pulled his arms free, dragged himself out from beneath the dead weight of the equally dead man atop him, and crawled over to join the others. The fire had been kicked to embers; night was nearly upon them.

But the slavers were dead. The hunt pack was free.

Gwawl looked at Kelyn and murmured approvingly, "It takes more than brawn to make a powerful hunter . . . or warrior. It takes a clever turn of mind. And you saved the clumsy for last."

Kelyn moved quickly into the clearing, using the last bit of fading light to grab knives from the slavers, and to snatch up the meat scattered beside the dead fire. She gave Gwawl one of the knives and they went to work on the ropes. She glanced at their stuporous pack mates. "Will they even remember what happened?"

Gwawl grunted as his ankle ropes parted, and stretched his legs with pleasure. "Who knows? Does it matter?"

"No," Kelyn said, settling in for a long night of huddling beneath the overhang to watch over her drugged friends, guarding against the return of the rock cat. "It doesn't."

Because she knew. And things would be different from now on.

Clumsy Kelyn could be her father's daughter after all.

DORANNA DURGIN

DORANNA DURGIN spent her childhood filling notebooks first with stories and art and then with novels. After obtaining a degree in wildlife illustration and environmental education, she spent a number of years deep in the Appalachian Mountains. When she emerged, it was as a writer who found herself irrevocably tied to the natural world and its creatures—and with a new appreciation for the rugged spirit that helped settle the area and that she instills in her characters.

Dun Lady's Jess, Doranna's first published fantasy novel, received the Compton Crook/Stephen Tall Memorial Award for the best first book in the science fiction, fantasy, or horror genre. She now has sixteen novels in a variety of genres on the shelves and more on the way; most recently she's leaped gleefully into the world of action-romance. When she's not writing, Doranna builds Web pages, wanders around outside with a camera, and works with horses and dogs. There's a Lipizzan horse in her backyard, a mountain looming outside her office window, a pack of agility dogs romping in the house, and a laptop sitting on her desk—and that's just the way she likes it.

You can find a complete list of fantasy books, franchise tie-ins, and action-romances at www.doranna.net, along with scoops about new projects, lots of silly photos, and a link to Doranna's SFF Net newsgroup. And for kicks, her dog, Connery Beagle, has a LiveJournal (connerybeagle) presenting his unique view of life in the high desert of Arizona. Drop by and say hello!

AN AXE FOR MEN

Rosemary Edghill

THEY CARRIED SLEEPING TAR'ATHA before them, borne upon Her golden lions. Ten kings followed Her—the Sacred Twins who had danced with the bulls within the walls of Saloe for Her fame and delight.

But Saloe was no more.

Since before the beginning of the world, the tricolored walls of Great Saloe had stood tall before the Reed Lake, beside the Blue River. Her pillars of red orichalcum called down Ut-ash-atha from heaven, all for the glory of Sleeping Tar'atha.

Saloe was changeless. But Saloe changed.

It was in rain-time, the season that turned the plains dark and lush with pasturage for goats and horses. But that year there was more rain than Sais could remember ever having fallen before. For month after month, Tar'atha hid Ut-sin-atha in the sky by night, hid Ut-ash-atha in the sky by day. There was only darkness, and clouds, and rain.

And then, one day, there was the sound of the world breaking.

Water rushed down into the valley in a great flood. It shattered villages. It drowned the beasts in the pastures.

But Great Saloe was not destroyed.

Not then.

The people came to the city as the waters rose, begging for refuge, and the Lady of Saloe admitted them. Sais was only a very young Priestess of the Temple then, but she cherished the way in which the Lady of Saloe spoke as the voice of the Sleeping Goddess. Perhaps someday, if she too bore twin kings to Tar'atha, she would stand where the Lady of Saloe stood now and rule over the people with the same calm justice.

That had been three turns of the seasons ago.

Before the Reed Lake had turned entirely to salt.

Before it grew to cover the villages, the grazing lands, the fields. Before it grew to rise over the outer terraces of Great Saloe itself.

The rain had stopped, but the water kept rising.

And soon they realized that they must leave Great Saloe . . . or starve.

The Lady of Saloe dreamed an oracle and chose the most propitious day. They would leave at high summer and build a new city in the south. So Tar'atha ruled.

All the remaining people of the city gathered together their animals and their possessions. They built beautiful wheeled carts to carry them and wove lovely clothes to wear.

On the first day, the Ten Kings had led the sacred bulls, garlanded in wreaths of beaten gold, through the great gilded gates of the city. They were followed by a glorious procession: the shadow-women of the Sleeping Goddess, dressed in their most ornate gowns, their most elaborate aprons, bearing the golden image of the Goddess on their muscular shoulders.

Behind them walked the Lady of Saloe, with the gold Crown of the City upon her head and the knotted Belt of Sovereignty about her hips, and behind her, Sais and the rest of the Priestess-brides.

But the sacred bulls had never been outside of the city in their lives. They balked as they were led down the long ramp outside the city gates, and when the feet of the first pair sank into the muddy ground outside the city, the creatures panicked.

Bawling and shaking their heads in terror, the sacred bulls stood fast and would not be moved.

It was a terrible omen. Sais could not see it, but she could hear the bellowing, and heard the whispered descriptions of the sight at the head of the column.

"Their throats are to be cut here," the Lady of Saloe said at last. "Tar'atha requires this sacrifice to bring us good fortune on our journey."

Sais felt a cold chill of dread creep over her. This was not the ancient ritual. Yes, the sacred bulls died for Tar'atha's favor, but the Twin Kings danced with them first, bringing them to the place of their death with stave and noose before slitting their throats with the stone knife, for no metal must ever touch their flesh. This was . . . wrong.

But the word was passed, and eventually the bellowing stopped.

The people moved on.

The beautiful gowns were quickly draggled with mud and water, for all the earth outside Great Saloe was wet and marshy now, salt-poisoned and dead. The ground was too wet for the wheeled carts to be able to roll over it, too wet for the people to simply drag them through the mud. At last they loaded as much of the food and their possessions as they could onto the horses and any other animal that could carry a burden, and left the rest behind. The sucking mud quickly stole away one of Sais's glittering golden sandals, and in a fit of temper she unlaced the other one and threw it as far as she could.

The golden image of Sleeping Tar'atha they kept with them.

They did not know where to go, or what they must do. They had lingered long, protected by the walls of Great Saloe, while others fled before them. The land had changed.

Tiny streams were great rushing rivers of bitter undrinkable water. Fertile grasslands were dying swamps, the grass yellowed and sere.

By the time Ut-ash-atha sank toward the Halls of Sleep the people were all sick and weary with walking, but a shepherd named Neshat had found a stream of water that was still sweet enough—just barely—to drink.

That night they finished all the cooked food they had brought with them out of Saloe. They lit their lamps, but the wind blew out the flames. It did not matter. Soon the oil would be gone as well.

That night Sais Dreamed.

She had not yet been admitted into the Sanctuary, where the Priestess-brides courted the wisdom of the Great Mother in sleep. Only last year had she begun to bleed as a woman. If the Salt had not come, this year she would have taken one of the Young Kings as a lover in the soft meadows of spring, courting the favor and fertility of Sleeping Tar'atha.

She was still virgin, and so she should not Dream.

But she Dreamed.

She stood within the walls of Great Saloe. Water filled the streets, rose over the steps of Tar'atha's Temple. In the distance, the villages that had once looked to Saloe for wisdom could no longer be seen: only the waters of the Reed Lake, growing vaster with each death of Ut-sin-atha. The Younger Son shone down into the Sacred Courtyard, turning the sacred pillar to a dull bronze.

And she was not alone.

A figure stepped out from behind the orichalcum pillar. It was a man unlike any Sais had ever seen.

He wore the dancing-kilt of the Young Kings, but his beard was the long red beard of a man. In his hand he carried the Axe of Sacrifice, which only the Lady of Saloe might wield. And upon his brow . . .

It was as if one of the Young Kings had grown to manhood and wore the horns of the sacred bulls upon his own brow.

She did not know what to do. This was a vision, Goddess-sent, but this was not the Goddess.

The Sleeping Goddess was the Mother of All, and in token of that, they depicted Her with Her sons, Ut-sin-atha and Ut-ash-atha—the Tar'athanis, the Sacred Twins who watched by day and night. And since Sais's world was but a mirror of Her dominion, the Lady of Saloe had Twin Kings as well: five pairs, like the fingers of a hand.

But never did the Young Kings live into the fullness of bearded manhood. Should one be taken by the Mother from the bull-court, his brother must accompany him to Her sky-hall at once: it was the Law of the City. And the bulls were fast, and agile, and clever. Only the young could dance with them, and live.

"You do not know Me, Sais," the Horned One said. "I have danced for your pleasure and My Mother's many a time, and still you do not know Me. But you will. You will need

Me, and what only I can teach you. Call upon My Name, when you are ready."

With a startled gasp, Sais awoke, staring into the darkness. The images burned strong in her mind and her heart.

But they made no sense. A man? A god-man? A man who was a god?

It could not be. There was only the Mother, alone and One. The Mother and Her suckling babes.

But sleep did not come again that night.

Another day, their progress southward slower still. When they stopped at midmorning to eat—slaughtering the young and the weak of the herds to feed themselves—it took a long time to find fuel to cook the meat, and the people lingered over the food. Worse, they made the water palatable by mixing it with the jars of beer and honey-wine they had brought, and so they slept after they had eaten and did not move on again that day.

But Sais was too frightened to sleep.

When the sheep and the goats and the cattle are gone, what shall we eat? When the grain and the fruit are gone, what shall we eat? Why do not the Great Mother and the Lady of Saloe tell us what we must do?

She knew she should tell the Lady of Saloe of her vision, but she was afraid. She sat among the slumbering Court and watched the herdsmen as they moved among the surviving beasts, trying to find them palatable grazing. Here and there a tuft of hardy new growth arose in the blighted earth, but most of the grass was yellow and dead with the salt that had risen through the soil. Among them she saw the shepherd Neshat, standing among his beasts.

Sais could look back the way they had come and still see—faintly, in the distance—the gilded towers of Saloe. And along the way, the swath of broken grass that marked their path. It glittered with those things her people had carelessly dropped or discarded—a sandal, a painted fan, a shawl, a child's ball.

The day is warm, she thought. *But winter will come again. Our looms are behind us in Saloe. How shall we clothe ourselves when the cold winds blow?*

"You will need Me, and what only I can teach you. Call upon My Name, when you are ready."

They had been on the road a handful of days when the first of the Young Kings died.

Sais had not Dreamed again since that first night, but she seemed to feel the presence of the Horned One with her always, waiting for the moment when she would do something she could as yet barely imagine. She was the youngest and most-untutored of Great Saloe's Priestess-brides. What could she do?

The way before them led through a marsh. They had looked for a way around it and found none. They must cross it or turn back. By driving the animals ahead, Neshat said, they could find the driest ground and the easiest way. And so it was: where cattle went, men could follow.

But one of the Young Kings turned aside, just for a moment, to pluck a clump of yellow flowers as a gift to the Lady of Saloe. There was so little beauty in the world now, but here in the marsh, flowers grew everywhere.

He put his hand upon a fallen tree to steady himself, and as he did, the trunk rolled aside, and an adder darted out from beneath it, sinking its fangs into his foot.

He died in seconds, gasping out his life, as his brother watched in horror.

The Lady of Saloe waited until they had all crossed safely to the far side of the marsh. Then she called for the Axe.

The Axe of Sacrifice and Tar'atha's golden image were all that they had managed to keep of the sacred things that had been Saloe's. The Axe was older than Great Saloe itself, it was said: its head was polished gray stone, smooth as a woman's skin, and its edge was sharper than any metal.

The dead king's twin came before her. He had known his fate from the moment his brother died. He knelt before her, consenting, and leaned back, offering his throat to the blade. In the shadow of Sleeping Tar'atha, the Lady of Saloe struck, sending him to the sky-hall to join his brother.

Their replacements should have been anointed at once and sent to dance with the sacred bulls in the bull-court. But the bull-court was gone and the sacred bulls were dead.

Things are changing, thought Sais uneasily.

She did not mean their lives—those had changed on the day the Salt had come. She meant the way in which they were held upon the Mother's knees, and that was something Sais had not thought could change even if the Salt covered all the land below the Mother's sky-hall.

That day, when they stopped, she resolved to tell the Lady of Saloe of her vision and beg for her comfort.

But that comfort did not come.

"These are virginal fancies," the Lady of Saloe told her implacably, when Sais had stumbled through her tale and brought it to its close. "What you speak of is not possible. An axe for men? It cannot be. Who have you told of this?"

"No one," Sais said, stunned and surprised. To whom should she speak of such horrors, save the Lady of Saloe?

"Speak to no one—or never speak again. And Dream no more."

But though she could promise not to speak, Sais could not promise not to Dream.

That night He came to her again. Once more she stood in Drowning Saloe, in the Birth-Room of the Young Kings. Their bodies were painted with the red ochre and the yellow, their faces painted as white as Ut-sin-atha's. Their bodies were bound with strips of fine cloth for their journey to the sky-halls, but she could still see the marks of the adder's bite upon the one and the mark of the Blade of Sacrifice upon the other, for his head had been carefully set upon his shoulders again with a collar of white clay set with the teeth of bulls.

And He was there.

He is no man, Sais thought rebelliously, for the Lady of Saloe's scorn still lay heavily upon her. *He is the Son of the Mother.*

"Do you know Me yet?" He asked.

"You are the Mother's Son," Sais said. She knelt before Him in reverence, though when she did, she knelt in icy water that came to her slender waist.

"My Mother is the Lady of All Beasts, and all that is wild and tame does Her reverence. Yet she has kept for Herself that which is tame, and given to Me that which is wild. You go now into My realms. Call upon My Name when you would accept My gifts."

Once more Sais awoke in the night, her heart fluttering in terror.

Her gown was sodden to the waist, as if she had been wading in a pool. She wrung it out and sniffed at her fingers.

Salt.

But I do not know Your Name, Horned One! How shall I call upon You?

The darkness gave no answer.

They had been a full cycle of Ut-sin-atha upon the road. He had gone down into the Halls of Death and been reborn victorious. In honor of his rebirth, two bulls had been sacrificed in the name of Tar'atha, and the people had feasted, though there had been no incense, no oil, and only brackish water to drink, mixed with the blood of the slain bulls.

Since the death of the Young Kings, Sais was in disgrace, and so she heard things that others did not.

The Court—the surviving Young Kings, the Lady of Saloe, the Priestess-brides, the shadow-women, the great nobles and all their slaves and households—all grumbled constantly about the privations of the journey, but they trusted in their hearts to the wisdom of the Lady of Saloe, she who was the Hand of Tar'atha, and went on as if Great Saloe would rise again.

The others—the herdsmen, the farmers, the craftsmen—those who did not eat from the first cut of every sacrifice, but must make do with what the Court left . . . they doubted. They wondered if Tar'atha was displeased with them, if She had sent the Salt to scour them from the face of the world.

Neshat was first among them. He had even dared to speak out against the sacrifice, saying that if it was done there would be no bulls to put to the cows in the spring, for they had been the last.

For that, the Lady of Saloe had had him beaten until the

blood flowed, until he groveled for her favor and wept for her anger.

He had been foolish to speak, Sais thought. It did not matter. There would be no cows come spring to stand to a bull. They would have eaten them all long since, just as they had eaten the goats and the sheep. The horses remained—for Tar'atha would not allow the killing of horses, or of dogs, even in sacrifice—but the horses were thin and sickly, and the dogs grew daily more anxious for meat.

And where Neshat had spoken and been rebuked, others would eventually follow. When there were no more cattle. When there was nothing left to eat.

Sais was in disgrace, so she had not been permitted to attend the feast of the bulls. She stood in the darkness and watched as the Court ate its fill, and then watched as the remains were dragged on flayed skins to the fires of the herdsmen and farmers.

She thought long upon the words of the Mother's Son. And as she waited in the darkness, she made her plan.

That which she bore, she carried wrapped in her shawl like a child, lest any see it. She walked boldly to the fires of the herdsfolk, though her mouth tasted bitter with terror.

"I come seeking the herdsman Neshat," she said, stepping into the firelight. "I come to claim my bride-right, by the Law of Saloe."

A Priestess-bride might claim any man she chose to be her lover. It was the Law.

"You have come to the wrong fires, little Goddess," one of the men said, not unkindly. "Turn, and choose again."

Almost, her courage deserted her then. But fear and her visions drove Sais onward. "I come to claim my bride-right.

I come for Neshat," she repeated, hugging her bundle tightly to her chest.

The men and women around the fire spoke among themselves, too low for Sais to hear. At last one of the women pointed. "He is there, little Goddess. He is yours."

Sais did not bow or thank her—that would have been wrong—but her heart leaped with gratitude. She turned and hurried off in that direction.

She found Neshat lying facedown beside a fire upon a fleece. One of the other herdsmen was pouring water over his wounded back from a jug. Sais knelt beside Neshat, cradling her bundle carefully.

The herdsman looked at her in surprise—and then in more than surprise when he saw who she was.

"I have come for Neshat," Sais said, summoning up the last of her courage. "I bring that which it is not proper for you to see. Leave us now."

The herdsman leaped to his feet and bolted into the darkness, his eyes wide with awe and fear. Now Sais was alone with Neshat.

He slept—or seemed to. Carefully she unwrapped her bundle. The most important thing she set aside, out of harm's way. The immediately necessary items she took into her hand to use at once.

Even a virgin Priestess-bride knew the secrets of the Temple, and so she knew that the base of Tar'atha's statue was hollow. She knew that it was filled with those things that the Lady of Saloe treasured—not gold and jewels, but things more valuable.

Medicines.

Sais had plundered that store ruthlessly.

A wooden box held an ointment of lamb-fat, honey, and distilled poppy-juice: she had compounded it herself many a time. It was sovereign for all hurts, dulling their pain. Now she laved it gently over the weals the shadow-women's whips had left upon Neshat's back. He began to stir to wakefulness at her touch.

Into the sacred agate cup—which she had also stolen— she mixed poppy-juice, honey, and wine, adding a little water from the jug the other herdsman had left to thin it, and stirring it with her finger to mix it well. As she stirred it, she whispered the spells she had been taught, praying for the Mother's aid in healing—and for Her blessing upon what else Sais would do this night.

Neshat was awake now, watching her with glittering dark eyes.

"Drink this," Sais commanded. "It will ease your pain."

He sat up stiffly and reached for the cup, drinking its contents quickly. Then he reached for the water jug and drained its contents as well. When it was empty, he wiped his mouth with the back of his hand and stared at her unspeaking for a long moment.

"Why do you come here, little Goddess?" he asked at last.

"I would claim you," Sais said. "It is my right," she added, when he said nothing.

"Are the Young Kings all dead, that you must come to me?" Neshat said. "Or have they cast you out of the Temple?"

"There . . . is . . . no . . . Temple," Sais said. Suddenly she felt sick with despair. He spoke the words of the Young Kings, of the nobles, of the Lady of Saloe. Somehow she had thought he would understand what she herself did not.

"No," Neshat agreed. "There is not. But woe to him who

says there is not." For a moment he smiled, then suddenly he looked past her, at the other thing she had brought with her, and his face grew very still.

"It is death for you to touch that which you have brought here," he said, gazing at the Axe of Sacrifice.

"We are all dying," Sais said simply. "Come. Be the bull to my cow. It is my right—and it is you I would have, above all the kings and princes of Saloe."

I will raise you up—My Son, My Lover, My Consort—

The Voice echoed through Sais's mind. She felt as if she were borne upon the wings of the storm and did not know if she spoke the words aloud.

I will give birth to You, I will take You to My golden bed, I will slay You in the harvest year—

Neshat rocked between her thighs. Sais's nails dug into his shoulders, reopening weals. His blood was on her hands.

The blood of sacrifice—

She felt the Horned One—near, so near—the Great Mother's Son, but sons grow to manhood. To father children, and to care for them. To teach them what they needed to know to survive in the world, no matter how harsh the world was.

His hand reached out to her, to lift her up. And in that moment she knew His Name—hers to call upon, to seal a new covenant.

If she dared.

"Nis! Your Name is Nis, Son of Tar'atha! Nis, help us!" Sais cried.

Afterward, when Neshat lay upon her, spent, Sais took his hand and clasped it about the haft of the Axe.

He did not die.

*   *   *

She Dreamed, and in her Dream, Nis came to her again. This time he did not come to her in Drowned Saloe, but in a great forest filled with beasts of every kind, and Neshat was beside her.

"Now I shall teach you what you need to know," Nis said to them. "You know My Name and may call upon Me. The first meat of the kill is mine, as the blood is My Mother's, but the rest is yours, to nourish your bodies and your hounds. I shall lead you to a land of sweet grass and tall trees, and there you will flourish, but you must never forget Me."

"We will always honor You," Neshat said. "This I vow, upon Your Horns."

Before the dawn, all among the herdsmen and farmers heard the story of Nis, Son of the Mother, from Neshat and Sais both. They hid the Axe carefully, for it had passed from the Mother to the Son.

It was too late now to return it to the Sleeping Goddess. Too many would see. The Lady of Saloe's wrath would be as bitter as the Salt.

And it was no longer hers to own.

The loss of the Axe of Sacrifice did not go unnoticed. At the beginning of Ut-sin-atha's feast, it lay before the golden statue of Tar'atha. When Ut-ash-atha took his brother's place in the sky, it was gone.

No one could say how it had happened. It was impossible that anyone should lay hands upon the Axe of Sacrifice and live. The shadow-women set up a great wailing, and the Priestess-brides added their lamentations, and the wives of the nobles and all their households howled like dogs.

In so much confusion, it was possible for Sais to replace the cup and the box and the medicines she had taken from the base of Sleeping Tar'atha's golden statue without being seen.

At last the Lady of Saloe gave her pronouncement: she had Dreamed, and in her Dream, Tar'atha had come to her and taken the Axe of Sacrifice, saying She would leave it for them as a sign in the place they were to build Her new city.

She lies! Sais thought in shock. *She lies about a Dream of Tar'atha! She puts words into the mouth of the Great Mother!*

She had not thought it could be so. But it was.

The Court was quieted, but the Lady's eyes rested keenly upon Sais's face.

"Do you say I do not Dream true?" the Lady of Saloe said softly, for Sais's ears alone.

"You forbid me to speak of Dreams," Sais said quietly, casting her gaze down upon the earth. *But Nis would have me speak, and what I speak of is no Dream.*

To hunt was a small thing for herdsmen who had tracked lost sheep and goats through the high grass. To kill with the sling and the stick was a simple thing for farmers who had driven cows from the field and shepherds who had driven wolves from the fold.

At first their attempts went unrewarded, but they quickly learned. For a time—a very short time—their successes went unnoticed by the Court.

Each night now Sais slipped away from the Court to go to her lover. Together they dreamed of Nis, and of the southern forests where they would raise His altar beside Tar'atha's own. From the horns and hide of the last bull of sacrifice, the artisans had fashioned for Neshat a Nis-crown, so that he might properly offer Nis His due portion of each kill. And

Nis rewarded them, showing them new ways to reap His bounty.

But when Ut-sin-atha had gone down into the Halls of Death once more and the nights were dark and filled with stars, Sais was summoned before the Lady of Saloe's face.

"The dogs no longer howl with hunger in the night," the Lady of Saloe said. Her voice was mild. In the red light of the fire, Sais could see her face, painted just as it had been in the halls of Saloe, though not even the shadow-women still painted their faces, nor did the Lady of Saloe paint her own face every day.

But tonight her face was as white as the face of Ut-sin-atha, and her lips and her cheeks were as red as the face of Ut-ash-atha. Her brows were as black as the hair of Tar'atha Herself, and the lids of her eyes had been carefully blackened as well.

"The dogs do not howl in the night," Sais agreed, though suddenly her heart beat fast with fear.

"And the smoke of the cookfires of the herdsmen and farmers is black with fat and savory with roasting, though they have no meat to roast," the Lady said.

Sais did not answer. Two of the shadow-women stood close behind her, and in their hands were knives of the red orichalcum.

"They grow sleek and full of flesh while we starve and dwindle. Why should this be?" the Lady of Saloe asked.

"It is so because I wish it to be so," a new voice said.

Neshat stepped into the fire's light. Upon his head he wore the Crown of Nis. In his hands he bore the Axe of Sacrifice.

The shadow-women stepped back, gibbering in horror. The knives of red orichalcum fell to the earth.

Sais stepped to Neshat's side.

The Lady of Saloe stared at them both from behind her painted face, and her eyes were terrible to see. She stretched out her hand.

"That is mine. Give it to me."

"It is not yours. It is not yours to give. It is not yours to take. It is the Mother's to give—and She has given it to Her Son: Nis." The fear Sais had felt was gone now. She knew that she spoke Truth—and Truth had once been honored in the Courts of Great Saloe.

"I know of no Nis," the Lady of Saloe said. But her voice quavered like that of an old woman, and she could not meet Sais's bright gaze.

"You know Him," Sais said, and now her voice was as hard as the Lady's once had been. "He has danced for your pleasure with the bulls. He has lain with Tar'atha in Her golden bed, and gotten Ut-sin-atha and Ut-ash-atha upon Her. As a goodly gift, She has given Him rulership over the wild things of the world. It is He Who gives the duck and the hare into our sling and our snare. Now it is time for Him to lead us."

A faint moan of fear escaped the Lady of Saloe's lips, and Sais knew that at last the Lady knew in her heart that Saloe was no more.

"But the Axe," the Lady whimpered. "It is Tar'atha's Axe."

"No," Sais said, more gently now. "Now it is the Axe of Nis. Now it is an Axe for men."

ROSEMARY EDGHILL

ROSEMARY EDGHILL's first professional sales were to the black-and-white comics of the late 1970s, so she can truthfully state on her résumé that she once killed vampires for a living. She is also the author of over thirty novels and several dozen short stories in genres ranging from Regency romance to space opera, making all local stops in between. She has collaborated with authors such as the late Marion Zimmer Bradley and science fiction grand master Andre Norton, and has worked as a science fiction editor for a major New York publisher, as a freelance book designer, and as a professional book reviewer. Her hobbies include sleep, research for forthcoming projects, and her Cavalier King Charles spaniels. Her Web site can be found at www.sff.net/people/eluki.

When the editors of this anthology approached Rosemary about doing a story, she immediately thought of the mythological Amazons. New research done in the Black Sea area (where her story is set) indicates that, oddly enough, the theories of the long-discredited anthropologist J. J. Bachofen may be a more accurate model of the culture of 5000 BCE than we ever thought possible: he theorized that the ancient world was run as a utopian matriarchy at one time. But in times of great catastrophe—such as a great flood—things always change. Rosemary knows a good story when she sees one. There's not much drama in perfection. But there's a great story to tell in a changing society, and in the young heroes who see the need for change.

ACTS OF FAITH

Lesley McBain

MY NAME IS BRIDGET RILEY. *I did not come here to waste away and die.*

Bridget bent her head, knees throbbing as she scrubbed the tiled floor furiously. Sodding nuns, working her worse than her ma had before she'd been sent away as a charity case. And they called this a *school*? Workhouse, more like.

Her auburn braid dipped low over her chest, swinging dangerously near the wet floor. Before she could toss it back over her shoulders, another young, roughened hand did it for her.

"Bridey," her friend Maire said, "almost time for lights-out. Sister Fiona sent me to tell you. Punishment duty *again*?"

"Sodding Sister Margaret," Bridget growled, sitting back on her heels and looking up.

Maire grimaced. Sister Margaret had called her narrow-boned face devilish when she did that; Bridget didn't think so. Maire was just smart, that was all.

Bridget studied her more intently. Her friend's blue eyes

shone with a conspiratorial light she recognized. "All right, let's have it. You didn't come just to tell me it's almost time for lights-out."

"Sister Fiona *did* send me, but . . . I heard her and Sister Maureen and Sister Cecily talking. There's a new girl in our room." Maire looked down the long, dim, empty corridor. "Let's get your wash water dumped. Terrible heavy, this bucket is. Going to take two of us to carry it." She winked.

"So it is," Bridget agreed as she got up, stretching her aching back. She was fourteen. She felt forty. "Come on, then. Let's be about it." She picked up the scrub brush and stuck it into her deep apron pocket. "Wouldn't want to be late for lights-out, would we now? Jerry might get us. Or the Brits."

The two girls lugged the sloshing bucket to the main building's back door. Only knowing the hallway by heart kept them from tripping; the knowledge had been paid for in bruises.

As they eased open the door, a sliver of moon greeted them, along with the familiar smells of night air and peat smoke. The Irish city was battened down for the night. With coal rationed—along with everything else—peat was what made the trains run. When the trains ran, that was. Rationing had taken its toll . . . even on *tea*.

"The name they're giving her is Anne Smith," Maire whispered as the two walked a little way down the alley behind the main building to dump the dirty water into the convent school's tiny garden. "But Sister Maureen was telling Sister Cecily it's not her real name. And that she'd have to be taught the prayers."

"What, is she a bloody Protestant?" Bridget asked in surprise.

"Shhh, not so loud!" Maire stopped. As the two upended the bucket, taking care not to muddy their shoes, she whispered, "She's from abroad. The nuns are hiding her."

Bridget shook her head. "I don't believe you."

" 'Tis true, Bridey. When have I ever lied to you?"

Bridget paused. Maire never lied, but she had a fey, fanciful streak to go with all her book learning, so Bridget took everything her friend said with a grain of salt.

"Sister Margaret wouldn't allow it. She'd rather see Hitler win the war than the bloody Brits."

"Sister Fiona said what Sister Margaret didn't know wouldn't hurt her. Sister Maureen and Sister Cecily agreed."

"Have they gone daft?"

Maire shrugged. "Sister Fiona said other convents took in refugees. I think those were Catholic girls, though. She said it was a holy cause."

Bridget shook her head. "Grand. If they *are* breaking the law, we'll all be in gaol together soon. Not that we're not already."

My real name is Miriam Cohen. I came here so I might live.

Miriam sat on the narrow bed, waiting for the other girls—her new roommates, Sister Fiona had told her as she'd whisked Miriam upstairs and down the hallway lined with closed doors.

There were no mirrors in the room. Sister Fiona had said there were mirrors aplenty in the shared lavatory down the hall. Just three beds with thin blankets, a small washbasin with stand tucked into the corner, and crucifixes hung over each cot. The Glimmer Man, Sister Fiona had explained, patrolled nightly, checking for blackout violations, so only candles were used at night. The lone candle burning on the washstand cast an eerie, flickering light. It made the crucifixes look almost as if they were sneering at Miriam.

She didn't mind the dark. And the spartan accommodations were a luxury compared to what she'd gone through to arrive here.

Shema Yisroel, Adonai eloheinu, Adonai ekhod, she thought defiantly, staring at one crucifix.

I may have to hide here and pass as a Gentile, but I will not forget who I am.

Miriam closed her eyes and remembered her mother's face: dark eyes, dark hair, new lines on her forehead . . . holding back tears as she kissed Miriam's cheek. "Go, my little Miriam. You speak English better than the rest of us. The money will get only one of us out, so it must be you. But don't worry, my darling. We will be together when the war is over . . . and you'll tell us of your travels."

Miriam prayed her mother's words would come true, even though part of her knew her mother had been lying. She was the oldest daughter—fourteen, a woman already. Her mother had sent her away so that *one* Cohen female would survive to carry on.

She bit her lip. She couldn't, mustn't think of it. Even here in this so-called neutral Ireland. Sister Fiona had warned her only moments ago: "Our leader has said he'd turn Jews over to Germany," she had whispered in Miriam's ear. "The government will imprison anyone threatening our neutrality. You must be careful . . . for *all* of our sakes."

"Then why did you take me in?" Miriam had whispered furiously in return, unable to help herself.

Sister Fiona had reached out as if to hug her, then drawn back. "My child, we serve God, not the government." She drew herself upright. "And though I'm a loyal Irishwoman and a loyal Catholic, I won't be consenting to what's going on in the world without a fight. Let them imprison me if they like. After all," she said with an unexpected scapegrace smile, gesturing at their surroundings, "a gaol cell and a nun's cell aren't furnished that dissimilarly, are they now?"

Miriam shook her head at the recollection. Her name was Anne Smith, she recited silently. Her father's cousin was Sister Fiona. After her family died of influenza, she had remembered Sister Fiona and had made her way by bribes, by stowing away—at least *that* part was true enough—to this convent school.

The door creaked open. Two girls near Miriam's age stood in the doorway. One of them was tall, buxom even in her loose gray dress and apron, with red hair tied back in a braid. The other was small and pale, with wavy black hair escaping from her braid.

Miriam rose. Sweat ran down her back. The tall girl's shoulders and arms were broad and muscular. If Miriam had to fight, she'd have to cheat. She didn't reach for the knife hidden in her dress pocket. Yet.

The smaller girl smiled. "I'm Maire; this is Bridget. And you're the new girl?"

"Anne," Miriam said, after a moment of deciphering the accent. "Pleased to meet you."

Bridget didn't answer. Instead, she shut the door and walked to the bed closest to the window. She fished two candles and saucers out from under the mattress and set them on the nightstand, lighting the candles from the already burning candle. "The blackout curtains'll hide this." Her contralto was melodious, and Miriam wished suddenly for her long-gone piano. "Let's have a proper look at you."

Miriam brought her chin up. "Excuse me?" She pivoted to face Bridget. The innocent, sheltered girl she'd been was long gone. She'd seen things, done things—she pushed the thought aside to focus on Bridget.

The two stared at each other, not quite challenging.

"We haven't had a new girl for a while," Maire said to appease them. "The war and all."

"Sister Fiona saw us downstairs. She says you're kin to her." Bridget's tone was neutral. Miriam didn't show her sudden fear. Was her cover story *that* flimsy? Or was Bridget just a bully?

"My father's cousin," Miriam lied. She hadn't been told what the connection was that had brought her *here*, of all places. Sister Fiona's desire to help seemed sincere, but Miriam didn't dare trust sincerity very far.

"Ah, then you'll be Sister's pet," Bridget said tonelessly, then sat down on her bed. "Maire, blow out the candles. The morrow'll come soon enough for me to see Sister's pet by daylight."

"Good night," Miriam ventured as Maire did Bridget's bidding. Neither girl answered.

O Brigid, hear me now, Maire prayed. *Give me strength to follow your path.*

She had been orphaned and taken in by the convent school last year. Her mother had believed in the *old* ways, not the Church's ways. So did she.

The bed to her left creaked. The new girl was restless. Maire wasn't surprised.

They try not to tell us of the world, but the world tells us things.

One day, she would break free to see the world for herself. But where could a sixteen-year-old girl with no money or family, but more education than was good for a girl in the eyes of the world and the Church, go? While there was a war on, no less?

O Brigid, Maire prayed before sinking into her own restless sleep, *please, show me the way.*

She dreamed of a featureless gray plain where she walked hand in hand with a tall woman wrapped in a blue cloak. Maire couldn't see the woman's face, but the long auburn hair streaming from under a white veil reminded her of her mother's hair.

"Where am I?" she asked softly.

The woman squeezed Maire's hand; the contact was reassuring. "No matter, my daughter. Look within, not without. See your way."

"See my . . . I don't understand."

The woman let go of her hand. "You have the Sight. See your way clear." She gestured at the plain in front of them, then vanished abruptly.

Left alone, Maire turned in a circle to stare fearfully out at the plain. Then she shook herself. *Look within, whoever it was said. So I'll look within.*

She closed her eyes and stood very still, emptying her mind of thought. The image that surfaced in response was double: an old, tattered book, and a building filled with hurrying people that didn't look like anything she'd ever seen.

Just as she thought she could see the book's title clearly, a hand shook her. Her eyes opened wide.

"Time to get up, Maire." It was Bridey; her auburn hair fell loose around her shoulders just as the woman's in the dream had, and Maire blinked.

Bridey. Brigid.

Goddess, if this was Your answer to my prayer, please let me be worthy of interpreting it.

The ruler smashed across the backs of Bridget's hands. "Insolent girl!"

Bridget's back stiffened. She blinked hard, her gaze downcast, to keep the tears of pain from showing. Then she mentally damned Sister Margaret for a sodding cow. *She's no true servant of God—just a bully in nun's clothing.*

Silence was the only way to win. So she kept quiet, head bowed in apparent acquiescence. And eventually Sister Margaret sniffed. "Learned your lesson, have you then? Good." With a swish of her habit, she turned away. "Lunchtime, girls."

Bridget's hands hurt, but she forced herself to ignore the pain. Sister Margaret had taken the ruler to them before for the "insolence" of asking questions. The scars on Bridget's knuckles testified to that.

Maire and the new girl, Anne, caught up with her as they left the classroom and began the walk downstairs to the refectory. The other girls looked curiously at Anne. Inspecting her by daylight, Bridget saw a faint resemblance to Sister Fiona in the shape of the girl's dark brown eyes and wide mouth, enough to make the story passable. The girl's nose was larger and higher-arched than Sister Fiona's, and her wavy chestnut hair didn't resemble the dark hair Bridget had seen once when a wind gust had disarranged Sister Fiona's head-covering.

So much for Sister Margaret knowing everything, Bridget thought in irreverent satisfaction.

"Are you all right?" Anne asked quietly.

"Fine, thank you." The question surprised her, but she didn't let it show.

"Sister Margaret," Maire said in an undertone, "has the heaviest hand with a ruler."

Anne's dark eyes narrowed. Bridget recognized anger held in check—and suddenly began to like the girl despite herself.

"Thank you for telling me," Anne said.

"Shhh," Maire whispered. "No more now."

They filed into the refectory in silence, took seats at the long trestle table, and bowed their heads. Sister Maureen—a round-faced, bright-eyed nun all the girls liked, even Bridget—presided over the table.

As Sister Maureen began to lead the pre-meal prayer, Bridget glanced surreptitiously at Anne, who sat between her and Maire at the end of the table farthest from the nun. The girl only mouthed the prayers. Her sign of the Cross was fumbled.

It's true, Bridget thought in mingled excitement and wonder at the confirmation of Maire's information. *And if she got* here, *maybe she knows how to get* out *of here.*

Miriam scrubbed the floor hard enough to wear away the tiles, out of pent-up frustration. Her fingers hurt from gripping the scrub brush. Backbreaking chores and rigid discipline she could stand; it was better than being dead. She bore the unceasing worry about her family silently.

The overwhelming dread of exposure had lessened to a muted, constant presence after several weeks of adapting to the environment. Maire—and Bridget, which had surprised Miriam—had coached her after lights-out on the words and gestures of the Catholics' prayer rituals. She knew the other two were bursting with curiosity but were smart enough not to ask questions. She appreciated it. Given that she'd grown to cautiously like them, she didn't want to lie to them more than she could help.

"Annie," Bridget said from the other end of the room, "you're exhausting me to watch you."

Miriam looked over at Bridget. The other girl's auburn braid swung almost into her bucket of soapy water.

"Sorry." Miriam shrugged and kept scrubbing. Her biceps ached.

"Besides," Bridget said more acerbically, "no matter how clean it is, it won't be good enough."

Miriam nodded, frowning. She'd learned that lesson quickly at the hands—and ruler—of Sister Margaret. And when Sister Margaret had discussed Judaism in Church history lessons today, Miriam had bitten her lip to keep her mouth shut. *Lying, prejudiced*—Miriam scrubbed furiously.

If she weren't hiding for her life, she'd teach Sister Margaret a lesson or two about Judaism and Jews. And if she didn't suspect the nun of trying to bait her into exposing herself.

"Annie," Bridget repeated impatiently, "I *said*—"

"Ah, isn't that a precious sight, Sister Fiona's little pet on her knees," another voice interrupted.

Miriam tensed. Deirdre O'Fain, the class bully, had taken an instant dislike to her. So far she had avoided confrontation.

"I'm talking to you, *Annie*," the fair-haired girl said with a sneer.

Miriam kept her head down but stayed alert. When Deirdre bent down to snatch at her braid, she uncoiled upward. She hadn't grown up knowing how to fight, but recent experience had taught her. Brutally.

She punched the other girl hard in the stomach. As Deirdre doubled over, Miriam tackled her, knowing that if she didn't win decisively, Deirdre would only be more trouble.

Deirdre—caught off guard—went tumbling to the floor. Water spilled from the bucket. Deirdre managed to keep her head from rapping too harshly against the tiles, but that was all.

Miriam landed on her and locked her long, piano-playing hands around Deirdre's throat. Memories of the German soldier she'd stolen the knife from, the men who had . . . they all swam in her head, along with her rage at Deirdre's bullying and Sister Margaret's cruelty. Her hands tightened.

"Sweet Jesus, Annie, you'll *kill* her!" Bridget frantically hauled her backward. That broke the spell. Deirdre lay limp, but wide-eyed and breathing. Bridget shoved Miriam aside and knelt beside the fair-haired girl.

Miriam's knees shook. She *would* have killed Deirdre. *What's become of me?* she thought in mingled shame and fear.

Deirdre coughed and tried to sit up. Bridget held her down. Miriam tensed again.

"Deirdre," Bridget said coldly, "I didn't stop Annie from wringing your fat neck because I *like* you. We're in a house of godly nature, and blood oughtn't to be shed here. But I swear, if you don't leave Annie alone, the Sisters will know about the American you've been sneaking off to see. D'you understand?"

"He loves me!" Deirdre said raspily.

Bridget's mouth turned down. "They'll *all* say that. But if you say a word about this, or if you bother Annie again, you won't be hearing more fancy words of love from your American. D'you understand?"

Deirdre's face flushed. After a moment, she nodded.

"Your word as an O'Fain," Bridget pressed.

Anger sparked in Deirdre's hazel eyes. "My word as an O'Fain," she finally snarled. Bridget released her. Deirdre got to her feet, touching her throat and looking at Miriam with fear and hatred. Then she turned and stalked down the corridor, wet dress clinging to her plump frame.

Miriam and Bridget faced each other across the water-splashed floor.

Bridget shook her head, smiling slightly. "Annie, you're a corker. Your brothers must be a handful if you're such a scrapper."

Miriam blinked back sudden tears. "My brothers didn't teach me to fight." *Oh, Jacob, oh, Isaac . . . where are you now? Be safe, please,* she half pleaded, half prayed.

Bridget's eyes—green as the emerald ring Miriam's mother had sold to buy her passage—darkened with what took a moment for Miriam to recognize as sympathy. "The world taught you, then." The questions behind the statement lay unspoken.

"The world's teaching all of us," Miriam said quietly.

"Ah, but Ireland's neutral and they'll keep it that way, no matter how many they have to arrest." Bridget's gaze stayed on Miriam's. "And some, like Deirdre or Sister Margaret, would be more than happy to go bearing tales."

Miriam nodded at the warning. Then she shivered.

"Ah, you're soaking wet and I'm blathering. C'mon, let's get this mopped up before lights-out."

Bridget lay awake long after lights-out, thinking. She'd grown up brawling. A girl fighting didn't surprise her. *That cow*

Deirdre had it coming for a long time. From someone other than me.

But . . . when she had pulled Annie away, there'd been a killing rage in those dark eyes of hers. *That* Bridget hadn't seen often.

Maire slipped into the room. Bridget turned her head. "Where have you been?" she whispered. Maire had warned her she'd be late and not to worry, but she couldn't help it.

"In the library." Maire sat carefully down on Bridget's bed, trying not to make it squeak. "I found a book while I was cleaning. An *old* book."

"Maire . . ."

"*Listen.* If we can find out where to go, I can get us there."

"How?"

"*Magic.*"

Miriam listened silently. Maire's arrival had awoken her from a light doze.

She knew there was no such thing as magic. But hiding in Ireland, she'd learned the Irish believed as fiercely in magic and mystery as she did in the Torah.

"And how are we going to find a place to go?" Bridget didn't sound convinced.

"Bridey, I can't think of *everything*. Can't you help?"

"How am *I* going to find a place to go? I've never been outside the city!"

I have, Miriam thought. The convent felt less secure every day. If she was discovered, she'd be deported. Which meant her death. She'd tried to blend in, but she knew she was conspicuous. The growing suspicion in Sister Margaret's eyes told her that. Deirdre watched Miriam closely now too. So did others. If Sister Margaret, or Deirdre, or someone else, guessed the truth . . .

"Annie has," Maire whispered in a strange, toneless voice that sent shivers up Miriam's spine. "And it's farther she'll go before the war's over, 'cross the water to 'scape the death looking for her . . ."

Miriam sat up without thinking.

"Farther she'll go, in the smoke and fire," Maire continued, as if she hadn't heard Miriam's bed creak. "With kin not her own and naught but her wits, to fox the hunters and make a new den."

Miriam drew the blanket tightly around her, chilled to the bone.

"Jesus, Mary, and Joseph," Bridget whispered.

"What?" Maire's voice sounded normal again.

Miriam heard scrabbling sounds; then candlelight bloomed. Bridget looked pallid, even in the dim light. "You never told me you had the Sight, Maire Riordan," she whispered. Her voice shook.

"I . . . what happened?" Now Maire sounded frightened.

"What have you been *playing* at? And in a house of God?"

Maire drew herself up. "I do not *play*," she said with knife-edge precision. "My mother had the Sight, and her mother before her, and *her* mother before *her*, I'll have you know, Bridget Riley. There are more things on this earth than the Church teaches."

Bridget crossed herself.

Miriam sat watching, trying to reconcile everything she knew with what she'd just heard. All she knew of magic was folktales and faint whispers she'd heard about kabbalah lore—

but she knew only that it wasn't "proper," as her father had said when Isaac had asked once.

"Annie," Maire asked, "what did I say?"

"You don't remember?"

"No." Maire tucked her knees up under her chin. "It's not the way with me to remember."

"You said . . . I had farther to go before the war's over. Across the water. To escape a death looking for me." *That could be a guess. She* is *very smart.*

"And?"

"You talked about smoke and fire. And . . ."

" 'With kin not her own,' " Bridget continued, " 'with naught but her wits, to fox the hunters and make a new den.' "

"Ah," Maire said.

"Ah, *what?*" Miriam asked impatiently when Maire didn't elaborate.

"Ah, as in . . . shh!" Maire blew out the candle and scrambled into her own bed.

Miriam lay down quickly, trying not to make the bed creak. She heard soft footsteps along the corridor. Her hand crept to the knife under her pillow.

The door opened a crack. Miriam feigned sleep, her senses stretched taut to catch every sound.

"Sleeping," she heard Sister Fiona whisper.

"I smell smoke," Sister Margaret whispered in return.

The candle, Miriam thought in alarm.

"I was poking up the fire before; it's me you smell it on," Sister Fiona whispered.

"Hmph." The door eased shut again, but not before Miriam heard "Troublemakers, all three" from Sister Margaret.

If only you knew, she thought grimly.

*   *   *

Maire rubbed tired eyes. Every chance she'd had, she'd been poring over the musty tome she'd hidden in a corner of the library. She'd found it buried on a disused bookshelf. Something besides neatness had drawn her to dust that corner. When she saw the spine jutting out slightly from those of the other books, she had remembered her dream with a shiver of mingled excitement and fear—and pulled the book out, knowing she'd found what she sought.

Sister Fiona tolerated her reading so long as the library remained spotless. Maire felt a pang of guilt. The good Sister would be appalled at her reading. But . . . Needs must when the Sight drove.

She thought she could cast the spells—powerful ones, from the way they made the hair stand up on the back of her neck. The first was for protection, should they need it.

And now she knew where they were headed, so she could cast the second spell, the journey one. *Bless Deirdre and her American. All it took was an armlock from Bridey and Deirdre repeated all his tales of New York City, and all the names of his family and friends, that lonely he was for them . . .*

They. Bridget's going with Maire had never been in question; Maire had come to love her like a sister, for all the younger girl's gruffness.

Anne . . . Well, that had been a surprise. But the Sight had told Maire more than the other girls had realized, once they'd repeated her own words back to her.

" 'Kin not her own,' " she murmured. " 'Naught but her wits.' " She smiled slightly. "Describes all three of us, now doesn't it?"

The night exploded. Maire screamed as the library walls shook.

" 'Smoke and fire,' " she breathed, eyes wide. Then she grabbed the book. And ran.

Pandemonium reigned. Girls streamed from their bedrooms, down the stairs, calling out in fright, praying, or weeping. "They're *bombing* us!" Sister Margaret screamed, ruler forgotten beside her as she knelt in the middle of the center hall, habit askew, crying hysterically. "We're *neutral*! They're not supposed to—"

Bridget—who'd been on punishment duty again, this time long after lights-out, and had just come from dumping her water out and admiring the full moon—stood stock-still as terrified girls careened into her.

She heard air-raid sirens. *Jesus, Mary, and Joseph, they're using the* full moon *to bomb us by!* Part of her wanted to drop to her knees with Sister Margaret. Part of her wanted to run. Somewhere. *Anywhere.*

"It's her, that dirty Jewess new girl—" Sister Margaret gabbled.

You'll not betray Annie! Bridget's slap to Sister Margaret's face, delivered with all the pent-up anger she had kept in check for so long, sent the nun sprawling. Sister Margaret scrabbled for the ruler, but Bridget got to it first. Other girls scattered, wide-eyed.

The third blow she slashed across Sister Margaret's back and hands splintered the ruler. Grinning ferally, Bridget snapped it between her hands and flung it aside. Someone—Deirdre?—cheered. Before the dazed nun could recover, Bridget hauled her up and pinned her against the wall by the throat.

"It's hysterical you are, Sister Margaret," Bridget said

loudly, staring into her hate-filled eyes. "Aren't you supposed to be setting a godly example for us? Not blathering on about fancies?"

"You little—that little—"

Bridget's grip tightened. "There *are* no Jews here, Sister. *We* know that. *You* know that." *Only my friend. And I'll fight you or anyone for her, you Nazi-sympathizing cow.* "You're daft."

Sister Fiona stormed up the hallway, habit billowing, dark hair exposed. She cut across the crowd to pull Bridget's arm away from Sister Margaret's throat. The older nun slumped to the floor, coughing. "Go on with you!" Sister Fiona ordered.

"But—"

"*I'll* deal with her." Sister Fiona pressed a quick kiss to Bridget's cheek. "God be with you, Bridget Riley, wherever you go, and take care of your friends!"

Bridget ran upstairs as dust shivered from the ceiling. The air-raid sirens howled frantically. Explosions resounded ever closer, ever closer . . .

Anne was in their room, throwing clothes into a satchel. Maire paced by the door.

"There you are," Maire said. Her eyes were a more brilliant blue than Bridget had ever seen them. "I packed your bag." Two satchels sat on Bridget's bed.

"Done," Anne said, turning to Maire. "What door do we use?"

Maire smiled serenely. "We'll leave from here."

She took Anne by the shoulders. "Your ways are not our ways," she said, voice changing to the same strange whisper Bridget had heard before. "But it's believe in this or die. Your God, my Goddess . . . both of them will understand. Do *you* understand, Miriam, daughter of Rachel, granddaughter of Susannah?"

Miriam froze, Maire's hands cool and firm on her shoulders. The people arranging her escape had given a second false name to the nuns. No one in Ireland knew her or her mother's name, let alone her *grandmother's*. Her grandmother had died when Miriam was five. There was no logical way Maire could have found those names out.

That left . . .

Miriam swallowed hard. Screams sounded downstairs and outside. The blackout curtains rippled as impacts struck closer and closer. Window glass shattered on the floor.

She prayed for guidance, staring into Maire's fathomless night-blue eyes.

And smelled her mother's perfume.

She brought her hands up to cover the other girl's. "What do I do?"

Maire drew the other two girls close. "Hold hands. Put the satchels over your shoulders. They may not come with us. Anything you really need, leave in your dress pockets."

"Already did," Anne—Maire continued to partly think of her as Anne, though the Sight had told her the girl's true name—said tautly.

"You didn't need to tell me," Bridget quipped, trying to smile. "My brothers kept *everything* in their pockets. Made laundry terrible."

Maire took Anne's cold and trembling hand. *"Macushla,"* she said gently to the dark-eyed girl, "it'll all be well, you'll see." Then she took Bridget's warm, reassuringly solid hand.

Brigid, hear me now. Miriam must escape the death waiting

for her. She needs Your help. But . . . please, if You will, let us go with her. She needs us. Her family is gone.

In the same moment the Sight had shown Maire Anne's true name, it had shown the terrible details of what had happened to her family. Maire took a deep breath and cleared her mind.

Then she began to chant the words she had memorized. The room darkened with smoke—from outside, or from within? The words came strong and true, in a voice she recognized as her mother's more than her own.

First, to shield this place. I owe the nuns that. They took me in. And the other girls deserve protection. Even Deirdre.

Brigid, bless this place. Keep it safe. Even Sister Margaret— her Sisters will deal with her.

The explosions marched closer. Maire chanted harder, sweat beading on her brow, fiercely envisioning an impenetrable shield of air inverted over the building. *Brigid, hear me now. Keep this place and its inhabitants safe from harm. I ask this in my name, in my mother Nuala's name, and in her mother Sorcha's name.*

The building stopped shaking.

"Praise be to God!" Sister Maureen called from the corridor, voice high with wonder. "The bombs are *missing* us! God's hand is shielding us!"

Maire smiled. *Blessed be Brigid's grace.*

Now to carry us away.

New York City. She let the image grow in her mind as the American had described it to Deirdre: Pennsylvania Station, where the trains came in . . . Greenwich Village, where he'd been born and raised, with its crooked twisting streets and houses jammed so closely together they looked like gossips huddling . . .

Something popped. A bluish glow filled the room. Anne's and Bridget's hands tightened around hers.

The girls vanished . . .

. . . to reappear, dazed and with satchels missing, in a shadowy corner of what Maire, blinking frantically, recognized, she thought, as . . . Pennsylvania Station. People hurried to and fro. *Just as in my dream.*

Bridget's mouth hung open. "Sweet Jesus," she whispered, and let go of Maire's hand long enough to cross herself. Then she took it again, as if afraid to be without contact.

Anne murmured under her breath. Maire knew she was praying to her God, and smiled.

Thank you, Brigid.

Hello, America.

My name is Maire Riordan. My friends and I have come here to live.

So shall it be, Maire heard a voice say inside her skull— a caressing whisper like a mother's lullaby. *So shall it be.*

LESLEY McBAIN

LESLEY McBAIN is a writer/consultant who currently lives in the South. Her short fiction can also be found in *Turn the Other Chick*, edited by Esther Friesner.

The inspiration for her story, "Acts of Faith," partly comes from growing up surrounded by Scots-Irish warrior-types—both male and female—in and out of uniform. (Both her parents were naval officers; all her uncles served in various branches of the U.S. military. And then there was her god-father, the Air Force chaplain who sometimes jokingly called himself "the Mad Monk." . . .)

The story's inspiration also derives from her being a Jew-by-choice interested in both Jewish and Celtic history. But mainly "Acts of Faith" was drawn from knowing that warriors emerge in unexpected places and guises. Plus from a healthy dollop of a "what if . . ." reworking of history.

SWORDS THAT TALK

Brent Hartinger

THE PROBLEM WITH TALKING SWORDS, Brinn decided, was that most of the time they didn't know when to shut the hell up.

Now, for example. Brinn was deep in the middle of a maze of narrow, echoing canyons, methodically searching for a terrifying monster. But his sword wouldn't stop talking.

"You know how you rubbed pig fat into my blade last night?" the sword was saying. "Did I happen to mention how good that felt?"

"Yes!" Brinn whispered urgently. "You mentioned it! A lot! Now would be you please be *quiet*?"

Most warriors got to prove their valor by going to war. For Brinn, there was one problem: no war. Didn't it just figure that he had been so unlucky as to have been born in a time of enduring peace?

But Brinn was sixteen years old now—well past the age when he should have proved himself a great hero. So he had had to come up with another plan: the Troll in the Labyrinth.

That's what these endless, twisting canyons were called—the Labyrinth. And somewhere within this wasteland of blackened canyon walls, there lived a vicious troll that guarded a hoard of fabulous treasure. Or so the legend went.

Brinn had come to kill the troll and claim the treasure. True, the creature hadn't exactly attacked the village. Not lately, anyway. Maybe not ever—at least not in Brinn's lifetime. But the threat was always there. Constantly looming. Hanging over everything.

When Brinn brought his village the horn of the Troll in the Labyrinth, they would realize just how dire their situation had been. And when he showed them the creature's treasure, they would be downright overjoyed. After all, the village was poor. The whole kingdom was poor. People would come for miles around just for a glimpse of all the gold and jewels—and the great warrior who had claimed them for his village. No one would even remember that Brinn hadn't had permission to borrow the talking sword known as Irontongue from the town armory.

Speaking of Irontongue, the weapon was quiet at last. But not deferential-quiet. Sulking-quiet. Brinn could tell the difference.

"Look," Brinn said to the sword. "I'm sorry I yelled at you. But it's important that we have the element of surprise. These canyons echo enough as it is. We can't make any noise."

"You want a quiet weapon?" the sword said. "You should get yourself a mace."

Brinn stopped right there in the middle of the canyon and sighed. The sound echoed back at him like a dying gasp.

"Now what?" the sword asked.

"Nothing," Brinn muttered. But it wasn't nothing. The truth was, he hadn't counted on how long it was taking to find and dispatch the Troll in the Labyrinth. He'd been searching these corridors of stone for *days*—and he was quickly running out of water. He'd had no idea that proving your worth as a warrior would be so *hard.*

Glancing at the ground, Brinn caught a glimpse of something sharp partially covered by the sand.

He bent down for a closer look. It was a sword—or part of one, anyway. He kicked it loose and saw that it was the tip of a broken—and very rusted—longsword. Where had it come from? This was the third old discarded sword he'd found in the last three days (one night, he'd even unwittingly placed his bedroll on one!). He'd also come across six arrowheads, two horseshoes, and the remnants of a very rusted helm.

"I wonder . . . ," Brinn said.

"Yes?" Irontongue asked.

But before Brinn could answer, a grinding sound echoed out from the canyon up ahead.

Brinn could barely believe his eyes. The Troll in the Labyrinth! It was roughly human-like—though eight feet tall, with pale blue skin and a big gray horn jutting up from the middle of its forehead. It had yellow eyes, a massive misshapen head, warted like a gourd, and giant hands with twisted fingernails that looked like they hadn't been trimmed in years. And hanging between its legs was—well, let's just say it was definitely a *male* troll (funny how the stories never mentioned such things!).

He had made his home in the end of a box canyon, where the walls of the gorge widened into a round open area of sorts, almost like a small coliseum.

So the stories were true. The Troll in the Labyrinth *did*

exist. And if the stories about the troll were true, the stories about the troll's *treasure* also had to be true!

Crouched down at the entrance to the open canyon area, Brinn saw that the troll had gathered a large mound of boulders. It looked like he was now in the process of using the boulders to seal up the entrance to a cave on the opposite side of the canyon. The troll's stacking of boulders was the grinding sound that Brinn had heard before.

"Well?" Irontongue whispered. "What are you waiting for?"

What *was* Brinn waiting for? Wasn't this why he had come all this way—to thrash the troll? But Brinn hadn't expected the creature to be so, um, tall.

Suddenly the troll swung around to stare right at Brinn. Somehow he had sensed Brinn was there, or maybe he had heard Irontongue's whisperings. Either way, Brinn had been spotted. There was no turning back now.

Brinn drew Irontongue from its scabbard—a little fumbly, he hated to admit—and stepped out into the open area.

"Head of the troll?" he called.

The creature's yellow eyes narrowed disdainfully.

"Say farewell to the body of the troll!" Brinn finished.

"Good one!" Irontongue said.

But the troll didn't respond. Instead, his eyes widened again and got glassy, seeming to lose their focus. The creature swooned a little, then staggered to the nearest boulder, which he used as a seat.

Brinn wasn't sure what to do. This wasn't the reaction he'd expected.

"Prepare to lose your head!" Brinn said to the troll.

"Wait," the sword said to Brinn. "Didn't you just say that?"

But even as the sword was talking, the troll was swooning again. Yellow eyes quivering in their sockets, the troll swayed left, then right. He lifted a hand full of twisted fingernails up to his forehead.

Then he toppled forward into the sand. The troll made no effort to break his fall. He smacked against the ground facedown, with what had to be a very painful thud. A big cloud of dust exploded upward at the impact.

Brinn could only stare. What had just happened? This was obviously a ruse of some sort. But as the dust slowly settled, Brinn saw that the troll was sprawled across the sand like a gutted carp.

There was dead, and there was *dead*. That troll was *dead*. Not a single muscle on the creature stirred; none of his fat quivered from an intake of air.

Even so, Brinn approached cautiously, sword drawn. It could still be a trick. What did he know about trolls, anyway?

He kicked the body of the creature. It hurt his toe—a lot. It felt like he'd kicked solid stone.

Up close, Brinn was still in awe of the monster. And yet something didn't seem right. The skin, for one thing. Was healthy troll skin supposed to look so washed-out? And the tone was off—way off. The flesh literally sagged. Somehow the troll managed to look both flabby and emaciated at the same time. And sixty seconds after collapsing, he already had the stench of death.

Could it be that the troll was old? Is that why he had died? Was he teetering on the edge of death when Brinn had come upon him, and had Brinn's sudden appearance been just enough of a fright to push him over?

It didn't matter. Brinn had vanquished the troll—hadn't he? No one needed to know the story of what had really happened here. He could still cut off the troll's horn and take it back to the village.

"Well, that was anticlimactic," Irontongue said drolly.

The sword, Brinn thought. It saw what had happened; it knew the truth. Would it talk? No. Talking swords weren't like that. They were magically bound never to betray their wielder; they were the ultimate yes-men. And each time they were picked up by a new person, their memories were wiped clean. So Irontongue's lips were sealed, so to speak.

"The treasure!" Brinn said, remembering the legend of the troll's fabulous hoard. It had to be in the cave!

Stepping around the body of the troll, Brinn faced the entrance to the cave. The troll had already sealed it halfway up with boulders. But the rocks were large and solidly placed. Brinn sheathed his sword and easily climbed over the obstruction.

Once he was inside, it took several moments for his eyes to adjust to the dark.

Then they adjusted. And what a treasure confronted Brinn there! Golden bowls brimmed with sparkling jewels and rings, ropes of pearls, and even a crown or two. Wooden chests spilled forth with coins. Even the dust of a canyon cave couldn't dim this treasure's luster.

"It's incredible!" Brinn whispered.

"It was too easy," Irontongue said. "Quests aren't supposed to be this easy."

"It wasn't *that* easy," Brinn said, piqued. "I've been searching these canyons for days. And I have a blister on my heel you wouldn't *believe*." But the truth was, Irontongue had said aloud what Brinn was feeling inside. The quest *had* been pretty easy—which meant that maybe he hadn't proved his worth as a warrior at all.

"Getting here was not an easy feat," a voice said. "But the real test lies ahead."

At first, Brinn thought it was the sword that had spoken. But no, this was a new voice, one from outside the cave.

Brinn whirled back toward the entrance. Standing in the middle of the open area outside the cave, on the other side of the troll's corpse, was a man—a stout-looking warrior in full armor, with a polished shield and sword by his side. But the angle of the sun must have changed, because the glare from the man's shield and armor made it difficult to look directly at him. And something must have kicked up the dust again, because there was a haze in the air, further obscuring the figure.

"Uh-oh," Irontongue muttered. "I *knew* it was too good to be true."

Brinn ignored the sword, staring out at the warrior in the sun. "What do you want?" Brinn called to him.

"I came about the treasure," the man said.

The treasure! Brinn thought. Of course! Brinn wasn't going to be able to claim it after all—at least not yet. He had a competitor now: this warrior. And from the look of things, he would not be so easy to vanquish as the dying troll.

"Go away!" Brinn shouted, and his voice reverberated inside the cave. "The troll's treasure is *mine!*" But how had the warrior known about the treasure, anyway? It hadn't been visible from outside the cave. Had he been watching from somewhere too, waiting for the troll to die?

"Oh?" said the warrior.

"It *is!*" Brinn said. "I have vanquished the troll!"

"I see," said the warrior, and from the tone of his voice, Brinn knew he knew the truth. "But for the record, the treasure did not belong to the troll. He was merely guarding it."

Brinn wasn't going to be drawn into this game of verbal
cat and mouse. Why was he even talking to the warrior, anyway? He was going to have to fight him, so he might as well
get it over with. Brinn wouldn't *necessarily* be slaughtered. He
wondered what the odds were of the warrior having a heart
attack right then and there.

Brinn drew his sword. This time, he wasn't clumsy at all.
In fact, as it slid smoothly from its sheath, the sword actually
rang. That had to count for something.

"Attaboy!" Irontongue whispered. "Go get 'em!"

"The question is," the warrior went on quietly, almost as
if talking to himself, "who *does* the treasure belong to? That
was never really clear, you see. Different people laid claim.
Whole kingdoms, in fact. It changed hands many times.
Many battles were waged for that fortune."

Brinn squinted, still trying to make out the warrior. But
the glint of sunlight was particularly strong off his helmet. He
couldn't make out the face at all.

"This is your last chance!" Brinn shouted, using Irontongue to underline each word. "Desist, or I shall be forced
to defend my spoils!"

The warrior kept talking, as if Brinn had not spoken at
all. "Many great battles," he mused. "This area all around us,
this wasteland, is the result of those wars."

"I *mean* it!" Brinn said. But at the same time, he thought,
What was it the warrior had said? Something about the
surrounding area being a battlefield? Brinn couldn't help but
remember the remnants of weapons and armor that he had
discovered over the past few days. And the black marks on
the canyon walls—could they be the scorch marks of wizard
and dragon fire?

"But it was very long ago," the warrior said. "Almost the life span of a troll."

A troll? Brinn thought. What did *that* have to do with anything?

"Two vast armies." The warrior kept on talking, softly, confidently. "Both thousands of swords strong. An army in yellow and an army in purple. Together, that made red. Again and again they clashed, and the red ran deeper still."

Brinn ignored the warrior's words and stomped his way to the cave's entrance. Brinn would have to climb over the boulders again but he wasn't about to sheathe his sword, no matter how hard that made it for him to clamber over the rocks. He would need to be ready for battle the instant he touched down on the other side.

But the warrior didn't take advantage of Brinn's vulnerability as he climbed. The warrior just kept talking. "There were survivors of the wars, of course," he said. "The strongest was a troll—a mercenary for the army in purple. Some people said that he took the treasure for himself and hid it in this cave. But others said that even a troll has a conscience. And that this particular troll had grown very weary of war."

Leaping down from the top of the stacked boulders, Brinn shouted victoriously, "Aha!" He looked up at the warrior, but the canyon dust had not yet settled—which was strange, because now Brinn could feel that there was no wind outside, or even a breeze. He could still see the man within the haze, but his face didn't seem any clearer than before. How was it, Brinn wondered, that the dust did not block the sun's glare?

"But now the troll is dead," the warrior said, "and the treasure has been found again."

"Yes!" Brinn said. "By *me*!" And with that, sword swing-ing, he charged the warrior.

A few moments later, he stumbled out from the other side of the cloud of dust. At no point had his flailing sword found the warrior's flesh.

How was that possible? The dust was thick, but it wasn't *that* thick. Brinn had run right for the man, and he had been swinging wildly. Had the warrior stepped out of the way at the last second, obscuring himself in the swirling haze?

Confused, Brinn spun around to face the cloud again. The gleaming warrior had turned to face Brinn too, but otherwise didn't appear to have moved at all. It was almost as if Brinn had passed right through him.

"And if you take that treasure back to your village," the warrior said casually, as if Brinn had not just attacked him, "you think it will change everything?"

"Yes!" Brinn shouted angrily. "Of course it will!" His vil-lage was desperately poor. But even as he thought this, Brinn remembered that the surrounding villages were poor too. The whole kingdom was poor. And if word got out that one vil-lage had acquired a great treasure, what would stop the other villages from wanting a portion of it? But there hadn't been war among the villages since—well, Brinn had *never* heard of such a war. For the most part, they were all equally poor, so what would be the point?

Sure, he thought, there might be some scuffles, some inter-village conflicts. But that was the consequence of wealth. Besides, maybe Brinn could leave some of the trea-sure here for a while—after he defeated the warrior, that is. It was true that his village didn't need *all* of the gold and jew-els. It wasn't like his village was *desperately* poor. No one was starving, exactly.

"But will they believe you if you tell them there isn't any more treasure?" the warrior asked. "Can you be sure they won't come into the Labyrinth themselves, looking for the rest?"

Brinn knew the warrior was right. The villagers *would* come looking for the rest—and eventually they would find it.

Wait a minute, he thought. Brinn hadn't said that part about not taking all of the treasure out loud. So how had the warrior known what he was thinking?

Once again, Brinn squinted at him in the haze. "How did you *do* that?"

"Do what?" the warrior asked, as if he really didn't know.

"You knew what I was thinking!"

At that, the warrior did not speak. Brinn glanced over at the half-sealed entrance to the cave, and at the pile of boulders outside.

Now it was Brinn's eyes that lost their focus. "The troll knew he was dying," he whispered. "So he was hiding the treasure so that no one would ever find it. To make sure no one ever fought over it again."

Again the warrior did not speak. In the blur of his own eyesight, Brinn suddenly thought he saw other figures gathered in the haze before him, glints of sharpened swords and polished armor, pennons of purple and yellow.

Brinn gasped, raising his sword. But when he looked more closely, he saw that he was mistaken, that it was only that single warrior alone in the dust.

"Huh?" he said. "Where did they—?"

"Who?" the warrior asked.

Brinn lowered his sword again. "But if I don't take the treasure," he said softly, "won't you? Then there will be war anyway."

"I am not here to take the treasure," the warrior said. "I couldn't even if I wanted to." And somehow Brinn knew without question that the man was not lying.

"Who are you?" Brinn demanded suddenly. "Why *are* you here?"

"Let's just say I have an interest in where the treasure ends up. I happen to think it should stay exactly where it is."

"Maybe I *will* leave the treasure here," Brinn said, oddly relieved. "Who needs it, anyway? Wealth makes one a king, not a warrior. What I came for was the horn! And I can still take *that* back to the village!"

"And then people will know the Troll in the Labyrinth has been defeated?" the warrior asked.

"Yes!" Brinn said proudly. "And then they will be able to come safely into the Labyrinth, and . . ."

And eventually someone might still find the treasure, Brinn thought.

"Oh," he said.

"Yes?"

"But if I return empty-handed—" Brinn started to say.

"Yes?"

He didn't finish what he was thinking: *Then people won't think of me as a great warrior!*

"You never answered my first question," Brinn said. "Who *are* you?"

But when Brinn looked again, the warrior was gone.

"Wait!" Brinn said, turning all the way around in the coliseum-like canyon. The dust was settling at last, and the sun was setting too, beginning to dip down under the rim of the canyon. But the warrior was nowhere to be seen.

Brinn looked down. There were footprints in the sand—

his own. He could trace them from the side of the canyon, where he had hidden, to the dead troll and the cave. Then from the entrance of the cave through the place where the cloud of dust had been.

But from the warrior there were no footprints at all. It was as if he had never even been there.

"He wasn't here?" Brinn asked aloud. "He was only a . . . ?"

"Ghost," Irontongue said, speaking aloud the word that Brinn wasn't sure he would ever be able to bring himself to say.

It was a long walk back to his village, so Brinn set out that very evening. He wished there had been some way for him to seal the treasure inside the cave. Unfortunately the boulders were too heavy for human arms. But he had buried the fortune in the sand as best he could. And the story Brinn was formulating—a horrifying tale of defeat and woe about his encounter with the Troll in the Labyrinth—would act as a barrier of sorts. For a few years, anyway.

Brinn had only just begun the journey out of the Labyrinth when Irontongue asked him, "But now how are you going to prove you're a warrior?"

"Don't laugh," Brinn said. "But I think maybe I just did."

"That's just what I was thinking," said the sword, who, as usual, insisted on having the last word.

BRENT HARTINGER

BRENT HARTINGER has been writing books since he graduated from college in 1986, but he didn't have any luck getting them published until 2001. That year, his luck definitely changed, and he has since sold nine novels to various publishers, including three teen novels (*The Last Chance Texaco, Geography Club,* and its sequel, *The Order of the Poison Oak*) and two fantasy novels (*Dreamquest* and the upcoming *The Fifth Season*). Brent also writes screenplays and plays, some of which are adaptations of his novels.

Of all the genres and mediums in which he writes, Brent most likes writing fantasy—preferably fantasy for young people—which is why he is so thrilled to be included in this anthology.

Brent lives outside Seattle, Washington, with his partner, novelist Michael Jensen. He loves meeting people and talking about the process of writing, and often speaks at schools, seminars, and conferences. Visit his Web site, "Brent's Brain," online at www.brenthartinger.com.

ɊFTERWORD

◆◆◆

Josepha Sherman

Is THE IDEA of young heroes and heroines strictly fiction? No, it certainly isn't. The fictional heroes and heroines in this book definitely have their parallels in history and folklore. In fact, in many of the world's cultures, young people, boys and girls alike, were expected to become warriors, to help protect their tribes and sometimes to show their worth as potential husbands or wives.

The pre-Christian Celts of Great Britain and Ireland actually wrote into their law codes (or at least had the law codes memorized before the days of writing) that for the protection of each clan, every noble family must have at least one child trained to be a warrior. If a family had no son, the daughter was trained to be a warrior. There seems to have been no taboo against a warrior woman marrying and raising a family, since there were always servants (or slaves) available to do the "traditionally female" daily work of cleaning, mending, and cooking. Indeed, women warriors could gain as much honor as the men. In the mythic cycle centering about the great Irish Celtic hero Cuchulain, the hero is trained in arms by the greatest warrior of all, the woman Scathach. Some scholars even think that at one time Scathach, too, had a cycle of stories about her, but none of those stories still exist.

The Vikings of Norway, Sweden, and Denmark also had a long tradition of teenage warriors. Boys were more often trained to be warriors than were girls, but there were girl warriors as well, who were sometimes called Shield Maidens. One of these young female warriors is Hervor, who learned how to fight while still a girl living in her maternal grandfather's house. Hervor avenges her father's death, then joins a band of Vikings and has many adventures as a warrior before finally settling down and taking a husband. Other young women warriors who sailed with the Vikings ran away from home rather than be forced into marriage. Among those were Sela, Stikla, and Alvid.

In ancient Greece, the boys of the land of Sparta were trained from birth to be warriors. Any weak baby was left in the mountains to die. The surviving boys began their military training at age seven. It was a harsh training, teaching the boys to be hardy and resilient, able to live off the land and ignore hardship. Girls were trained to be hardy, too, not as fighters but as the mothers-to-be of a warrior race.

The Cossacks, a martial people from the steppes of Russia, trained their boys in the warrior ways from birth. In fact, when a boy was born, his parents placed a weapon in the newborn's hand. By the time he was three, he would be an expert rider. Cossack boys would fight war games on horseback, and any boy who showed bravery and skill was praised.

India has its share of legendary young heroes, but three women stand out among them. The first of these is the historical Rani (or queen) Chennamma. Born in 1778, she was trained as a warrior from childhood and, after her marriage to Raja Mullasarja of Kittur, became leader of the women's wing of the royal army. The rani died in 1829. The second historical figure is Rani Laxmibai of Jhansi. Born in 1834, she fought against the British and their attempts to take over Jhansi, which was then an independent Indian province. Rani Laxmibai was raised as a warrior by her raja father and was as a child already an expert rider and sword fighter. She died in combat against the British in 1858, at the age of twenty-four, but is still remembered in many Indian folktales and ballads. A third young warrior woman is Jalkari Bai, also from Jhansi, who came from a poor family and had to teach herself how to fight so that she could protect herself. She is said to have killed a tiger with her ax when she was about ten. Tradition says that Jalkari Bai looked very much like Rani Laxmibai and was taken under the rani's wing.

Mongolia is the birthplace of one of the world's most famous warlords, Genghis Khan, who conquered almost all of Asia and much of Eastern Europe. He was born Temujin, son of a tribal leader, somewhere between AD 1150 and 1170. But his father was poisoned by an enemy when Temujin was about ten years old, and the boy was made a slave. Temujin refused to give up. He escaped when he was a young teen and, through courage and sheer willpower, began uniting the other Mongol tribes. By 1206, he had united them all, avenged his father's murder, and become known as Genghis Khan, or "Universal Ruler."

In the nomadic tribal groups of North America, where food was found, not raised, and other tribes were always potential dangers, boys were trained to be hunters and warriors almost from the day they could walk. In fact, a boy's first toys often included a toy bow and arrow. Girls were trained to take care of the family and to gather whatever vegetables and fruits were available. However, whenever there are groups of people, there are exceptions to the rule. Some tribes, such as the Cheyenne, had a role for the bedarche, who was a gay boy or man who lived by choice as a female. The tribes who had this custom accepted gay people without any problem. Other tribes did not. In all the tribes, some girls chose to be warriors, either to escape marriage or because they felt a drive to protect their people and gain honor. The Oneida—who are one of the Six Nations, also known as the Iroquois Confederacy, comprising the Mohawk, Oneida, Onondaga, Cayuga, Seneca, and Tuscarora—have a legend about a young woman warrior named Aliquipiso. Although captured and tortured by the Mingo, an enemy of the Oneida, Aliquipiso remained brave, pretended to give in, and deliberately led the enemy into an Oneida trap. The Cheyenne people tell of a historic brother-and-sister team of warriors who fought together and protected each other in battle.

The heroes and heroines in this book may, indeed, be fiction—but they do, indeed, have an honorable link to the real world.

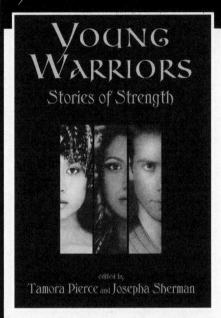